Dervla Alarms the Nanas

D.R. Ransdell

Fiction:

Sofi & Cenzo Mysteries

Party Wine (also an audiobook)

Andy Veracruz Mysteries

Mariachi Meddler
Island Casualty
Dizzy in Durango
Substitute Soloist
Brotherly Love

Campanello Travels

Amirosian Nights
Thai Twist
Carillon Chase

Non-Fiction:

Secrets of a Mariachi Violinist

Dervla Alarms the Nanas

D.R. Ransdell

Author's Note:
Any resemblance to real persons is coincidental.

To David Loeb

For always believing in me

Chapter One

I dragged my cousin toward the tourist shop. "Just one more."

Keevah held me back half-heartedly. She knew I would wrestle away. "Dervla, enough!"

Even though I'd promised her a drink on Bourbon Street before she escorted me to the airport, this was the fifth shop I'd dragged her into. "Maybe I'll find something here."

"Emil does not need a souvenir. You've only been gone a few days."

A jealous partner might have given me a guilt trip about leaving him behind. I wanted to pick up one small thing as a thank-you, but nothing was cute enough or New Orleans enough. The real problem was that it was always hard to come down to earth after Mardi Gras. Party dust was still in the air. Who could focus?

I shook the snowball and watched as flakes settled over Jackson Square.

"That's nice." Keevah wasn't watching me. Her eyes were on the bar across the street.

"Not allowed for carry-on." I pointed to a stack of sweatshirts dotted with saxophones. "One of those?"

She fingered the thick fabric. The cinnamon color complemented our hair color. "Isn't that too hot for Tucson?"

"Emil always jogs in the morning. It's not too hot then. But he never listens to jazz."

We headed for the exit, but we halted simultaneously before a shelf of little dolls. The four-inch figures were wrapped in yarn. Their eyes were mismatched buttons.

"That one's cute," she said. "It looks like a dog."

We'd honed in on the same doll at the same time. I picked it up carefully and turned it around. The gray yarned bristled in the artificial light. The tongue was a triangle of red felt. The eyes were the same size, but one was blue and one was green. The tail was a snippet of black pipe cleaner that pricked me, not enough to hurt, but enough to hold my attention.

I held the figure eye level. "A dog? Really?"

"Or a cat."

"I can't tell whether I like it or not."

The doll was sweet in a goofy way. I turned the critter upside down and checked the price tag on its paw. "Thirty-five dollars! Are you kidding me?"

I set the figure on the shelf, but Keevah picked it up again. She examined it from all sides. "Local handicraft. The residents are still recovering from the hurricane."

"That was years ago."

"Recovery is a slow process. They have to make a living somehow."

"Not off me, they don't!" I laughed.

"But these dolls are special."

"They're specially priced for tourists."

"They have magical powers."

"They do not."

"I'll get it for you. An early birthday present."

"Gee, thanks." I wasn't sure I wanted to celebrate turning thirty, but my cousin had beaten me by two months and survived without any loss of confidence.

She indicated the clerk behind the cash register. "We used to bartend together. She'll give me a discount. Wait outside. Go!"

I moseyed to the front door, which was open, and breathed in fresh air. The night before, the same space had been a madhouse of partiers. By now bacchanalia had yielded to reality. Lots of people passed by, but they walked in straight lines. Another year, another Ash Wednesday.

I loved the routine. I saw my parents and siblings for some Christmases, the occasional Easter, and sometimes in the summer. But I never missed a Mardi Gras with the only fun member of my family. For four hedonistic days, we caught beads thrown by parade crews, pushed our way into crowded bars, and stayed up talking until one of us fell asleep.

A kid ran down the pedestrian street in my direction. He might have been fourteen. What he needed most was a trim for his straw-like hair. A yellow handbag that bounced over his shoulder contrasted with neon orange running shoes.

That was part of Mardi Gras, too. The strangest costumes you could imagine. People who didn't have money for luxuries improvised. So did those who liked looking weird, which was everybody else. I'd been a green fairy myself.

Farther back, a stout lady ran up as fast as her legs would carry her. "My purse!"

I wasn't hungover, but it took me that long to catch on that the purse wasn't part of the kid's outfit. And to react.

I hurried toward the youth, watching him sideways. I hadn't played college soccer for nothing. As he passed me, I stretched out my left foot and cheered with pure joy when he tripped over it.

The thief flew through the air and landed on his stomach. His chin bounced on the concrete like a ping pong ball. A large man turned and slammed his foot on the kid's back to convince him to stay where he was. The purse landed several feet away.

The passersby huddled as they took in the sequence of events.

I bent to the ground. "What were you thinking?" I yelled in his ear.

He squirmed, but by then a young man grabbed his legs while an older man took ahold of his arms.

"How dare you?" asked the older man. "People like you ruin our city!"

"I—I—"

That's all the kid managed to say before the purse owner caught up. She kicked him in the side so hard that she stumbled off like a clown on a tightrope. She would have landed on her rear if a bystander hadn't steadied her.

Another bystander called 9-1-1. Half a dozen shot videos.

"Please don't call the cops," the kid squeaked.

"Too late," I said, stepping away. By now the first man had straddled him

The purse owner nearly squeezed the life out of me with a hug. "Thank you so much! I had the last pictures of my grandma in that purse!"

"Glad I could help."

"Dervla!" my cousin called from the shop entrance. "What are you doing?

"Nothing. Let's get you that drink." I took her arm and herded her away from the crowd.

"You tripped that guy?"

"He was snatching a purse."

Keevah stopped. "You had to dive into things?"

"I didn't dive. I merely stuck out my foot. The lady got her purse back."

Keevah turned and looked back on the scene. "We should stay. The police might want to talk to you."

"That's all right."

"You never see things through."

"Sure, I do."

"Prove it."

"Six years with the same man?"

"I know. It's a record for you. But don't get cocky about it."

"Wouldn't dream of it."

Before she could give me any more trouble, I led her into the nearest bar and ordered a couple of Sazeracs.

***

I shut my notebook as Emil entered our office at World Lingo, our language school. The Tucson native nearly stopped my breath. His light brown body lit up the door frame: tanned muscular arms, strong legs beneath thin dress pants, brown eyes that darted around mischievously.

I squelched the impulse to jump up and give him a bear hug. At work we kept our distance even though our students were adults. Mine were about to arrive. "I hope I didn't wake you last night?" It wasn't my fault that I'd arrived after midnight—the bad weather had been in Dallas.

He set down the canvas laundry bag that he used for his laptop. "Good trip?"

"Terrific."

"That's nice." He paused as if trying to remember something. "I have bad news you won't like."

I turned to my schedule, which was written on a big erasable calendar on the wall by the desk. My English classes were listed on the left side. Emil's Spanish classes were listed on the right. "Another cancellation?" I had a private class of beginners at eleven a.m., a trio of Japanese business executives at noon, and Basics from two to four, which made it one

11

of my lighter days. If students cancelled at least twenty-four hours in advance, we didn't charge them.

"I'm moving out," Emil said.

"Or is the cancellation for tomorrow?"

"I mean it."

I looked over in slow motion. "Did I leave the cap off the toothpaste again?" I was teasing; Emil never noticed details.

"I signed a lease for an apartment."

"What?"

"It won't be ready until next week."

"You're — moving out?"

"I was going to tell you before you left for Mardi Gras, but I didn't want to ruin your vacation."

I pushed back from the desk. "You're leaving me."

"That's why I'm moving out."

I pulled on my ear lobes. I hadn't heard right. I was in a movie. A bad one.

"Sorry," he said.

"Sorry? You're breaking up with me here? Now?"

"There wasn't a good time to tell you."

I felt like the purse thief who had ping ponged across the pavement. The wind had been knocked out of me with such force that I could barely breathe.

"So we're through," I said.

"That's one way to sum it up."

I was too stunned to move.

"Well?" he asked.

"Where is this coming from?"

"No one place."

I snapped my fingers. "You're moving out. Just like that."

"Right."

I'd met Emil when we started grad school. We began dating soon after. He moved in with me halfway through our degree program. Once we graduated, we opened our language school. Emil was my lover, my confidante, my friend, and my business partner.

Or so I thought. I breathed deeply. I'd read in some self-help magazine that extra oxygen could cure almost anything. My biggest breathing, however, did nothing for shock.

The World Lingo office was flanked by a classroom on either side. Antonio came in through the building's front door, waved to me, and proceeded into the room for English class. As usual, my most earnest student was a few minutes early.

I waited until he was out of earshot. "Do you want to tell me what I've done wrong?"

"Nothing. I'm moving on. That's all."

I held his gaze without gleaning anything from it. We never fought, but we glossed over difficulties.

Lily and Ginger, my young Taiwanese students, shouted "hello" as they walked by.

"You have class," Emil said.

"You're breaking up with me five minutes before I start teaching for the day?"

"Like I said. There was no good time."

No. There was never a right moment for shaking up someone's world. I sat blankly as the tsunami washed me up on the beach.

"Well, I guess you have class now," he said.

"Now I'm supposed to walk in and teach?"

"I'll pay you for the hours, of course," Emil said. "We'll work out a salary."

The second wave of the tsunami tossed me into the nearest palm tree.

"What do you mean, salary?"

"It's my business. But I'll hire you, of course."

"A business we started together! I'm not hired help. I'm your partner. We created World Lingo together. Remember?"

13

"I covered the initial start-up costs. I paid for the advertising."

"You did not. The nanas loaned us the money." They weren't both his nanas, but his grandmother and her sister lived together. Within the family, we always referred to them as such.

"My name is on the business license. World Lingo is my business. Period."

"Hi, Mrs. Dervla," Ahmed called out.

I ran through a list of "Reasons Why I'm Not Good Enough" as if they were names on a Rolodex. I didn't jog. I never cooked. I didn't hand out compliments like they were free flyers at a church gathering.

Emil looked away long enough for me to sense that he had pangs of regret. Or guilt.

"Who is she?"

"No 'she.'"

I imagined my eyes as swords. "Emil Arellano, if you know what's good for you, you'll change that tune before you whistle another bar."

He backed up until he knocked against the door jamb. He nearly fell. "I'm sure we can work things out. I'll stagger the classes so that we're never in the office at the same time."

I was stunned by my own incompetence. I'd ignored every damning sign. Whenever he slapped his laptop shut as I entered the room, I assumed he indulged in porn.

"Well, I wanted you to know." He spoke as if the subject had been successfully covered, so now we could move on.

"Counseling?"

"I already decided."

As if the wall of my office were a movie screen, my mind conjured up pictures of romantic dinners we'd enjoyed on our own balcony. Weekend getaways to San Diego. Longer trips to Mazatlán. Joyous holiday dinners with his assortment of relatives. Movies we'd watched on the couch arm in arm. Long conversations about literature, life, aspirations, growing old together. Emil completed me. I thought I returned the favor.

I almost wished I were the kind to burst out crying, but I held things in like a popcorn popper. First there was nothing. Then the faint sizzling of oil. Then one kernel popped. Then another. Then all of them at once.

"Maybe you're leaving me for a 'he'?" Emil was firmly heterosexual, but I hoped for a rise.

He lowered his voice as if the volume softened the message. "I'm not discussing it."

That was it.

Had he admitted to falling out of love, I would have accepted such a situation as unpleasant but pardonable. If he'd apologized. If he'd pointed to a concrete issue between us that could not be solved. No, he'd switched off his emotions and handed down his pronouncements. As he lorded his secrecy over me, I fantasized about whether he would see another tomorrow.

"I'll let you prepare for class," he said. "Don't worry about starting a bit late if you need to take a few minutes."

I didn't routinely make life-changing decisions on a moment's notice, but the former love of my life had given me no choice. He'd shaken me right from complacency onto the soccer field, and what I needed to do was kick, kick, kick.

I slid my laptop into its faux leather cover, set my sweater around my shoulders European-style, and snatched up my purse. Then the pretty coaster caught my eye, one done in needlepoint by Emil's great-aunt. Mari had written my name in cherry pink against a flowery background. Because she hadn't known the

Irish spelling, Dearbhla, she'd written my name the way she heard it: Dervla. When Emil and I started World Lingo, I borrowed her spelling. I swooped up the coaster and waved it in Emil's face.

"What did you tell the nanas?" They were the center of the family, and all the important gatherings happened at their house.

Emil looked down.

"Oh," I said. "Nothing. Coward."

"I'll tell them later. When the time is right."

"As you said, there's no right time." I indicated that he should stand aside.

"Where are you going? You have class now."

"You think you're going to pay me by the hour?"

"How else would I pay you?"

"I don't know. But if you're so clever, let's see you teach English and Spanish at the same time."

"You can't walk out."

Was I strapped to the desk? I was not.

"I'd dance across the floor," I said, "but I'm not wearing the right shoes."

"Dervla, be reasonable!"

I pushed past him on my way out of the room.

Chapter Two

I drove the short distance home, taking deep breaths to calm myself down. I wanted to ask "why, why, why?!," but I didn't have time. I needed to use my temporary upper hand.

My narrow house was on Eighth Street between Norton and Norris, one of the infrequent two-story structures in the neighborhood. A sturdy oak tree shaded the creamy white stucco. A balcony paraded outside the master bedroom. In back, a patio hugged the back door.

The fifteen hundred feet was perfect for two people, but the place was overly crowded with furniture because we hadn't reorganized when Emil moved in. He'd come over from his mom's place bit by bit. First he'd brought the retro lamp with five arms of colored lights. Then a stained coffee table with a crack in the glass lid. Then, although the rust color clashed with my greens, his favorite beanbag chair.

Within minutes those items rested on the pebbles outside the house. Since the day was bright and sunny, they were safe outside. Thieves had better taste. I proceeded to empty my living room of anything else related to Emil even though I was fond of his Escher *Relativity* print and the poster with the Dublin doors had been his first present to me.

The living room extended to a dining area with a large picture window. The potted cacti? They all had pointy tips. I didn't need them. The bar between the dining area and the kitchen? Emil had bought the stools, but I needed them. I would pretend they were mine. The knickknacks on the shelves above the bar? I'd never liked the statuettes of singing frogs that he'd bought in Jamaica or the yellow vase he'd been given by an aunt. I set them on the coffee table along with a note that said FREE.

By the time I hit the kitchen, I picked up speed. Emil's striped plates? Out. His Day of the Dead bottle opener that took up too much room in the drawer? Out. The cheap hot dogs that I said weren't worth eating? The processed orange cheese with no flavor? Out, out. His Coronas? Completely out. I was a Guinness girl. Breakups had their advantages.

The postman walked up. The lovely fellow was an outdated hippy-type who always gave me a few extra seconds if I was finishing a letter when he arrived.

The situation was too drastic to ignore. "Spring cleaning," I said brightly.

"It's always good to shake the dust off things." He handed me a bundle of junk mail. "Anything for me to take?"

"No. Nice day, isn't it?"

"It is." He smoothed a wrinkle from his pants. "I thought it would be cooler, but it must be sixty-five degrees already."

The temperature was perfect, but I wasn't sure if my own temperature was hot or cold. Maybe both at once? Cold blood, perhaps. Hot head.

The postman reviewed the abandoned furniture. "Are you all right?"

"Emil's moving out."

"I see. That would be Mr. Arellano." The postman's face reddened. I understood exactly. I was often caught in such situations myself. Students came to my office hours with the excuse of needing help with past irregulars, but suddenly they were explaining about their high schooler who quit school or the demotion their boss handed out.

I tapped the mailbox. In my honor, Emil had painted it green, but by now plenty of beige showed through. "The mail for Gallagher will come here as usual."

"I, uh, I'm sorry if there's been a problem."

I appreciated his discomfort only as proof that a breakup was disruptive and alarming, and I wasn't crazy for thinking so. "Sometimes you have to shake the dust off your relationships too."

"Right! Well, have a good day." He waved as he hurried on.

Good day, I muttered as I traipsed upstairs. Toiletries? Out. I balked at the clothes, however, because there were so many. Rather than make a dozen trips up and down the stairs, I went to the balcony and tossed out his garments by the armful. I tied the athletic shoes in pairs and threw them at the tree. Two pairs landed in the driveway, but third secured itself to a branch. I hoped they were his favorites.

The study was more problematic. The books that we'd bought together I would claim for myself. The books that were clearly his? No. I couldn't mistreat books. Our breakup wasn't their fault. I stacked them in sturdy Trader Joe's bags. The desktop was mine, but I honestly couldn't remember who paid for the printer. Best to keep it for myself. There was also a drawerful of legal documents. I might have been angry, but that didn't mean I could toss out a passport even if it belonged to a philandering—

I should have run across proof. I reviewed the files on the desktop. Nothing. I went outside and checked pants pockets. Sixty-five cents in small change. I was missing something, but what?

I loaded the car with Emil's books and important papers. I wasn't prepared to have them in my possession one more minute, but I knew the perfect place to dump them.

Coincidentally, that would be the best way to find out more about Emil.

***

The nanas lived in a comfortable ranch house on Third Street, a block and a half from the University of Arizona. An assortment of relatives had lived with them, but by now it was just the two of them and Orlando, Emil's younger brother, who was going to the U.

As was usual for mid-day, the nanas rocked on their front porch in frumpy housecoats as they watched the parade of students going to and from campus. But the nanas were never merely watching. They always had something new up their sleeves, and I loved them for it. Their killer cat, a dull black stray named Mordy, sat on the railing before them, ready to bite anyone who came too close. More than one unsuspecting passerby had discovered that the hard way.

Although the sisters resembled one another, they were easy to tell apart. Nana Lula, Emil's maternal grandmother, was a bit taller and three years older. The long white hair piled on top of her head contrasted with full black eyebrows. At eighty years old, she had a piercing glance that she usually reserved for naughty younger relatives. Her tongue was equally piercing, and she didn't hesitate to use it.

More petite than her sister, Nana Mari used makeup to create eyebrows she no longer had. She sported a pixie cut whose graceful white strands surrounded her round face. Patient and soft-spoken, she was a good listener, and she laughed at jokes whether they were funny or not.

Although they both waved as I pulled up in the drive, I couldn't bring myself to leave the car. My reluctance was simple. I didn't want to see them one last time. No matter the occasion, I adored spending time with them. They were fun and inventive, and they didn't let anything slip past them. More importantly, they'd always been on my side, something I would never say of my own relatives save Keevah. And the nanas were both special.

I'd learned early on that Lula could see through any lie. Once she latched onto a truth, she bullied her victims into confessions. The unsuspecting child or sometimes adult usually ran off crying. Lula wasn't mean, but she spoke plainly and loudly. Maybe that was why we had always gotten along. I favored clear speaking as well, no matter how little recipients wanted to hear the message.

Mari was special too. She saw auras, which she described as color vibrations. I'd never seen one myself, but she explained their basic meaning. Generally, when the shades were dark, people were upset. When they were happy, the shades were light. She used this skill to her advantage. Since she could perceive people's moods, she could judge the best way to make requests. The end result was that she could talk anyone into anything. Plumbing or yard work? She could coax a nephew into instant cooperation. Laundry or errands? Any niece would do. Pesky paperwork? That usually fell to Emil. Or me.

I exited the car before they rallied themselves to come investigate. Although the process would be painful, at least they would hear me out. They wouldn't like my version of the story, but they'd believe it and sympathize. Then I'd have to extract myself from their lives. What else could I do? They weren't my relatives. They were borrowed. I would have to return them.

Trudging up the six porch steps, I greeted them flatly.

"What's wrong, angel?" asked Mari.

When I first met the nanas, my name was too difficult for them. Mari called me "angel." Lula called me "honey." At first I'd resisted such endearments. Today I was thankful for them. The kind names took the edge off my burden.

"It's something terrible." Mari pointed to my head. "Your aura is deep red."

Since Lula was present, I didn't bother to sugarcoat the truth. "I came to say goodbye, but first I have to ask a favor."

"Goodbye?" they chorused.

"You can't be going on a trip," Lula said. "You just came back."

I rested my hand on the wooden handrail. The wide porch skirted three sides of the house, and I'd spent many happy hours sitting on it. Moisture gathered in the corners of my eyes, but I ordered it back. "Emil is leaving me."

The two women shot up as quickly as rockets. They embraced me with a couple of *"¡Ay, mi'jitas!"* before spewing Spanish in unending streams. They may have lived in the States, but for true emotion, and always for swearing, they used their mother tongue. That way the rest of us—and the neighbors—never knew exactly what they were saying.

I'd expected them to listen patiently as I explained my story. They did not. Instead the porch beams rattled with their movement. They swung their arms as they shouted. Their rising pitches could have been heard at the elementary school several blocks away.

Their attitude needed no translation. To my delight, they were furious. Even Mordy troubled himself to register their reaction before moseying off to a quieter spot.

"How could this happen? What's the matter with that boy?" asked Lula. "How could he turn into such a *cabrón?*"

I couldn't hide a huge smile. No matter what else she said, I knew that she had called her grandson a bastard.

Mari pulled over a chair even though it was so heavy

that she struggled with it. "Sit right here and tell us what happened."

"We want to know everything." Lula indicated a small side table. "Pour yourself some coffee first."

Their ritual was to drink weak coffee all day to avoid napping. By twilight they were wound up, but after dinner they drank decaf with brandy. Some of their younger relatives, including a nephew studying medicine, kept advising them to change their ways. They laughed at such advice by saying they wouldn't die young. That always ended the conversation.

Mari gently placed her hand on my arm. "Don't leave anything out."

I drank a sip of the tepid coffee and suddenly liked the taste of it. Maybe I would copy their drinking habits. "I was hoping you could tell me. Last night I got in late, and Emil was asleep. Come to think of it, maybe he was pretending. Anyway, he went for his usual jog before I woke up. I didn't see him until I got to school. Right before I walked in to teach, he informed me that he was moving out."

I waited while an extra blue streak of Spanish hit the air as a tornado smacking a house. I wished I'd recorded them. When they calmed down, I confessed my confusion. I thought Emil and I had an enviable relationship. I thought we were happy.

"Men," said Lula. *"Cabrones todos."*

"One or two men are worthwhile," said Mari. "Unfortunately, those aren't the ones I met."

Their delightful attitude shouldn't have surprised me after all. Although they were tight-lipped about details, within the family, their reputations preceded them. Emil's favorite theory was that Lula had paid a thug to cut off a piece of her philandering husband, but he misheard the message and offed the guy instead. More cheerful and loving than her sister, Mari might have called the police.

Her husband would have run away too fast and too far to find his way back.

Lula pounded on her armrests. "Men don't leave unless they have another lover picked out. What's going on?"

"I have no idea," I said. "That's one reason I'm here. Do you know anything that I don't?"

They shook their heads slowly.

"I was afraid of that. Anyway, would you mind if I left some of Emil's stuff with you?"

"Throw it away," said Lula.

"I only brought over the most important things. Everything else is sitting outside in my yard."

"As it should be," said Mari.

"You are by far the best thing that has ever happened to that boy," said Lula. "All through high school, it was one girlfriend worse than the last, young women dressed like hookers looking for a free ride. Not a decent one in the bunch. And then he met you. Wasn't it the first day of graduate school?"

"Maybe the second."

Lula rocked extra hard. "You enchanted him right away. It took him a while to give up—what was her name? The one who thinks she's an actress. Irene?"

"Isabel," said Mari. "Joachín's sister."

"Right. Isabel. Never mind. Once he found you—"

"We thought he was set," said Mari. "Finally he was dating a smart woman."

"That might be the problem," Lula said to her sister. "He's finally realized he's not the brains of the business. Who does all the paperwork? Dervla. Who keeps things organized? She does. He can't even organize his socks. Now what's he going to do?"

Mari shook her head. "The question is what has he already done? You're right. There has to be someone else. Otherwise he would never interrupt his comfortable life. But what about World Lingo?"

I set down my cup so that I could make fists. "He claims the school belongs to him since we started it up with his money."

"It was our money," said Mari.

"All ten thousand," said Lula. "And you paid it back. The business belongs to both of you."

"Yes, which is another reason why I blew up this morning. First he calmly says he's moving out, and then he explains that he's willing to keep me on as a teacher. He'll be generous enough to pay me by the hour."

Mari slammed her hand on her thigh. "You're his business partner!"

"Not according to him. Can you believe it?"

"That's not right," Lula said. "Not at all. "You have to get in there and fight. Tell him you don't accept his terms."

"What did you tell your students?" Mari asked.

"Not a darned thing. I was too stunned to think straight. I took my purse and left."

For the next half hour they suggested business strategies. I wanted to consider each one, but before settling down enough to think about teaching, I had to straighten out my personal life. "Mind if I give you Emil's things?"

They murmured approval.

"Since I won't be seeing you anymore—" I reached out to hug Lula, who was closer to me.

I didn't have the chance to finish the sentence. She gave me such a death-grip hug that she might have invented a new form of murder.

"You are part of our family," said Lula. "We won't let go even if you do."

Mari gave me a similarly life-threatening hug. "Everybody loves you! You brighten up family dinners with your stories and good spirit. We'll throw out Emil before we let loose of you."

I stepped back, dangerously close to tears. Perhaps in the long run they would let loose of me after all. Blood always turns out to be thicker than water in the end. But for the moment, which was when I most needed it, I relished the support.

"Let's show her!" cried Mari.

"Indeed!" Lula hurried inside, returning with a basket moments later.

"Sit, sit," said Mari.

I obeyed. "Still trying to read Tarot cards?" They'd worked on the process for a month, but so far their readings hadn't match any of their friends' situations.

Although Mari's eyes were dark, they twinkled. "We're onto something else!" She reached into the basket and pulled out a doll about five inches long.

It wasn't supposed to be pretty. The head was made from a small ball of multi-colored yarn, and the eyes and mouth, which were felt, had been glued on. The body was made from a scrap of green and yellow material that looked vaguely familiar, perhaps a retired tablecloth, and stuffed.

"That was the first one we completed," Lula said. "Show her the others!"

Mari pulled an additional doll from the basket. The head was similar, but its body was pink. The next was smaller and lopsided, its body dark blue.

"Voodoo dolls," I said. Leave it to the nanas to follow magic cards with magic dolls. I applauded their blind enthusiasm.

"It's not voodoo, exactly," Mari said. "But we're harnessing our energy."

I looked between them. They were mischievous cats with feathers sticking out of their mouths. "Are you mad at somebody?"

Mari dangled the dark blue doll. "They can be used for good magic as well."

"But usually they're for revenge," Lula said. "You should know that. We heard New Orleans is crawling with voodoo."

"It's full of voodoo shops," I said slowly. "I always figured the dolls were for tourists. In fact, my cousin bought me one."

"Where's the first doll?" Lula asked her sister. "The one you didn't finish?"

Mari poked around in her basket until she found a doll made from white terrycloth. The limbs and head were discernible, but the face had no features.

"I have just the thing," said Lula. "Wait right there, honey."

Mari pulled out a strawberry pincushion and a hand-written chart. "You see, there are different colors for different things. Blue is for love. Green is for power."

"So if you wanted someone to fall in love—"

"We're not sure yet. We've been googling it. Black is bad, though. We're sure of that much. Red might represent pain."

Lula returned with a photo of Emil and a pair of scissors. She proceeded to cut out his head and measure it against the doll. "Too big." She trimmed it down, cutting off most of his wavy hair and the tips of his ears, and measured again. "This ought to do."

As if swearing at Emil weren't good enough, they were prepared to arm me with the supernatural. I adored the silliness. I needed it.

Mari opened a small container of Elmer's glue. Together they attached Emil's face to the doll and held it until the photo head stuck.

Triumphantly, Mari handed me their creation. Then she selected pins with different colored heads, stuck them onto a piece of scrap paper, and handed them over. "Now you're set."

I wanted to whip out my cell phone and take pictures, but I was afraid of embarrassing them. "Thank you."

Lula picked up the red-headed pin. "When you want to punish Emil—" She jabbed the doll's foot several times.

"That's going to hurt him?"

"It sure will," Lula said.

Mari sensed my skepticism. "Well, it might. Go on. Try it."

"With the red-headed pin?"

Lula handed me the pin. "Why not?"

Indeed. I had nothing to lose by playing along. I gingerly pushed the pin into the doll's head.

"Try again," Mari said. "Use more *umph*."

I did as directed, but this time I enjoyed it. So I did it again, enjoying the action a little more. Then I stabbed the doll's head eight or nine times in quick succession.

"You see!" cried Lula. "Whether it works or not, who cares? It still feels good."

That it did. It felt great. It was nearly as much fun as throwing Emil's possessions out the window.

Mordy chose that moment to come back around and meow approval.

"Whenever you feel mad at Emil, you can punish— let's call him Emilito." Mari giggled. "Don't limit yourself to his head. Take a marker and draw on a—you know!"

"We should have thought of this years ago," Mari said.

"Your husbands?" I asked,

"Among others!"

"*Chingado*," Lula said.

"What?" I asked.

By the time I turned around, the *cabrón* had pulled up in the driveway.

Chapter Three

Mari quickly hid the dolls in the basket. When I tried to hand her Emilito, she wrapped my hand around it. "Oh, no, angel. You keep that."

I didn't have time to argue. I zipped the doll into my purse before Emil made it to the porch.

"Nanas, I . . . . " He saw me and stopped short. How he missed noticing a redhead before that moment, I'll never know. "What are you doing here?"

Mordy growled at him, and Emil took a step back.

"She came to do you a damned favor," said Lula, "not that you deserve it."

"You shouldn't be proud of being a *pendejo*," said Mari.

"Why are you breaking up with the only woman who's ever kept you in line long enough for you to make something of yourself?" asked Lula.

"The only woman who was patient enough to help you create your own business!"

"The only woman you ever brought home who was worth a damn!"

"The only woman with more brains than boobs!"

Emil looked from one nana to the next, completely startled. He had come for compassion, probably. A sounding board, maybe. Free coffee, also possible. He had not come to be yelled at, so I delighted in his confusion.

"I—I—" Emil muttered.

"Who are you sleeping with?" Lula asked.

"No, I—"

Mari took a pillow from behind her back and threw it at him. The pillow missed and landed out in the yard, but the point hit home. "There's someone and we know it."

Emil looked at me. "What did you tell them?"

"Don't look at me! You're the one moving out."

"Why are you here?" Lula asked. "Who wants to see you?"

"You should leave right now," Mari said, "before we really get mad."

"I thought . . . well, maybe an aspirin . . . ."

Lula stood on her tiptoes to gain her full height of five-nine. "Go!"

"But—"

"We don't want to hear it," said Mari.

"Some of your stuff is in my trunk," I said. "If you want your clothes, you'll want to get over to my place before some homeless guy takes everything."

"But—"

"Or not. See if I care. You're here why?"

He looked at his grandmother and then at his great-aunt, but neither offered a comforting smile. "Nanas, I thought I might stop by for dinner later."

Lula crossed her arms over her chest. Mari did the same.

"We're going out," Mari announced. "Tomorrow night too. And the night after that."

For a moment Emil stood motionless as if waiting for the dream sequence to end.

It did not. Sheepishly, he backed off. The three of us stood, arms crossed, as he transferred an assortment of bags from my trunk to his own. Then he sped off, nearly whacking a pair of pedestrians in the process.

Mari wiped her hands in the air. "He made a big mistake. Very big."

"The biggest in his life." Lula turned to me. "But don't think that changes anything between us. Would you please join us for dinner? We're not actually going out."

I smiled with unexpected satisfaction. The nanas represented the strongest form of female solidarity. I treasured everything about them right down to their crazy dolls. "I'll come another time. I appreciate your offer more than I can say. But right now I need to rescue my teaching materials from the office while Emil isn't there."

They nodded their approval.

"How can we help you?" asked Mari.

I loved the Arellano system. There was almost always some relative or friend who could help out, no matter what you needed, no matter your request. On the rare occasion that they didn't know someone appropriate, they called someone else who would have the right contacts.

"I might need help changing my locks."

Lula addressed her sister. "What time does Orlando get home today?"

"Usually around three-thirty."

"You don't think he'll mind?" I asked. "Emil is his only brother."

"Orlando will be pleased to help," Lula said. "We'll send him over as soon as possible."

The nanas made me promise to return within a couple of days, which I readily agreed to do. I made a last attempt to return the doll, but they insisted I hang onto it. The gesture was as ridiculous as it was good natured. As soon as I got home, just for fun, I would give Emilito a few more hearty jabs.

I would savor each one more than the last.

***

I was cramming my new references books—all the ones Emil wouldn't be using—onto the bottom shelf of my bedroom bookcase when the doorbell rang. I looked over the balcony to be sure the visitor wasn't selling anything, but then I grinned like a naughty child who had been caught letting the pet Collie into the fancy living room. Joachín was on my front doorstep.

"Go around to the back," I yelled. "Be right down."

As I slid past the bar, I waved at the dog-cat doll. I unlocked the back door to admit the slim, twenty-three-year-old. He was as lithe as if he spent all morning doing yoga exercises, and his ready smile suggested he had a joke for every occasion. Even though he wore sweat shorts and a ragged tank top, he would have been welcome at the most exclusive disco. Given wavy black hair and sky-blue eyes, he might have been a model. He was that good-looking. Better yet, he never let on that he knew it.

He gave me a brief hug. "Orlando has a big test tomorrow, so he sent me."

Of course. The Arellano way. You can't help? You get someone who can.

I'd always loved spending time with Joachín anyway, but now we shared a strange kinship. He too was an honorary Arellano, an honorary nephew. At the time Isabel started dating Emil, she was often assigned to babysit her younger brother. She would drag Joachín over to the nanas' house with her. He was a year older than Orlando, but the boys became close friends. By the time Emil broke up with Isabel to date me, Joachín was a regular part of the family.

"Thanks for coming," I said. "Something to drink?"

"Let me change the lock first. Nana Lula said you're no handyman."

As I sighed, my shoulders drooped.

"I'm sorry. That didn't come out right."

"It came out fine." I'd relied on Emil for the carpentry and gardening as well. "I'm not much of a house anything." I handed him the set of locks I'd picked up at Ace.

Joachín examined the package, nodding. "Have a Phillips screwdriver?"

"If I knew what it was, I might know if I had one."

He grinned and fetched a toolbox from his car. Within minutes, he disassembled my current lock, slid the new one in place with the slightest help from me, and tightened the screws, explaining each step as he did so.

"Did your dad teach you all this stuff?"

"Some of it. The rest I learned from on-the-job training down at the theatre."

"I thought TTC hired you as an actor."

The Tucson Theatre Company was a small local outfit that promoted theatre within the community by offering classes for kids and modest ticket prices for shows. The actors received a stipend, but most held day jobs.

He tightened the final screw. "Between shows, they pay me to build their sets."

We walked around to the front so that he could repeat the process on the front door. I felt mean for acting so quickly, but I didn't want Emil barging in whenever he felt like it. He would have no reason to return inside the house, and he'd already liberated his possessions from the front yard.

Changing the locks was an excuse. I wasn't worried that Emil would try to sneak in. I needed to prove to myself that I'd made a choice, and this was an easy way to prove it to myself.

Joachín removed the old equipment as if the job were routine. He whistled a tune, maybe a salsa number, as if he hadn't noticed the seismic shift in my life. Around the Arellano dinner table, he'd always been one of my favorites, and I sat next to him as often as possible. Not only did he liven the atmosphere, but he'd read almost as many Irish plays as I had.

He wiggled the old door handle out of its socket. "Sorry to hear about Emil."

"Thanks."

"I mean it. He was lucky to have you."

I handed him the replacement lock. "I thought we were lucky to have one another, but somehow I was wrong."

"Breakups are never that easy, but then, neither are relationships. Hold the lock?"

As I steadied the new piece, he inserted the long screw and tamed it with a few quick twists.

"Emil took me off guard," I said. "I should have sensed that something was wrong, don't you think?"

"That's what we always think afterwards. Then we make lists of our mistakes: the odd comments we overlooked, the excuses we dismissed at the time."

"I feel like such an idiot."

"Emil should have talked to you at least. Never mind. You have to move on."

"You sound like a marriage counselor."

"Do I? I've had bad breakups too." He inserted the Phillips — at least now I knew what it was — and tightened the last screw. "You know the nanas' saying: *Mejor sola* — "

" — *que mal acompañada*. Better alone than in bad company. Even I know enough Spanish to remember that." The nanas used the phrase every time an unwitting younger relative suggested they look for boyfriends.

"It's a phrase to live by." He tested the lock, which worked perfectly. "You should be set."

"So to speak."

He packed up and closed his toolbox. I walked with him as he deposited it in the trunk of his perky blue Kia.

Then I panicked. Once Joachín left, I'd be alone for the first time I could remember, which was like having a whole night to review my shortcomings. I nodded toward the house. "Can I get you a drink? Coffee? Beer?"

"I'm a boring drinker."

"Water?"

"Sure."

I led him through the decimated living room straight through to the kitchen. Then I prepared two glasses of ice water and sat next to him at the bar.

"How are you really?" Joachín asked.

In high school I'd had a memorable breakup. Two more as an undergraduate. Each time I'd gone through cycles of anger and sadness and loss before making sense of things. "Ask me a few days from now. I'll have a better idea by then. Right now I don't know how to think things through."

"I can't blame you. But you know what? Never mind about Emil. Nana Mari said you might need a job."

For a nanosecond I wanted to curl my fists and yell at the nanas for sharing so much information. Then I realized that Joachín had not been sent over as a locksmith, but as a life coach.

The first night Emil took me over for a family dinner at the nanas,' they'd spent the main course arguing that Mari's daughter Flor, recently divorced, should move back in with them. Flor tearfully insisted otherwise. I assumed the sisters were stubborn and commandeering until I learned that the divorcée was a step above bankruptcy. The nanas had a big enough house, and they thought they offered the most logical solution.

By now I knew better than to judge the nanas' advice too quickly. They kept out of the way when they could. When they needed to step in, they did that too, sometimes laterally, as was happening now. I should have asked for more dolls so that I could send positive vibrations their way.

"Sorry," Joachín said. "I was supposed to be subtle."

I clinked my glass against his. "With me subtlety is neither expected nor appreciated. I do indeed need a job. Emil kicked me out of his business, or maybe I quit. I'm not sure which it was. And I'm not sure I'm leaving without a fight."

"You might need a lawyer. You could call Cousin Ronny."

"He would side with Emil. Besides, doesn't he do real estate law?"

"Not very well, if you can believe what he claims he paid in taxes last year."

Ronny was the only family member who was a lawyer, but Orlando would be starting law school in the fall. That wouldn't be soon enough to help me any.

"I don't know if I want to run a business with Emil or not," I said. "This breakup came out of nowhere."

"He might change his mind. He ought to."

"About me? Doesn't matter. I have a strict rule. Only allow a person to break your heart once. After that, erase him from your life. Which is why I'm not sure I want to work with him even though, well, I thought I had my career mapped out. For the time being, it would be great to have options up my sleeve. What have you got?"

"The seamstress for the theatre needs wrist surgery, so she's out of commission for a while. Nana Mari said you're great with a sewing machine."

Mari exaggerated. My formal training consisted of classes I was forced to take in high school where I made ugly garments I never, ever wore. Thanks to Flor's dire finances, though, I'd discovered an aptitude for making Halloween costumes. By now I routinely outfitted the youngest Arellanos: princess dresses, usually, or monster suits. I had as much fun as the kids, finding the material, choosing the design, adding unexpected feathers or buttons or sashes. Not only were my creations pleasantly unique, but by accident I found that I could accurately guess sizes without taking measurements.

"I would love to design your costumes. What do you need?"

"Our new play takes place in England in the 1950s. We started rehearsals this week."

"Tell me when you want me down at the theatre, and I'll come right over." I held my arms out wide. "All of a sudden my schedule is empty."

"Dervla . . . ." He stared so intently through his water glass that I knew he wanted to ask something indiscreet. I could have prompted him, but instead I waited. "Is this your first major breakup?"

He wasn't prying. He was concerned.

"I've had plenty of ruined relationships, but I'm usually the one to bail. I've been with Emil longer than anyone else. Don't laugh, but we were so tight together that I assumed he was the one. Growing old and strolling into the sunset and all that. Silly, huh?"

"I'm not about to laugh."

"One minute you have a solid relationship, and the next you're tossing Old Spice out the window."

Joachín swiveled toward the front window, which was above the couch in the living room.

"You tossed cologne out the window?"

"I tossed out everything. The postman was a bit surprised."

Joachín's blues eyes twinkled. "You didn't hurt anybody?"

"I played soccer, not baseball, although I would have happily aimed at Emil's head if he'd been here instead of teaching my classes. I've never broken up with anyone who was living with me. That's why this feels so different."

Joachín poked at an ice cube, and we both watched it shoot to the bottom of the glass and come back up again.

"Anyone on your horizon right now?" I asked. I couldn't remember the last time Joachín brought a girl to the nanas,' but I vaguely remembered a couple of crushes he'd told us about the year or so before.

"Maybe I haven't found the right girl yet. And you were taken."

"Very funny." Bless his heart. If Joachín wanted to make me feel better, he'd already succeeded.

He imitated a roller coaster with his hand. "Of course, I saw what Isabel went through."

I hadn't asked my former partner about his previous relationship. Emil and I had mutually agreed to move forward. Bits about Isabel circled back to us though, like dandelion seeds that swirled through the air without hitting the ground. "Emil said they fought a lot."

"Try all the time. Isabel ordered him around and got angry when he didn't do what she wanted. He gave in because . . . ." Joachín made a circle with his left middle finger and thumb and stuck his right index finger through the hole.

"When they weren't having sex, they were fighting," I said.

"Yes. Constant ups and downs."

And ins and outs. "Speaking of anger, check this out." I retrieved Emilito from my purse and dangled it in front of him. "Guess who gave me this."

"The nanas are into voodoo now?"

"They're playing around." I set Emilito next to my dog-cat, and they hugged one another like magnets. Must have been something in the yarn.

He picked the dolls up one by one, looked them over, and set them back down. "They're decorations?"

"Oh, no. They have a purpose." I wiggled the red-headed pin out of the piece of scrap paper. "The nanas realize it's all made up, but never mind. Basically, their advice was, 'Stick a pin in it. You'll feel better.' Watch this!" I jabbed Emilito in the head several times.

"Hey, don't stick yourself!"

Point well taken. I'd nearly drawn my own blood.

Joachín replaced the dolls. "Give yourself some time. You're pretending to be tough, but breaking up is a big deal."

I hated it when younger people expertly explained your situation to you. Joachín might have been seven years older than I rather than the other way around.

"It's okay to be upset," he said.

"I am upset."

"It's okay to let it out."

I grabbed Emilito and jabbed him three more times. "Right now I'm too mad."

"I know."

He stood behind me, put his arms around me, and squeezed. "Whenever you need something, let me know."

I patted his hand. "I will. You already helped me a lot."

"It was just a lock. But listen, I have lines to learn, so I better take off."

I let him out the back door. "Thanks for the help. And the job tip. And the chat."

"Anytime."

I carefully locked the door behind him. I poured myself a shot of Jameson as a defense against the queen-sized bed that would suddenly be both cold and huge. It would take more than one night to get Emil out of my system, but that's what I would do. I would get him out of my head as soon as possible. I would make sure he stayed out, too.

Chapter Four

The next morning the phone rang as I worked my way down the stairs. A series of five framed photos of Emil and me had graced the wall the day before, but I'd ripped my ex-lover from four of them.

"What's wrong, Nana Mari?" They never called in the morning. They stayed up late watching old movies and slept in until at least ten.

"We have a bit of an issue over here," she said slowly. "Could you come over?"

She sounded sluggish. Orlando would be at school, which meant the nanas were alone. "Are you all right?"

"Yes, angel."

"Nana Lula?"

"We're fine, but if you could come over, it would help us out."

The nanas rarely called in favors by phone. They were more effective in person. Of course, they knew my schedule was suddenly wide open. "Do you need me to pick up something from the pharmacy?"

"Just come."

I ripped Emil from the last photo and replaced the frame on the wall. Since the nanas only lived a few short blocks away, I threw on a sweatshirt, strapped on my helmet, and unlocked my bicycle from its spot on the back landing. During the entire eight-minute ride, I tried to remember any other time that Nana Mari sounded less than spry.

Emil got to them, I thought as I ran a stop sign. He begged and begged until they agreed to talk to me. Wouldn't I relent? Wouldn't I forgive him? I was gratified that he understood his mistake so quickly, but why would I consider taking him back? Since he'd been sleeping around, he wouldn't even be safe. Uff. We had sex the night before I'd gone to New Orleans. So I cheated, he would say. So what? I pedaled harder. Take him back? Not for any reason.

I had nearly reached the nanas' when I turned and went around the block instead. I needed a few more moments to prepare myself to meet up with the weasel who was probably at his nanas' right now, waiting for me, maybe with flowers, to tell me how darned sorry he was.

Steeling myself, I vowed to keep some things firmly in mind. He'd betrayed me. Unfairly stolen the business. Acted miffed that I was sitting on his nanas' doorstep when he'd gone to them for comfort. Cheater! As soon as I returned home, I would draw an itty-bitty penis on Emilito and prick it until the stuffing came out.

As I went yet another block out of my way, I considered going straight home. I was disappointed the nanas hadn't supported me a hundred percent. I thought they respected sisterhood a bit more than that, but honestly, as I'd realized the day before, blood is thicker than water. You can count on that.

I reached Tucson Boulevard, still unsure of my direction. But I would have to confront Emil eventually. At a dinner, at one of his niece's or nephew's events, at Safeway. I might as well get that first awkward meeting overwith. The second one wouldn't be as bad. The third one even better, and so forth and so on. Seeing him again would be like doing any other chore. Like mopping the floor. Buying new underwear. Doing taxes. Yes, that was it. Emil was a 1040. No matter how long you put things off, in the end you got out the Pine-Sol, shucked out twenty bucks for a mediocre bra, and popped your return in the mail on April Fourteenth at 11:59.

I would pretend it was April and get past it. I would move on as quickly and efficiently as possible. That was by far the best plan. When I reached Tucson Boulevard, I peddled south to Third Street and turned west. I would comply with the nanas' request to come, but I would leave the premises as soon as possible. Even though they'd turned on me, they would understand. They wouldn't stand in my way. Out of a misguided sense of loyalty, they'd summoned me on Emil's behalf. So be it. That didn't mean I could be tamed.

I waved as I rode up the drive. No matter how angry I was, I would be civil. I could explain later, maybe to Flor, how disappointed I was. I merely had to survive the next few minutes. I parked my bike at the side of the house and joined the nanas on the porch. They rose to hug me as if nothing had changed, but if they could act, I could too. I'd specialized in contemporary Irish drama. Certainly I'd learned something from watching all those miserable characters.

"Have a little coffee," said Nana Lula. "And some cookies."

Caffeine and sugar, their basic bribes. Whatever. I chose a mug with a smiling Fox Terrier on it and snatched up a *bandera*, a tri-colored Mexican sugar cookie. They came from La Estrella Bakery, and they were always delicious.

The nanas wore their normal housecoats, but Lula still wore slippers. Mari hadn't painted on her eyebrows. Their eyes held no sparkle. Maybe the voodoo business wasn't going so good. Ouch. I knew better even when thinking to myself. Going so *well*. "So where is he?"

Nana Lula's eyes were moist. It was a pretty good act. "Emil wasn't with you this morning?"

I assumed I hadn't heard right. The question was ridiculous. "I threw him out, remember? You sent Joachín over to change the locks, which I really appreciated."

"I told you," Mari told her sister. Next came a stream of Spanish expletives.

I tried to peer through the front door, but the screen was too dark. "Emil?"

The nanas looked at me questioningly and spewed a few more Spanish words.

"What's going on?" I asked.

I looked anxiously between them. They were old enough that dementia might be creeping in, but it wouldn't happen all at once, and not to both of them at the same time.

"He wasn't with you at all last night?" Lula said slowly.

"Of course not."

"He didn't call?" asked Mari.

As usual I'd turned off the ringer before going to bed, and I'd forgotten to turn it on again that morning. I took out my cell and checked the call log, but the last one had come from Keevah, who was checking on my flight status. How could so much happen in such little time?

I sank into my regular chair. "The last time I saw Emil was right here."

The nanas conferred at length in Spanish. This was unusual, too. Usually they conferred in two or three words.

"Was he in an accident?"

"There's no easy way to explain," said Mari. "Emil's in jail."

Usually he was a careful driver, but on extreme occasions, he had more Coronas than he could handle. Since Coronas weren't that strong, he had to drink quite a few to achieve a buzz. "A DUI, huh? Serves him right."

They shook their heads.

"Worse?"

"Worse," said Lula.

"Totaled the car?"

As if in pain, Lula closed her eyes.

"He—he hit someone? Oh, God. Did they die?"

"Tell her," said Lula.

"He's in jail on suspicion of murder."

It would have happened near the university. At night students strutted across the street wearing dark clothing. I'd had several close calls myself, more than once on my bicycle.

"He only hit one person, I hope?"

"No cars," said Mari.

I'd never seen him get drunk in public, much less start a fight, but there was always a first time. "Bar brawl?"

Lula put her hand to her head as if to soften a headache. Mari clasped her hands.

"Out with it," I said. "You're scaring me."

"Do you know a Miss Twinkle Witherbottom?" Mari asked.

I laughed. "Nice stage name."

"No?"

"Trust me, a name like that one I would have remembered."

"Evidently that's Emil's new girlfriend," said Mari.

The louse. He hadn't wasted any time setting up a new squeeze. I wondered how many months he'd been planning his escape. Was that why his Christmas present to me—a better frying pan, of all stupid things—was so impersonal? I'd expected a bracelet or at least a pretty blouse. A frying pan. And I never cook.

"Okay, I'm ready. What's so special about this new girlfriend? Great body? Fancy car? Rich family?" I was dead set against a daily run, but I biked and lifted weights and did squats. I was too athletic to have curves where, purportedly, most men wanted them. I had a regular car, a beige Chevy Prizm just like all the other ones on the road. My parents, with whom I had an uneasy relationship, never gave me any money, but they never asked for any either.

Mari rubbed her thumb and index finger on something she picked up from the table. When the object caught a glint of sun, I knew what it was: her Oaxacan worry stone. The smooth quartz piece was supposed to help her through emergencies. "I'm afraid it's serious."

The last time I'd witnessed her fingering the stone was when her grandson, a baby at the time, caught such a bad flu the doctor wasn't sure he would pull through.

Lula picked up a worry stone as well. They worked their fingers as furiously as young texters.

"Emil got her pregnant," I said slowly. "How do you like that? We'd agreed to wait for another three or four years, until World Lingo was firmly established."

The nanas rubbed harder. I noticed lines under Mari's eyes; she hadn't used moisturizer or makeup either.

"Stop torturing me and tell me what happened."

Mari shifted the stone to her other hand. "This morning someone murdered Twinkle in her own bed."

I shot to my feet out of sheer surprise. "There's a serial killer on the loose?"

"No," they murmured.

"She was shot?"

"No," they choroused.

"Blunt object?"

Lula drew her hand under her chin. "Evidently somebody cut right through her pretty little neck, maybe with a saw. Well, I'm sure it wasn't pretty by the time they finished."

I shuddered as I saw white sheets, splotches of blood on otherwise pristine Ikea furniture, and a head hanging to one side of the pillow, half detached.

"Someone murdered this Twinkle?"

"Yes."

"In her own house."

"Yes."

I sank back down and picked up my coffee cup. I didn't mean to be callous, but I didn't have the patience to worry about the whole world. "That's awful and everything, but so what?"

Mari teared up. Lula reached for tissues.

"Well?"

"Emil spent the night with her," Lula mumbled.

"And the police think Emil did it," Mari continued.

Emil murder someone? Out of the question. Jerk, yes. Killer, no. Plus the logistics made no sense. "If Emil spent the night with her, how could anyone—oh. Around dawn he went out for a jog."

"Yes," cried Lula.

"Meanwhile, someone busted in and sawed into her neck," finished Mari.

When we started dating, Emil and I made love several times before he spent the night. That first time, we were too distracted to relax. We didn't know how to hold one another or which direction to face. I finally fell into such a deep sleep that I didn't hear Emil silently rise and leave. I was so angry to wake up alone that our first night together might have been our last. I was pondering a range of snarky responses when he bounded up the stairs, left a sweaty kiss on my cheek, and hopped into the shower. He had told me that he was a daily morning jogger; I was naïve enough to think that he made exceptions.

"This morning he went out for his jog," said Lula. "The neighbors reported loud screaming. The police arrived and found Twinkle's body. As soon as Emil arrived, they arrested him."

"That louse is no murderer."

"The police are sure he did it," said Mari. "He explained that this morning. He was allowed to make a call, and he chose to call us."

Emil's mother lived in San Francisco, Orlando was in his twenties, and his sister Miranda lived with three small children. The nanas were the logical choice.

"He asked us to contact Ronny, but he hasn't called back yet," Mari said.

I accidentally snapped a cookie in two. Pieces flew across the porch. Mordy inspected and then dismissed them.

Lula clasped her hands. "The good news is that her children were spending the night with her parents."

Mari genuflected.

"I'm so sorry to hear all this," I said. "I don't even know what to think. The situation is crazy, of course. But why did you call me?"

"The police say he's guilty," said Lula.

I couldn't blame them. The story sounded ridiculous: He spent the night with a lover, left her in the morning, and stayed away long enough that someone sneaked into the house and executed her. It would sound improbable to the most open-minded juror, but it made perfect sense to someone who had suffered years of Emil's jogging patterns.

The killer would have had between thirty-eight and forty-two minutes. Plenty of time to scoot in and kill someone if you knew what you were doing and were waiting for the opportunity.

"We need you to help Emil," said Mari.

"You want me to be a character witness. After all Emil has done to me, that's a lot to ask, but of course I'll do it." I wouldn't want to, but fair was fair. They guy was merely a coward.

Lula leaned so far forward that she briefly lost her balance. "We were hoping you might do more than that. You know him better than anybody."

Twenty-four hours earlier, I would have agreed. "As it turns out, I know nothing."

Lula picked up her coffee cup but then realized it was empty. "Neither do we. But you know his business. His friends. His contacts. We want you to investigate."

"Me? That's a job for the police."

"They're sure he's guilty."

"They'll never be able to prove it."

The nanas said nothing.

"He's harmless. Right?" I asked. "The police will figure that out."

Lula refilled her cup while Mari bit into a *bandera* as if it might break a tooth.

Three bicycles swooshed by.

"My grandson has been a *pendejo*," Lula said. "You don't have to tell me that. But he's no killer."

"Surely the police —"

"We'll pay you," said Mari. "By the hour. Or however you like. I'm as mad at the little *cabrón* as you are, but we can't let him stay in jail. Not for something he didn't do."

"But —"

"Eventually I'll forgive him," Mari said. "You will too."

I couldn't believe I was having such a crazy conversation. The nanas were delusional. They thought I had some weird power. They thought I could magically put my ear to the earth and conjure up what happened and find proof at the same time. I admired their optimism, but I wasn't the girl for the job even if they wanted me to be.

"I can't possibly help him," I said.

"Sure, you can," said Lula. "You're both intelligent and organized. You're far enough outside the family to perceive it better than the rest of us can. We'll help you, of course. You tell us what to do, and we'll bend over backwards, well, not with my back, but we'll do everything we can. But we need you. We don't know much about the Internet. We can get around town, but we're not fast."

"What about Amaia? Let her come down here and make herself useful."

After Emil's father disappeared down into Mexico, presumably with another woman and another family, his mother had moved to San Francisco as if to get a healthy distance away from the family. By then Emil was an undergraduate. Orlando had started high school, so he refused to go with her. He'd opted to stay behind with the nanas, which was probably the way Amaia wanted it.

"I don't want to worry her," Lula said. "She had a heart attack a few years ago, remember? We don't want her to have another one."

Wrong. The nanas should have called and gotten her on the next plane. She'd made a career of ignoring her kids, so it was time for her to step up.

"This is her son we're talking about," I said. "She'll want to help. She'll feel terrible if she doesn't get the chance."

Lula shook her head. "Do you know how many forty-year-olds die of heart attacks? A lot. Don't think I'm going to cause my daughter to have one."

The skimpy excuse suggested an ulterior motive. Maybe the nanas were afraid Amaia wouldn't come. I'd only met her twice, and she'd impressed me with her general lack of involvement with anyone in the family, including her mother.

"What about Flor?" Mari's daughter wasn't a responsible person either, but she lived in town.

"She'll fall apart as soon as we tell her, and then she'll be useless," said Mari. "I love my daughter, but she's weak."

"Miranda has both her hands full," said Lula. "No husband, two jobs, and three kids."

"Orlando has to keep up with school," said Mari. "He's worked too hard to throw his last semester to the wind."

"What about Joachín?" I asked. "He's probably as organized as I am, and he doesn't hate Emil the way I do right now."

Lula leaned forward. "We love Joachín. We're sure he'll help you. But he's a man."

"So?"

"He'll never understand how Twinkle thought," said Mari. "You can."

"Why would I want to?"

"So you can figure out who killed her," Lula said. "That's the only way to clear Emil."

"Angel, we're begging you," Mari said. "And we'll never, ever forget how much we're in your debt."

Before I could protest, they swamped me with full-body hugs.

I spent the next ten minutes assuring them that everything would be all right even though I didn't believe it myself. I would be happy to try to find some leads that I would turn over to the police, and then the officers would release Emil and everything would be all right again.

By the time I pedaled home, I felt the weight of the Arellano household upon my shoulders. How could my whole life have derailed while I was in New Orleans? Everything I knew was upside down. Worst of all, when what I most needed was to forget about Emil, I would have to spend my time thinking about him.

I wasn't sure he would appreciate it.

Chapter Five

I went straight to the police station only to learn that not only could I not see Emil, but he couldn't call me. I had to fill out a background check and pay for it if I wanted to hear from him. By then I realized another problem: no one would be arriving to teach the Spanish classes or the English classes, and the students deserved a warning. I'd barely walked in the door when the office phone rang, and I seized it more quickly than Mordy bit unwanted visitors.

"Hello?"

"Dervla! I've been allowed to call my office phone, but I have to be quick."

Emil. He sounded like his normal self. Maybe he was in such shock that his body wasn't registering his actual predicament.

"I spoke to the nanas. What happened?"

"I don't know! I went out for a run!"

"You spent the night with Twinkle Toes, and your new squeeze was fine and dandy when you left." I hadn't planned on attacking him, but the words skipped right out before I could stop them.

"Dervla, now isn't the time to —"

"Right, right. Go on."

"She was sleeping solidly when I went out for my run. When I got back, the police were there, and she was dead."

I sat behind the desk. "Why did you ask the nanas to call Ronny?"

"He was the only lawyer I could think of. He must have friends. I'm going to need someone fast. Maybe you could help find someone?"

"Maybe. What else?"

"Maybe you could fetch my car from Twinkle's place?"

"If the police let me, you mean?"

"It's on the street opposite the house. They didn't ask about it and I didn't tell them. I would feel better if you went for it."

"The police never asked how you got to Twinkle's?"

"Sure they did. But she'd picked me up."

"What?"

"It's a long story, but see, my car was already at her house. Then we went downtown together, but—"

"Never mind the details. Address?"

"She's on, I mean, she was on, Seventh Street between Treat and Forgeus. I forget the number, but you'll see the car. South side of the street. White house with green shutters. There are two houses next to one another with carports. Hers is the house on the left."

"I'll look into it."

"Thanks. And thanks for teaching, too."

"Teaching? No. I came here to warn the students there wouldn't be any classes. I was rather fond of most of them, you know."

"No classes!"

"Your problem. I don't work here anymore."

"Dervla, I need you to run the school for me! I need you to cover all your English classes and find someone to teach Spanish!"

I placed both elbows on the desk as I relished my prime opportunity. Not only did the police have Emil right where they wanted him, but so did I. "Run the school? Why would I do that? It's not my school. You made that clear."

"But, but I need you!"

Antonio waved and continued into the classroom.

"This business is rightfully half mine. You can't hire me by the hour."

"But it's my business given that—"

"Stop. Our business. Fifty-fifty."

"That's not fair!"

From the bottom desk drawer, I pulled out the notebook where I'd listed the classes we'd offered over the past two and a half years. I flipped to the first pages.

"It's exactly fair. You may have arranged for a loan, but every single quarter I've taught one or two more classes than you have. How do you make up for that?"

"I ran extra errands. I did extra cleaning."

"You cleaned for five minutes while I worked five times longer than you did."

Lydia waved happily and went in to join Antonio.

Why was I thinking fifty-fifty?

"The time is immaterial given that—"

"No matter whom you're jumping in bed with, this is still our business. To be fair, from now on we're splitting the profits sixty-forty, my favor. Or I walk out."

"You can't! Not after I've worked so hard!"

"Don't think you can run me in circles, Emil Arellano. You're not in a position to argue. I'll run your business, somehow. I'll find someone to teach Spanish and cover my regular sessions. But the school is more mine than yours, take it or leave it however you want."

"I'm getting the high sign," he said softly. "I have to end the call."

I didn't believe him for a moment. More importantly, I was having fun. A wrongful accusation couldn't have come at a better time. It was almost as if some higher force had planned it for me. "Sixty-forty or nothing, and I better have your word, and I better have it now."

"You can't expect me to make a smart decision under these circumstances!"

Lily and Ginger arrived with Ahmed.

"You haven't made smart decisions for some months now, as it turns out. Sneaking around behind my back. Lying like a coward! Sixty-forty, I don't care either way."

He actually paused. Even though he was in a tighter spot than a fireman on a broken tree branch, he feigned control.

"Tick-tock," I said. "You decide."

I heard grumbling in the background; maybe he wasn't lying about ending the call.

"Your choice, Emil."

"Have it your way, but keep the business going! And get me out of here."

Julio and Nayela went in with Yessica.

"Should I teach today's classes first?"

He hung up without answering. That much I could pardon him for. But now that I was a business partner again, it was in my best interest to do the best for our students. I pulled out the phone and called the nanas. When they complained that they'd never been trained as teachers, I complained that I'd never been trained as an investigator. They agreed to come in time to cover the next class.

Then I hung up and walked into mine.

***

I assured my students that I'd made a quick recovery from my sudden illness the day before and smiled through my lessons. I half listened as the nanas taught Spanish next door. They'd lied to me. Training or no, they were naturals. The students laughed and sputtered Spanish. What more could we want?

As soon as the last students left, I drove straight home, switched my medium-weight jacket for a lighter one, and walked toward Twinkle's house. The modest bungalow was a white stucco guarded by cypress trees. Bricks bordered the tailored lawn. Queen's Wreath vines, dead at this time of the year, clung to the wire fence that separated her property from her neighbors on the east. On the west, a modest carport sheltered a sedan. A red tricycle lay on its side in front of the picture window.

Bingo. No wonder Twinkle had gone after Emil. She was a single mom with at least two kids and maybe more. Emil had a moderate business and no responsibilities except to a partner he wasn't married to. He was perfect. Trainable.

I strolled past Emil's car without stopping. Twinkle's yard swarmed with police. Two patrol cars jammed the driveway, and another hugged the sidewalk. Officers entered and exited the front door. For a mad moment I considered jumping into Emil's car and taking off fast before anyone noticed, but the sun afforded complete visibility, and I had no reason to take risks for a two-timer.

I also considered waiting around a bit for the police to clear out, but there was no hurry about the car. The police were too busy with everything else. Although Emil had talked about taking care of the paperwork, the hand-me-down vehicle was in his mother's name. The neighbors were probably used to seeing it.

Aside from the beehive of activity at Twinkle's, the area was tranquil. The one-story houses were   not complicated. Typically residential for mid-town, the lots were big enough for the properties to breathe. Twinkle and her neighbor shared a carport, but twenty feet lay between their dwellings.

The yards were big enough to allow for creativity but small enough to be manageable. While Twinkle's yard was strewn with toys, her neighbors' was a pristine rock garden bordered by carefully trimmed bushes. The surrounding properties were similar. Filled with rocks, mesquite, or palo verde trees, they blended with the desert environment.

It was the kind of neighborhood filled with regular people with regular jobs. The younger ones rose early and went straight to work. The retirees had lived on the same block for years but kept to themselves.

Until they heard screaming.

On a block this ordinary, the neighbors should have noticed something. An unfamiliar car. A person dressed strangely. It was impossible that a madman—with a saw!—could sneak into Twinkle's house, carry out a horrible act, and leave undetected. At least one neighbor would know something.

It would be up to me to find out what.

Chapter Six

That evening I was clicking on yet another cheerful picture on Twinkle's Facebook page when my cell buzzed. Since it was Joachín, I picked up. "Have you heard?" I asked.

"Yes, but the news hasn't sunk in yet. You busy?"

"I'm trying to learn about Twinkle Witherbottom."

"Need help?"

"Well—"

He knocked on the back door.

"If you were already outside, why didn't you say so?" I asked as I admitted him.

"I didn't want to bother you if you wanted to be alone."

We exchanged our usual hugs. Never mind that he had invited himself. I was glad to have an ally. Freshly showered and shaved, he smelled so good I wanted to ask what brand of aftershave he used. The question seemed too personal.

"Can you believe they think Emil killed somebody?" he asked.

I liked the way Joachín's eyebrows scrunched up because they suggested total chaos. I'd never noticed before. "I don't know what to think. Come help me with this."

I led him to the bar and pointed to my laptop.

"Behold my rival," I said.

Although Twinkle had included a huge picture of herself, one that imitated studio quality with poorer lighting, she looked completely plain. Small nose, uneven ears, nondescript brown hair, short neck, dull brown eyes—and she had something more than I did? Not even the necklace around her neck, an old-fashioned cameo, held any appeal. How had Emil fallen for her? Or maybe he'd been snatched.

"Tell me I'm much better looking than she is," I said.

"No comparison. You're gorgeous."

"This is no time for hyperbole."

"I'm not kidding. Besides, she's overweight."

I would have called her medium. "That's highly subjective."

He pointed to a shot where Twinkle wore a tank top. "Look at her arms. You can tell. Extra layers all the way down."

In Mexican circles, layers were appreciated. I learned that the day I met Emil's mother. She followed "It's nice to meet you" with "You're too thin to ever be sexy." I had never figured out whether she was making a slur, giving a compliment, or stating a fact. Maybe all three.

"Emil fell for her somehow," I said. "Big breasts, do you think?"

Joachín's face was too caramel to redden, but his neck muscles tensed. Ignoring the question, he reached over me and tapped on her gallery of pictures. "Two small children."

"Yes." If the pictures were current, there was a toddler and a three or four-year-old. "The usual set of girlfriends. A vacation in Rocky Point."

Joachín scrolled through her profile. Associate's Degree from Pima Community College. Employment? None listed, although people weren't always honest. Hobbies? Hanging out with her friends and taking her children to the park.

"He left you for her?"

I shrugged. What did she have that I couldn't see? "The nanas want me to snoop around. They're afraid the police won't try since there's so much evidence against Emil."

"It looks bad. But if there's anything I can do, say so."

"Glad you asked. I was hoping you could cover some of Emil's Spanish classes."

He scooted a half inch back. "My Spanish is so-so."

"You'll be fine for Spanish 1. We can't expect the nanas to do everything. They're spry for their ages, but we don't want to wear them out. So if you could hop on over to the school tomorrow morning—"

"Dervla, we can discuss this later. I stopped by so we could go to the theatre together. They're expecting you at seven."

I checked the wall clock where a lucky black Irish cat pointed his long paw to the ten. "Now?"

"I assured Tommy you'd be happy to work with us."

A mere twenty-four hours earlier, I'd needed a job. Suddenly I had three or four, depending on whether you counted school administration.

"They're hoping you'll come take measurements."

Joachín had gone to the trouble of setting me up with a job I no longer needed, but I wanted to open doors, not close them. The thought of spending the evening with Joachín and his theatre friends was a lot more enticing than spending the night alone.

I fished a tape measure out of the cabinet beneath the bar. "Let's go, then. But I have a condition."

He smiled. "Don't tell me you need another lock changed."

I snapped the tape measure at him. The plastic red coil *pinged* as it tapped his arm. "No. But after rehearsal, I need you to help me rescue Emil's car."

Minutes later I followed Joachín into a small rehearsal room that was cheerfully decorated with posters of previous productions. Two men and three women sat around a table making notes on their scripts.

"They made it," said the oldest woman.

"Thank God." A thin man stood and shook my hand so hard I wanted to remind him I would need it if he expected me to sew any costumes.

"Meet our director," said Joachín. "This is Tommy Gunnerson."

Tommy performed a mock bow. Thanks to the receding hairline, I assumed he'd left his twenties behind. Despite black pants and a black T-shirt, he oozed positive energy. I'd seen his last three farces, but I'd never met him in person.

"I always love your choice of materials. I saw *Lend Me a Tenor* twice."

"And we thank you. Farce is us, as we say."

"I like most genres," I said, "but right now I need a laugh more than anything."

"That's most of us most of the time," Tommy said. "Who needs to take life seriously?"

"I agree. Better to get out there and live it up."

"Yes. That's the best plan by far. Speaking of which, this production will be exactly your kind of thing. You might think of *What's in Your Closet?* as a comedic version of an Agatha Christie play. Same time frame."

Since Agatha Christie had published over a period of five decades, that explanation didn't narrow things down, but I smiled as if it had. Directors were notorious for living in their own little worlds. I wasn't sure whether or not Tommy fit that category.

"I'm Willard," said the other man, who might have been in his late 40s. He stood and offered his hand but didn't shake as long as Tommy did. "Didn't Joachín give you a rundown of the plot?"

I could hardly say that we'd been too busy talking about Twinkle's murder to discuss their play. "Somehow he only made time to tell me about his own character."

The actors laughed appropriately while Joachín brought over extra chairs. We all settled around the table.

Tommy pointed to the woman seated next to Willard. She was around Willard's age, somewhere in her forties. Her delicate layer of makeup contrasted with the string of wooden giraffes bouncing around her neck. "Désirée?"

Désirée pointed to the woman across the table from her, who might have been a decade younger. "Darling, Holland does a better job."

I turned toward the cheerful woman. The orange roses in her blouse somehow blended with the pink and red ones. Matching bracelets jingled on her wrists. Her hair poofed up several inches above her head

"It's simple, really." She pointed to Willard and Désirée. "My friends own a beautiful country house. They invite Joachín and me to spend the weekend." She pointed to the woman, perhaps my age, who sat at the end of the table. The fake blondie hadn't bothered to greet me but made a half-hearted attempt to hide a yawn. "The maid, played by Laney here, tries to get Willard in bed. When she can't, she goes after Joachín."

"Things go downhill from there?" I asked.

"Exactly! We spend the rest of the play chasing one another in circles."

"Sounds delightful," I said. The sillier the better, as far as I was concerned.

Laney tapped her nails, which were green. "The play revolves around me."

Willard laughed. "Is that why you have the fewest lines?"

"They're by far the most important. If it wasn't for me—"

"If it *weren't* for you, darling," said Désirée.

Laney laid her hands flat on the table. "Where I come from, we say—"

Theatre types. Complete with egos. Rivalries were understandable but unhelpful.

"I realize there's nothing as important as costumes," Tommy said, twice as loudly as he needed to, "but we're short on time. Do you mind measuring while we read through the lines?"

"Be glad to."

I expected to go off to a different room, but instead Tommy was intent on the reading. While the actors held their scripts at arm's length, I duly rolled the tape measure around waists and chests. When it was her turn, Laney shifted uncomfortably, refusing to make eye contact, but the other actors ignored me. They were used to public exposure. They appreciated it.

While noting lengths and widths, I took in the plot: the jealous maid made both wives think their husbands were cheating, and the wives kept checking for lovers in the closets until the men thought the women were crazy and called the police.

Why hadn't I ever looked into my own closets? I'd failed my lover without the help of a scheming servant. I'd neglected him, bored him, or driven him off. I'd thrown away six years of my life on a relationship I'd assumed was permanent. Now I was back at the starting gate as a horse about to run in the wrong direction. As petty as a jealous maid watching an elegant dinner from the kitchen, I wanted to blame all my trouble on Twinkle.

I wasn't sure she was guilty. The guilt probably lay on Emil.

Chapter Seven

"Sorry that took so long," Joachín said as soon as we tucked ourselves into his car.

"I enjoyed listening to the script."

"You didn't enjoy listening to Laney."

"Because she stumbled over her lines or because she kept giving Tommy advice?"

"How dare she, right?" Joachín turned on the engine. "Unfortunately, she's all my fault. I begged Tommy to hire her instead of Isabel."

"Your sister is so terrible?"

"Half-sister. It was selfish of me, I know."

Joachín wasn't a selfish person, but he had his pet peeves like anybody else. He was completely loyal, though. As long as I'd known him, he'd always worked in complete service of the theatre.

Since I wasn't blessed with Lula's ability to pierce through lies, I had to face him straight on. "What's your real problem with Isabel?"

He accelerated. I didn't stretch over to see the speedometer, but I sensed we were exceeding the limit.

"She's nearly impossible to work with," Joachín said.

"To an extent, it comes with the territory. What else?"

"She's always had Dad wrapped around her little finger. Anything she wanted, she got. Anything I wanted was too expensive or what have you."

"She got special privileges for being the girl?"

"Worse than that. I think Dad regretted leaving her mother and marrying mine. Of course, he never expected to have to watch her die."

I couldn't remember the details, but Joachín's mother had been hit with brain cancer when Joachín was in elementary school. He didn't like to talk about it, and I never asked.

"By then Isabel's mother had moved on," Joachín said. "Dad might have remarried her. Instead he pampers Isabel. At least that's how I see it."

"That makes your family as messed up as mine."

"Your parents are still together."

"They stopped liking each other a couple of decades ago. Or more. Who can keep track?"

Maybe they liked each other but in a weird way. They bonded when they were mad at me or my siblings or the government or their bosses or even the weather. I'd tuned them out when I was a teenager and never tuned them back in.

"Maybe I was meant to be neglected." Joachín fake-sighed. "You forgot to take my measurements."

"Don't need to."

"I have to perform in the nude?"

I lightly tapped his shoulder. "I wouldn't mind."

He gripped the steering wheel. "You wouldn't?"

"Not a bit." I tried to sound casual. Was I flirting with my sort of almost nephew? Not really, but I liked the feel of it. "But I don't need to measure you."

He stopped for the red light at Tucson and Sixth. "I'm out of the play?"

"I don't need your measurements or anyone else's." I tapped my temples. "I can eyeball all of you."

"Just by looking?"

"No big deal."

He rolled past the intersection. "You're special, too. Like the nanas."

"No. I have good depth perception or something like that."

"Isn't that unusual?"

"Among seamstresses you would find it common. Anyway, I'll measure you at my place if you insist."

`   "I might."

I grinned. "But you'll be wasting your time."

I wasn't sure he believed me.

He slowed for a stop sign. "The house is off Treat, you said?"

I indicated a right turn. "South of Sixth. Past the intersection."

Joachín spotted Emil's white sedan before I had to point it out to him. He slid behind the car and cut the motor.

Across the street, Twinkle's house beamed with yellow police tape.

"I wonder which room is the bedroom," Joachín said.

I wondered what the neighbors thought. Nothing like a murder in a quiet university neighborhood to make you question your property value.

The house itself seemed small and unimportant, as if it were a realtor's afterthought.

"What do you think really happened?" Joachín asked.

"I've asked myself the same question all day."

"You don't think Emil—"

"No."

I tried to picture an intruder, but the only image that came to mind was Magritte's surrealistic *Empire of Light*. The bottom portion of the painting showed the nighttime view of a house. Tall dark trees filled the middle. The sky showed the clear blue of day. On first glance the picture was a simple dwelling in a quiet neighborhood, but the clash between day and night whispered that secrets lurked beneath the surface.

Twinkle's place had that same quality. Something lurked so far below that ordinary surface that Emil hadn't seen anything coming.

"You know what's weird?" Joachín asked. "If I wanted to murder someone, I wouldn't wait until daybreak."

"It was somebody who knew the routine. Someone so mad at Twinkle that they waited for Emil to leave the house."

"Unless they wanted to frame him. Who could have been that mad at him?"

"Don't ask me. I didn't even know about Twinkle."

Yet I couldn't believe Emil had angered anyone. He ran a language school. He paid bills on time. He was nice enough to his family members. What did that leave? He cheated on me. Crass, yes. Uncalled for? Yes. Murder-worthy? Not worth the trouble.

For a moment we listened to the sounds of the street: the buzz of the streetlamp, cars passing in the distance. Joachín sat quietly while I collected my thoughts. A murder had occurred under Emil's nose. He had to know something.

I took Emil's car keys from my purse. "What we're doing is probably illegal. I should let you go."

"I'm not in a hurry."

The enormity of the situation pounded on my head. Emil, in jail for murder. Me, his biggest defense. I didn't even like him.

A single tear ran down my left cheek. Before I could mobilize, Joachin caught it with his index finger.

I closed my eyes. "Sorry."

"I'd be upset too. I am upset. But you have perfect reason to be. It's a shock to be sitting just outside your boyfriend's lover's house wondering who murdered her. You can't anticipate a situation like this. You can only deal with it."

"I'm trying to, but I don't know where to start."

"We'll work on it together."

The first night I met Joachín, he and Orlando had flicked paper footballs at one another across the dinner table. Suddenly he'd not only grown up, but turned into my mentor.

I squeezed his hand. "Thanks."

He brought my hand up to his lips and kissed it. "I'll help you. We all will."

I nodded as I unhooked the seat beat.

"Need anything else?"

"Tomorrow, teach for Emil?"

He pushed hair away from his temples. "I can try."

"You'll be fine."

"I have zero training and not that much Spanish."

"Don't sell yourself short. Go in, be friendly, and do your best. That's all I'm asking."

"I'll do such a poor job that you'll want someone else for next week."

I refused to worry about anything so far in advance. "You'll be fine. I promise."

I gave him an awkward car hug and hurried to Emil's vehicle. I was thankful that the street was empty, the neighbors didn't pull back their curtains to watch us, and the car started right up.

As I breathed in as deeply as possible, I wondered how often Twinkle had ridden in the passenger seat.

Chapter Eight

I threw on a gray sweatsuit so ratty I didn't normally leave the house in it, pulled on striped Norwegian socks, and slipped into running shoes. It was only fifty degrees, chilly for Tucson, but a perfectly normal temperature for a February morning. Then I headed for Twinkle's.

I'd always been a walker. In Glouchester City we'd lived a block from Johnson Park, a large leafy area that made an L around Newton Creek. Because having four siblings meant having at least three too many, I took long walks to avoid controversies. My parents couldn't complain that I was spending money if I was out walking, and I could always claim that I needed a break from my studies instead of telling the truth—that the break I needed was from Mickey, who made a habit of pulling on my hair, or Roisin, who thought everything I owned also belonged to her, or Tully and Jan, who simply wanted attention. I didn't bother to complain to my parents because they didn't care or wouldn't listen. So I walked.

By the time I met Emil, we had developed different habits. He loved nothing better than to wake up, run a couple of miles, return home for a shower, and start his day. I'd tried joining him a few times, but I preferred easing myself into morning with coffee and emails. Instead I walked in the evening, usually without Emil, half for exercise and half to clear my head. Emil thought I was daft to wait until near dusk, but I preferred that golden time between day and night. I adjusted my schedule according to the sunset even though Emil ran, without fail, no matter our social life, at seven o'clock during the week and eight on weekends.

Today, however, I sought neither exercise nor peace of mind. Posing as a jogger seemed a reasonable way to reconnoiter. I walked with my usual brisk pace, but when I reached Treat, I jogged past Twinkle's quiet house and down to the end of the block. The only car that passed me contained a mom and three grade school kids. I turned the corner, prepared to continue for a few rounds if necessary.

On the third round, an elderly man approached from the opposite direction. He was walking a Great Dane that might have been fifty or sixty pounds. Pacing myself carefully, I reached Twinkle's ten seconds before he did. As I jogged in place, I stared at the yellow police tape as if seeing it for the first time.

"Morning," said the man. He might have been seventy or eighty. Sunspots dotted his hands.

I stopped running and placed my hands on my hips as if I confused. "I thought moving into this neighborhood was a step up, but now I'm not so sure."

The man gently reeled his companion closer to him. "It's generally peaceful on this street, but the whole world is going to rot."

"Know who lives here?"

He bent to pet the dog. "A mother and her kids, but I've never met them."

I strained my neck forward as if that would help me see inside the house. "Have any idea what happened?"

"You must have a day job, young lady! The police were here all day yesterday. There must have been ten officers going in and out."

"Ten? Was there some accident?"

"They say the lady was murdered," he whispered.

I stepped back as if his words had slapped me in the face. "By her own children?"

"The kids are real small." The man pointed to the house west of Twinkle's, the one that shared her carport, a brick square whose blinds were shut tight. "The Livingstons would know more about it. Judith heard screaming, and she's the one who called 9-1-1. Scared her to death. Blood-curdling, she said."

Judith Livingston. A name to remember. "Her husband didn't hear anything?"

"Geoffrey got mad and told her to mind her own business, but it turns out that she did the right thing." The man indicated the Livingston's pristine yard. "Geoffrey was out here doing yard work yesterday. Told me all about it."

"I don't know what to think." I shook my head as if I'd never heard worse news. "It's one thing when something happens across town. When it happens on your block, it's a whole other thing."

He readjusted the leash, which the animal had twisted around his feet. "Exactly. But what can we do?"

The Great Dane seemed ready to move on, and I didn't want to seem too nosy. What I needed was my own dog, but since I didn't have one, I started jogging in place. "I guess the world is full of crazy people."

"It certainly seems that way! But you have a nice day."

I assured him that I would and ran on.

Judith and Geoffrey. I needed to talk to either of them. I could pose as a friend looking for Twinkle, perhaps. I could pretend to represent any number of government agencies, as in, "Oh, I bring free food for the kids."

With any luck, Judith knew more than she thought she did. For the moment, she was my best lead.

***

After we reached the end of the section on irregular verbs, I put down the book. My eight beginning students sat on the edge of their chairs, unusually attentive. This was appropriate; those past participles were darned hard.

"Any questions?" I asked.

Lydia's hand shot up. "Why Mr. Emil go for police station?"

What? How had they found out? I scrambled to gather my thoughts, which had scattered like stray cats. If I lied about Emil's whereabouts, I risked losing their confidence when they learned the truth.

If they ever had to learn it.

They were adults, too old for high school and too busy to be bothered with the paperwork and restrictions of the junior college. They had come freely because learning better English was vital to their well-being. No one forced them to come. They didn't receive government funding or other aid because of it. Since they paid by the month, they could come and go as they pleased. If they knew Emil was accused of murder, they could clear out within minutes and never come back. They would only lose a week's classes. That would be a small price to pay for feeling safe.

Fudge or tell the truth? I was glad I hadn't taught them the phrase about the cat getting one's tongue.

"I cut the hair for a lady her husband has cousin is janitor at police station," said Yessica. "Say English teacher go for jail."

Lying was so tempting: Your friend was mistaken, Emil is at the doctor's, Emil is having car trouble, Emil would never do anything wrong.

My brisk morning walk had done nothing to prepare me for this situation. I considered the view from their desks: If I knew the owner of the school I attended was arrested for killing a lover, I would leave even if he weren't my teacher. I wouldn't be confident taking lessons from his girlfriend either since she must be a real idiot.

My students were decent, honest people. We'd started out together in September when most of them only knew a few words in English. They'd worked hard ever since. They'd taken my advice on TV shows to watch, newspapers to look at, and word lists to memorize. They'd trusted me to guide them through the challenging process of learning a new language, and I took that mandate seriously. I might be capable of deceiving them short term, but I didn't have a strong enough reason for it.

I sat behind the desk, pushed the book aside, and clasped my hands. I leaned forward, stared straight ahead, and mentally held my breath. "Mr. E. has been detained."

Their faces were blank; "detained" didn't appear anywhere in the Level Two English book. I went to the white board, drew a face, and drew lines over it. Then I turned and nodded. "Yes. Mr. E. is in jail now. But he's innocent."

"¿Inocente?" asked Lydia.

"Inocente," I repeated.

She sputtered a stream in Spanish. The other four Spanish speakers smiled.

"Police wrong!" Yessica said loudly.

Never had I been more delighted that a basic communication act had been successful. I might have faced empty seats. Protests over dangerous schooling. Scorn.

"Police bad to people!" yelled Lydia. "They take my aunt to Mexico!"

"They not listen!" shouted Ahmed. "Take away my cousin but he innocent too!"

Indignation spread through the room. Normally I would have countered their outbursts. Police were rarely wrong. Police were there when you needed them. Police risked their lives every day.

Now was not the moment to insist on an alternate viewpoint.

"Yes! Police wrong!" I echoed their sentiments and limited phrases. I gave up on the day's lesson as they shared stories about negative experiences.

I stood and thanked them, which was my usual way of suggesting that class was over, but Antonio raised his hand. "If we can help, we help."

Had my heart been made of butter, it would have melted. I hadn't expected Emil's incarceration to come up in conversation. I hadn't expected the students to immediately concur that Emil must be innocent.

Even less had I expected a single student, let alone my shiest one, to offer assistance.

The others nodded so vigorously they might have hurt their necks.

"I have time extra," said Lydia. "No working."

"You need car, I borrow you," Antonio said.

"I nurse," said Nayela. "I check you to see you okay."

"I doctor for the pets," said Julio. "I give you medicine for relaxing."

"I good for the computer," said Ahmed. "Can find informations."

The cat had grabbed my tongue so firmly that the most I could do was smile. Normally I maintained more separation between myself and my students, but when Yessica offered a bear hug, I squeezed her back. And so it went with the others. They each hugged me as they left while assuring me that everything would be all right.

I used every ounce of energy to refrain from crying. I thanked them profusely and promised to ask for help as soon as I needed it.

As a professional, I wouldn't take them up on their offers, of course.

Unless I really needed to.

Chapter Nine

As I reached the nanas' front door that evening, a tall woman opened it. She had long black hair, more mascara than a makeup counter, and red lips that puckered up like a tropical fish. Although I guessed her to be around my age, wrinkles underlined her eyes. The wire bra was at least one size too small. From the pinched way she held her mouth, I assumed the jeans were a size too small.

Normally I wouldn't have paid attention to yet another of the nanas' many visitors, but this one I'd seen in pictures now and again. She was taller than most Mexican women I'd met, and she moved deliberately as she scooted past me.

"Hi, Isabel."

She looked up; I had the impression she would have preferred to ignore me altogether.

For a moment she stared, and I felt cocky about having the upper hand.

"So you're the new ex." Her eyes traveled up and down my body, mostly resting on my droopy blue T-shirt. "I'm surprised you lasted this long. Is that red hair real?"

More real than all the paint on your face.

"No. I love having hair that doesn't go with blouses that are red, orange, or pink."

I could see the question in her eyes: Is she being sarcastic or not?

But she didn't take the bait. "They're all in the dining room."

"Thanks."

I would have never found the nanas otherwise.

Awkwardly, as if her gait didn't fit her body, she wiggled past me. I watched as she hurried toward her car. She pushed the remote several times before the vehicle honked and unlocked itself.

"Lucky me," I announced as I entered the dining room. I pointed at Joachín. "I finally met your sister."

He and Orlando sat across the table from Lula and Mari. The coffee pot breathed hazelnut, and the plate of sweet empanadas had been double loaded. The curtains covering the windows fluttered from a slight breeze.

"'Half-sister," Joachin said.

I gave hugs all around. "Is your dad all right?"

"His heart has been racing a bit, and Isabel convinced him to make a doctor's appointment. That's not why she was here."

"She needed a loan?"

Joachín and Orlando laughed.

"We wouldn't have given her one," Orlando said.

"Too complicated," said Joachín. "When she wants money, she wheedles it out of my father."

For extra clues, I looked to the nanas. Lula scowled while Mari frowned.

Of course. I should have guessed immediately. "She wanted to know about Emil."

"She came to gloat," said Lula. "Did we know when he might get out of jail? Did we know if he needed anything?"

"I'm surprised she didn't offer to go pay a conjugal visit." I sat at the head of the table. "I've always been curious to meet her. Now I have an idea."

What made people want to meet their rivals? Perhaps a misguided sense of survival. I wasn't jealous of Isabel because she seemed limited. She finished a B.A. in the university theatre program, but so far the degree hadn't much helped her. She might have found an acting job out of town, but she hesitated to leave Tucson. She'd dated several men since Emil, but none of the relationships had lasted.

At the moment, though, I wished she were the recent ex-girlfriend instead of me.

"She's simply a busybody," Lula said. "Needs more to do with herself. Does she still work at the Bisbee Breakfast Club?"

"Three days a week," said Joachín.

"See?" Lula asked. "That doesn't keep her occupied enough."

"They probably don't want to hire her any extra," said Orlando.

I poured myself a half cup of coffee. "I didn't get a warm and fuzzy feeling from her."

"We tried to like her," Mari said, "but we're not saints."

"You're close!" I nodded toward the plate of treats on the table. "Fresh empanadas?"

Mari served me one before I finished taking a breath. The tower of treats smelled fresh and sweet. I could see from the dirty plates in front of them that the boys had already sampled several. But I knew what the nanas were doing—bribing us. They needed our help, and they'd done an excellent job of roping us in. Now we were stuck.

"We had extra time for baking this afternoon," Mari said.

Lula nodded. "We like having little projects."

In the picture behind the nanas' heads, the poker-playing dogs tricked one another.

"Thank goodness you feel better," Mari said. "Your red aura has faded considerably. The other day you might have shot out like a cannon."

"I've rarely been that mad." Not true. I'd been that mad at my brother Mickey when he ripped up my chemistry homework for no good reason, when my sister Roisín told the boy I was dating that I thought he had an ugly chin — the list could have gone on. No wonder I had a short temper. Too many people in my life had taken advantage of me — and those had been friends and relatives.

"I'm in a better place." I nodded to Joachín. "Thanks for covering the beginning classes." I nodded to the nanas. "And the advanced classes. Your work has been a big help."

The nanas nodded complacently, which meant they were building up to something.

"Did you test out my theory?" I figured if my students were willing to help even though they had no specific ties to Emil, I could talk the nanas into anything.

"We went over to Twinkle's house around noon," said Mari. "We went straight up to the door and called her name. The neighbor lady came out and said she wasn't there."

"Judith? The neighbor to the west?"

"Yes. We told her exactly what you suggested about setting up a playdate with our grandkids."

"I felt bad lying to her," Mari said.

Lula cut an empanada in half, and red filling spilled out. "I didn't feel bad since it's for a good cause. But she wasn't honest with us. Her husband came outside before she had time to tell us anything."

"What about the kids?"

"The man said they were still at daycare and that we could catch their grandparents over there."

"You didn't ask which daycare?"

Mari picked a crumb off the table and put it on her empty plate. "She didn't say, so we pretended that we knew. We would, of course. If we really were her friends."

Fair enough. There was a fine line between asking questions and acting suspicious.

Orlando whipped out a tablet. "There are several daycares right around there. I'll make a list of the closest ones."

"Great," I said. "Did you guys discover anything useful today?"

"I swung by Twinkle's after class," said Orlando. "Nobody was outside. The whole block was a ghost."

Lula licked a drop of filling. "Old people don't go out in the strong sun. Maybe it was the wrong time of day."

I made a note. "Joachín, maybe you and I can try again later. Did you see any people out with their dogs? We might have to borrow one. Dog people like to talk."

"Miranda has one," Orlando said. "But he's so old I'm not sure he walks."

"We can borrow Tommy's," Joachín said. "He often brings Havie to rehearsals anyway."

"Excellent. If we manage to pass through Twinkle's neighborhood several times a day —"

The kitchen phone rang so loudly the neighbors might have tried to answer it. Orlando popped up and checked the caller ID.

"Nanas! I think it's Emil! It says —"

Mari snatched the phone away. "Emil! What is going on? No bail? Too dangerous? *¡Diós mío!* Easy conviction? *¡No, mi'jo!* We'll get you out somehow! Yes, you must keep your call short. I understand."

I beckoned for the phone so emphatically I strained my shoulder. "We need you to tell us everything you can about your little squeeze."

Whoops. The sarcasm was unwarranted, but it wasn't premeditated. It had jumped out before I could control it.

Silence.

"Hello? Hello?" I hadn't noticed any clicking sounds, but maybe the connection was poor.

"My relationship with Twinkle is none of your business," Emil said.

If the phone had belonged to me, I might have flung it across the room. There was a half second when I might have destroyed it anyway, but I caught myself in time. "Idiot! I'm working on your behalf. Tell us everything you can."

"Did you remind the students that tuition is due at the end of the week?"

"What?"

"I knew it. Since you forgot to send out reminders on Monday—"

"On Monday I didn't have a job."

"Today you should have sent out reminders. Do it this evening. Put the message header in red so that the students—"

"Twinkle! Tell us about this Twinkle!" What was the matter with the man? Emil was delusional. He'd lost track of reality, so his mind spun down rabbit holes.

"Also, the janitor was late yesterday morning, so I want you to put a note in his file and send him an email warning. This will be his second warning, so you probably should start looking for an alternative—"

"Emil! Did you lose your senses banging Twinkle?"

Whoops. More sarcasm. Hadn't meant to. I purposefully avoided eye contact with the nanas, but Joachín grinned at me as if he'd said the words instead.

Meanwhile the jailbird waited so long to respond that I might have gobbled a whole empanada in the meantime. "I did not, not even once, 'bang' Twinkle," Emil said.

I put my hand over the receiver. "You'll all be happy to know that they were not banging."

The boys hid laughter, but both nanas scowled.

Mari held out her hand. "Would you like me to try, dear?"

I addressed Emil. "We're all thankful to hear that what you were doing with Twinkle had nothing to do with banging. But if you don't cough up details, you can rot away in jail while you think about her."

"Ann Louise is three," Emil said. "Hunter is five. Ann Louise won't eat peas. Hunter throws a fit whenever he gets too tired. They're in daycare—some place that starts with an S."

Orlando nodded and tapped on his phone.

"Enough about the kids," I said. "Tell us about her."

"She sells insurance for Farmwell."

"Something personal."

"She divorced a couple of years ago."

"I'm going to need something more personal than that."

"Stop. Just because you think you can win over the nanas by nosing around—"

I reeled back to smash the phone into the wall, but Joachín came up behind me and grabbed it before I could do any damage. He stepped beyond my reach.

"What Dervla means is that we need clues that would lead us to Twinkle's killer," Joachín said. "We know it wasn't you, but we'll need evidence to convince the police otherwise."

I couldn't decipher the words Emil shouted, but Joachín frowned as he paced. "What do you mean, what am I doing getting in your business?"

More indistinct words.

Joachín ended the call and tossed the phone across the table. It bounced onto an empty chair and thudded across the floor.

"He called me a *metiche*." Joachín looked over at me. "A busybody."

Lula and Mari consulted one another. They exchanged a series of glances and nods in a secret communication they'd practiced since childhood. I assumed they would explode. Their grandson and nephew had managed to call them, and Joachín and I had snapped the lifeline.

Lula crossed her arms. "Maybe he likes jail."

"Maybe he'll learn something." Mari pushed the empanadas in my direction "Take another."

I wasn't hungry, but I took another one anyway. "He's embarrassed. He knows he should have played things differently. I have my faults — "

"Don't," said Joachín. "You're human like everyone else, including Emil."

Lula refilled my coffee cup. Mari handed me the sugar bowl.

"Yesterday you said I'd learn to forgive him," I said to Mari.

She sank back. "I may have been wrong."

"We all know what part of his body he's thinking with," Orlando said. "But down deep, he's okay. We still have to help him."

Lula watched her grandson as if he were growing a long nose. "You knew."

"I what?"

Lula turned to us. "He knew."

Orlando shook his head. "He never told me anything, but — "

Lula rose so fast that her chair fell behind her and rattled on the tiles below. "You're lying." She bore into

Orlando with eyes that were sharper than a wizard's wand.

"No, I—"

"Ly-ing." She drew out both syllables. "You can't fool me."

No one could. Once she'd sniffed out a falsehood, she was a hawk with a mouse between its claws. No matter how much the rodent squirmed, the hawk still won.

"Tell us now or you sleep on the street tonight," Lula said. She wouldn't have carried out such a threat, but in Orlando's shoes, I wouldn't have risked it.

Orlando trembled. He was usually polite and mild-mannered. "He didn't mean for me to find out."

"Proceed," Lula said.

"Twinkle's house? It's just a few doors down from Angelina's."

"Angelina?"

"A girl I was dating. A while ago."

"How long ago was that?" I asked.

Orlando paused as if he honestly couldn't remember. He probably couldn't. Telling another lie would be too dangerous. One confrontation with Lula per day was plenty.

"Think carefully," Mari said gently. She knew when to play a counterpart to her sister. They might have been a tag team with S.W.A.T. embroidered on their aprons.

"It was on December 12th. You know."

The others nodded.

"What? What's the 12th?" I asked.

"La Virgen de Guadalupe," they chorused.

Right, right. A special day dedicated to celebrating the miracle of the Virgen of Guadalupe. In Mexico the day was a holiday. In Tucson people celebrated any way they could. Emil had always told me it was an excuse to kick off the holiday season.

"Go on," Lula ordered.

"Angelina's family was having a party. When I arrived, I noticed Emil's car. I thought he was one of the guests since it's a big local family, but I never saw him. When I left a couple of hours later, Emil's car was still outside, but I couldn't figure out why."

I could. On December 12th I'd spent the night with a girlfriend up in Phoenix. Very clever. Clever indeed.

"I asked him about it a few days later," Orlando said. "I assumed he had car trouble. He said something about staying over with a friend since he was too drunk to drive."

"Except that Emil never drinks and drives," I said coldly. "Never, ever, ever."

"I know," Orlando said. "And then at Christmas—"

I didn't want to hear it. I didn't need to. We'd agreed; Christmas with our families. New Year's together. I'd flown back to Tucson on the 30th. I'd practically invited Emil to have an affair by attending to my own relatives, and I didn't even like them.

"—at Christmas I noticed the car there again."

"You asked him about it?" said Lula.

"Not right away. But when I needed a little loan, you know, for the weekend—"

Bravo. Blackmail right in the family. Where better?

"He made me swear not to say anything," Orlando said. "He was going to tell you, Dervla. He was waiting for the right moment."

He told me everything some twenty hours before Twinkle's head rolled right off her neck. The timing couldn't have been better. "He found the perfect moment, all right."

Lula sighed with her whole chest, which made her cough so much she had to reach for her water. Then she addressed me. "Please. We will have to forgive him temporarily. He doesn't know what he's doing."

"It's up to us to learn about Crystal," Mari said.

"Twinkle, you mean." I tore apart the empanada until goopy filling decorated most of my fingers. "She didn't get her pretty little head sawed off for nothing. Robbers aren't early risers, so it's not like a burglar entered the house and got caught. She was attacked because of something personal."

"Since you're a woman close to her age...." Lula muttered. She stopped there, but I knew what she and her sister were thinking. It was still up to me to unlock Twinkle's miserable existence.

I'd never met her. Since she'd stolen my lover, I could hardly dig up much compassion. How many boyfriends had she stolen? How many affairs with married men? Who had fathered the children?

In a worst-case scenario, Emil himself. Local family, local girl. They might have met in elementary school.

"Surely there's something you can do?" Mari asked softly.

Thank Twinkle's killer? Send congratulations to her parents?

I shook off my snarkiest thoughts. Twinkle had been a mom with two small children. She probably had a sound relationship with her parents since they were used to taking care of the kids. If Emil were correct, she'd held a regular job, making her a productive member of society.

She'd also robbed me of Emil.

Shades of red probably darted around my head. I'd funneled my anger into sarcasm, but I could feel darts bouncing around in my stomach, careening into the sidewalls. What I most wanted was the freedom to hate Emil any way I wanted to. I deserved that emotion.

At the moment, anger was a luxury. I didn't want to help Emil, but I couldn't avoid it. I couldn't wait five years until I felt better about myself to trace Twinkle's last steps. I had to act now, while the trail was hot, and while the information was still of potential use to Emil.

Instead of hiding in a corner, my only option was to plow ahead through Emil's betrayal. As soon as I could point the police in a viable direction, I could erase Emil from my life. Whenever I visited the nanas, I would be able to spot Emil across the room, ignore him, and hold my head up high. I could keep friendships with Orlando and Flor. With Joachín. Even with Mordy.

I licked filling off my fingers. Gooey in a good way. Sweet but not too sweet.

"You can take some home," Mari said.

Bless them. They understood all about my emotional predicament. They also knew that no matter how I felt inside, I would take the high road.

For now.

"I'm not a detective. I don't have connections down at the police station. I don't know anything more than the rest of you do. But I think the Livingstons know something. Maybe the other neighbors do too. Who wants to walk around Twinkle's neighborhood with me tonight?"

"We don't like to walk after dark," Lula said. "It's too easy to trip on the sidewalk."

"I have a study session. It might last until midnight," said Orlando.

"Unless you think I could get away with walking Mordy—"

"I have rehearsal," Joachín said. "I can't skip it. But as soon as I'm done, I can catch up with you."

The nanas murmured thanks and approval. Orlando patted his friend on the back. I reached for another empanada. Maybe if I filled myself with enough sweets, some of the sugar would rub off.

That should help me tackle Twinkle's killer.

Somehow.

Chapter Ten

When Joachín honked, I locked my back door and went out to his car. I winked as I slid into the passenger seat. "I expected you a half hour ago." I was giving him a hard time. Out of the whole Arellano bunch, he was the timeliest. If he were late, he had a decent reason for it.

He gripped the steering wheel as if grounding himself. "Had a fight after rehearsal."

I looked for bruises or other marks on his face. He wasn't a fighter, and I wasn't sure he could defend himself. "Are you all right?"

"The fight was verbal. I made the mistake of offering Laney a piece of advice."

An error in judgement, then. She wouldn't be the kind to accept advice no matter how good it was.

He reached Sawtelle and turned south. "Guess what I told her. Since she raced through her lines too fast to articulate any of the words, I suggested she slow down."

I put my hands to my ears. "Ouch, ouch, ouch! How can you expect anyone to accept such raw criticism!"

"I know, right? I didn't say it loudly or anything. We were on break, and I waited until we were out of earshot of everyone else."

"That was kind of you, although I'm sure the others thought the same thing."

"They kept their mouths shut. Laney ambushed me after rehearsal to tell me to mind my own business. Gave me a list of my acting faults, of which there are many."

That was precisely why I started my own language school. When you had your own business, you could avoid working with difficult personalities — unless you'd hooked up with one.

"If you can't take criticism, you can't last in theatre," I said. "Not here, at least. Maybe not anywhere." No wonder beginning English students were so lovely. They never questioned your authority. They knew you knew better than they did.

Joachín waited for two passing cars before turning onto Seventh Street. "Laney claimed that the only person she would listen to was Tommy, but she won't listen to him either. Why try to help her? Last time I make that mistake."

"That's how I feel about helping Emil. Maybe we shouldn't bother investigating after all."

"Maybe, maybe not." Joachín slowed down. "Where do you want me to park?"

"Go past the next intersection. That puts us on Twinkle's block."

"The family appreciates your helping out, you know."

"Emil doesn't."

Joachín parked three properties past the corner. "Emil was rude to me too. He's crazy with worry. You can't blame him."

"I can blame him plenty, but never mind. How am I supposed to help? I obviously didn't know him half as well as I thought I did."

"You still know him better than anybody else."

"Lucky me."

Joachín tapped my shoulder blade until I squirmed. "You have to let it all go."

"I know. And I'm sorry to whine. Emil isn't your problem."

"He's our problem collectively, and we're doing our best. That's what counts." He pointed down the deserted street. "What are we doing here?"

When I got out of the car, Joachín copied me. "We're getting a feel for the neighborhood. Greeting some neighbors. The best thing would be to accidentally on purpose run into the Livingstons, but I haven't figured out how to arrange it."

I marched toward Twinkle's, and Joachín hustled to keep up. I didn't want to help her, dead or alive, so the quicker the better.

We continued until we were opposite Twinkle's dark house. Not even a porchlight graced the driveway. We stared at the empty windows as if they could tell us something.

"You should have brought the doll with you," Joachín said.

"Because it has cosmic energy?"

"Something like that."

I dug through my purse. "It's right here. I was going to show the nanas, but I forgot." I fished out Emilito and held him up as if giving him a view of the crime scene.

"Tell me what happened," I told the doll. "Don't leave anything out." I paused. "Nothing to say? Then you're worthless." I tossed him down and stomped on him.

Joachín laughed.

"I know. Stupid. But cathartic." I picked Emilito back up and blew off imaginary dirt.

Joachín pointed to the figure. "Excuse me?"

With a red Sharpie, I'd drawn a tiny penis.

Joachín nodded. "Trying to say something?"

"No. He was all right in that way." I shook my index finger. "Not, mind you, that women are hung up on size or that bigger is better." I took out a pen, which was my best weapon, and jabbed the baby penis several times.

"There! That's what I think of you!" I pointed down the street. "Keep walking?"

We reached the corner in silence and started back again.

"Maybe he didn't see her that many times," Joachín said.

I halted long enough to jab the doll with my pen again. "He was leaving me for her."

"Yes, but —"

Jab, jab, jab. "He gave up a solid relationship to be with another woman. He knew her pretty well. Although honestly, since I didn't even suspect anything, he must have seen her in frequent bursts. Or maybe he texted her all day long. I don't know."

"Mid-life crisis?"

"He's not old enough." I stopped opposite Twinkle's house and stared. "Sorry I dragged you out for a goose chase."

"I don't mind."

The lights were out at the Livingstons' too. It might take weeks for me to run into them legitimately, but I doubted we had that much time.

But Twinkle's property was empty. And dark.

I eyed the driveway. "We could take a look-see."

"Dervla! It's a crime scene."

"Maybe the house is. Not the driveway. Or even the carport. We could look in through the window."

"Dervla!"

The best way to get your way is to keep your head down, do your own thing, and ignore anyone who tries to stop you. I crossed the street.

Seconds later, Joachín followed.

By the time I reached Twinkle's beige Dodge, Joachín caught up. He shined light from his cell phone through the windows.

"Crumbs and kids' toys," he said. "Nothing exciting. Unless you think she smuggled drugs somehow?"

Possible. Somehow it seemed unlikely. I strode past the Dodge and the coiled-up garden hose to the side of the house, but it was too dark to see inside the other windows. I continued around to the back. A tricycle lorded over a plastic toy chest. A patio table hugged three chairs. I sat in one of them.

"Dervla."

I crossed my legs to get more comfortable. "What?"

"We can't hang out here."

"I'm drinking in the atmosphere. Sensing Twinkle."

A light went on inside the house, and we both jumped.

"Could anyone—" I asked.

"Do you think—" asked Joachín.

We ran to the window, crouched down, and peered through the blinds. No movement anywhere.

"What do you think?" I whispered.

"Timer."

"Oh. Right." A lover who had spirited Emil away should be famous or infamous, but not ordinary.

I'd been beaten out by ordinary. It was embarrassing.

"Joachín, I want to ask you something."

"Shhh."

"You don't have to answer."

"Quiet!" He pointed in the direction of the street. "Hear that?"

A car door slammed. It might have been two houses down. Then we heard two sets of footsteps. Men's, probably. They were coming our way.

My heartbeat accelerated. They wouldn't be visitors, not at this time of night.

A friend, maybe. A murderer?

I pointed to the back of the yard. "Run?" I whispered.

Joachín shook his head. "Too noisy. Get down!"

We sank beneath the window.

Moments later, the footsteps continued onto the carport.

"They came in through this door here," said a man.

He wouldn't have been the murderer.

"A burglar?" asked another man.

He might have been a neighbor.

"The lover. Revenge I guess."

Revenge indeed! I wanted to shout out that the revenge should have been on my part.

"What about the children?"

"An aunt or something."

"Who'd expect a murder in our neighborhood?"

"Lock your door. Even during the day."

The steps retreated. Car doors opened. An engine fired up.

I pulled myself up with the help of the window ledge. "What do you think?"

Joachín stood as well. "Locals, I'd say. One was a native Spanish speaker."

"Voyeurs, then?"

"Naturally curious."

If a similar murder happened on my block, I'd want to know more too. That didn't mean I was a busybody. People naturally wanted to understand their surroundings. It was a form of survival.

One that had eluded Twinkle.

***

After I drove home, I rummaged through Emil's car hoping to learn the smallest detail about Twinkle. The trunk held tools and a spare tire. The only receipt was for gas at the Circle K on Broadway and Campbell, paid in cash two weeks earlier. A single word graced a piece of scratch paper: tissues. The scrawl was Emil's.

I sat in the driver's seat and stared ahead without seeing anything. I'd never questioned the nights Emil claimed he wanted to return to the office to finish paperwork or his long trips to the hardware store where he could never find the exact tool he wanted. I didn't consider myself inattentive. I imagined our freedom meant that we were happy together.

Between staying with girlfriends, attending a teaching conference, and spending five days back home, I'd given Emil plenty of freedom in the fall. Those were just the special events. On Tuesday afternoons I had coffee with buddies from graduate school. On Fridays I played tennis. I spent even longer at the Irish singalongs on Sundays evenings. At first I'd been reluctant to give up the time, but Emil had encouraged me. "Singing is a way to release emotions," he said. Sure it was. The other way was to hop in your car and visit your favorite squeeze.

Why had he bothered with the secrecy? He wasn't a prisoner. He could have broken up with me at any time. Presumably while I'd lived it up with my cousin in New Orleans, he'd spent every moment gathering up the courage to claim independence.

I slapped the vinyl seat. How often had Emil taken Twinkle around or made out with her in the backseat? Had she hired babysitters or introduced her new friend as "Uncle Emmy?" Did their fathers come around, or did she know who they were?

A more intriguing issue was what Emil had told her to justify leaving me. That would be my next question when the silly jailbird called again. He would lie about it, but I'd still want to hear what he said.

I swallowed wrong and started coughing. I reached into the glove compartment and felt around for a hard candy. Usually a peppermint lurked under the maps and registration papers.

First I came upon a plastic triangle, a piece of the drink holder that had fallen apart a few years ago. Then a pencil. Finally, a faded Goofy at the end of a keychain holding a single key.

I recognized neither.

The key was ridged, like most housekeys. I got out my own set and compared. The nanas had given me their key long ago in case I should pop by when they were out and wanted to wait for them. Goofy's key did not match the nanas' or mine either.

I fingered the four sharp ridges while I asked myself why Emil would fill his glove compartment with an extra key.

He might have a copy of his mother's, but she lived in San Francisco. When he visited, he flew. His sister's? Possible, but Emil and Miranda weren't that close.

I rubbed Goofy so hard part of the red paint on his arm flaked off. Who paid attention to cartoon characters? Parents of small children.

I was holding the key to Twinkle's place. If using it meant finding useful information, I couldn't afford to hesitate.

Chapter Eleven

I released the lever for the driver's seat and slid back until it clicked. "We shouldn't have long to wait."

Seated beside me, Lula gave half a nod.

"Are you sure we should do this?" Mari asked from the backseat.

They'd begged for my help, but now that I needed them, their feet were cold. I nodded toward the daycare, which was to our left. The one-story building was the biggest in the neighborhood, and the ample parking lot provided distance from arriving parents. "There's no law against asking a couple of questions."

"We're not even certain this is the right place," said Mari.

Sunny Day was a mile and a half from Twinkle's. "We're ninety-nine percent sure," I said. "That's pretty good."

Lula cleared her throat. "Ronny says the case might get thrown out of court. Some procedural thing."

I'd met Emil's cousin Ronny on a couple of occasions. While he'd helped the odd cousin with immigration issues, his career was based on housing, not homicide.

"Nanas, a dismissal could take months. In the meantime Emil sits in jail for no reason, you and Joachín have to cover Spanish classes, and we might lose the business anyway."

"Yes, yes," said Lula. "We'll try. Are you sure you can recognize the grandparents?"

"If not, you'll recognize the kids."

In between classes that day, I'd studied Twinkle's profile. She'd grown up in Tucson. Chances were that her parents lived here as well. The only other Tucson Witherbottoms had owned a laundromat south of campus, which they'd sold three years earlier. It was not farfetched to think that they had retired when they became grandparents and that they were helping right now with two kids who didn't have anyone else to take care of them.

I pulled up Facebook on my phone and handed it over. The shot of the parents was fuzzy. They were crouched behind a boy about to blow out candles, but the bright light of the flame distorted everything else. The parents were fair, as Twinkle, with similar brown hair. Malcolm had a jaw too angular for his short neck, but he had a bright smile. Next to him, a petite Henrietta filled her cheeks with air.

A group shot included Ann Louise, the little sister. Henrietta held the child while Malcolm pushed a stuffed bear up to her face. The caption read, "Two years old."

Both children seemed happy and well cared for, so I silently awarded Twinkle brownie points. On the surface, she was a caring mother. I was nearly jealous.

"Game on." I pointed to the school entrance, which had opened. Several parents ascended the short flight of stairs and disappeared inside.

Lula gripped my arm. "Any special questions we should ask?"

"There's no script. Get a sense of them. Ask about their daughter."

"Those poor, poor people," said Mari. "I'm not sure now is a good time to bother them."

Lula tightened her grip. "Perhaps you could ask instead?"

I didn't need to see auras to sense their alarm, but our window of opportunity was tight. "Do you want to help Emil or not?"

They murmured "yes."

"People like to talk to people who are their same age. My striking up a conversation would seem intrusive. You can do it naturally. I cannot. We went over this."

"We don't want to do it wrong," Mari said.

Normally I would have gotten a kick out of their unusual hesitation, but today we didn't have time for it. "We're going. Now."

We headed up the sidewalk that led toward the school. As agreed, I veered off. The nanas continued onto the grounds and stopped by the playground fence. I wanted to be far enough away to seem unconnected but close enough to hear the conversation. Not only were the nanas a bit deaf, but they were stubborn about asking people to repeat things. They often pretended to understand when they hadn't.

I spotted Henrietta and Malcolm moments before the nanas did. We nodded our acknowledgement. The couple exited their car and slowly headed to the school entrance. Malcolm might have been six feet, his wife a foot shorter. They bent over as if their shoulders carried the weight of their daughter's death.

I felt terrible for them. They might have been sixty or seventy; either way they would probably be assuming custody of two young children who would someday find out about the violence of their mother's demise. Somehow, the kids would have to find a way to push past the awful facts. How long would they need—a few decades and years of therapy?

The plan was for the nanas to ambush the elderly couple after they fetched the children. Hence we waited three, five, eight minutes. I worried they'd slipped out another door, but finally they emerged, Henrietta tightly holding the girl's hand, and Malcolm stooped over to walk with the boy.

For a moment neither nana moved, and I worried they'd chickened out. Then they made their way over, feigning tender joints.

"Henrietta, Malcolm. We're so, so sorry to hear," said Lula. Once she'd gotten their attention, she reached to embrace them, and Mari did the same. The couple didn't seem surprised. No doubt they had received similar responses from other friends.

"How did you know?" asked Malcolm.

"We ran into the Livingstons at Safeway," Mari said. "Terrible thing. I guess you don't know what happened."

Henrietta's face clouded over. Mari, who was about her same height, gave her a second hug, and this one lasted for several long seconds because Henrietta didn't let go.

The woman finally released Mari from the death grip. "Thank you so much. We're too shocked to know what to think."

"I told you. It's best not to think anything at all," said Malcolm. He strengthened his grip on the boy. "We're at a loss. We didn't know she started dating again."

"We're never prepared for tragedy when it strikes." Mari crossed herself. "Who can explain the things God sends our way?"

Henrietta put her free hand over her heart. "We never thought God would give us such a trial and yet—well, He has. I thank Him that we are strong enough to carry on, Malcolm and I. What if these children didn't have us to fend for them?"

"They are so, so blessed," said Mari.

Henrietta clasped her hands. "It's a big help that we live nearby."

"You don't know anything about the attacker?" Lula asked.

"No," Malcolm said sharply. "We have no idea at all why some man would comfortably spend the night in our daughter's bed and be so deranged that he thanked her by murdering her."

"But surely the man — well, the police don't know —" Mari stuttered.

"A deranged lover. That's the only explanation."

"Not her ex-husband?" Lula asked.

"No, no, no," said Malcolm. "He left because he wanted to and moved five hundred miles away. The killer was this new guy we never knew about. The police caught him red-handed, so at least that's a satisfaction."

"The children —" Mari said.

"With us that night, thank the Lord," Henrietta said. "He's watching over you even when you think He isn't."

"We better let you go," said Lula. "We wanted you to know that you're in our prayers." More hugs. Then goodbyes. Then the nanas toiled their way up the short flight of stairs and into the school.

Henrietta and Malcolm smoothly placed the children in their car seats as if they were used to doing so. They quickly secured the children and drove away.

I returned to the car to wait for my spies, who shuffled out of the school moments later. "Good work," I said. "You're hired."

Lula fastened her seatbelt. "They think my grandson is guilty."

"Their auras showed horrible pain," said Mari. "You have to find out what happened so that we can put everything behind us."

"Red auras?" I asked.

"Dark purple. They're bewildered because they can't understand what happened to their baby."

At thirty-something, the woman was hardly a baby. Boyfriend thief, yes. "Nice touch about God and all."

Mari nodded. "Henrietta wore a small cross. As I spoke to her, she touched it."

I eased out of the parking lot. "Nana Lula, what did you learn?"

"Of course I am not an expert."

Not true. She knew more about character than St. Peter, and she'd had years of practice at reading people.

"Do you think they were telling the truth?"

"Not exactly. The woman was. She is absolutely astonished about what happened to her daughter. But Malcolm knows something. Not a lot. I'm not saying he slipped in and murdered his daughter himself. No. But he suspects something."

"Information he wouldn't share with his wife."

"Correct. Perhaps Twinkle was closer to him or confided in him more easily."

"Should we approach him again when Henrietta isn't listening?"

Lula squinted as I turned west. "Not yet. We should let things settle for a few days. It takes people a while to order their thoughts."

"You have to double your efforts though," said Mari. "Don't do anything dangerous or illegal, but we need Emil back. We're not teachers. Today was difficult."

While I'd limped through my own classes, distracted and preoccupied, I'd heard frequent laughter from across the hall. "The students had a great time."

"Yes, but we couldn't think what the *pluscuamperfecto* was. A student had to look it up for us."

"Who knows grammar terms by memory? Don't worry about it. The students are nice, right? They're happy to be learning."

"They had laughing fits when we didn't know who won the Super Bowl," Lula said.

After I stopped for a yellow light, I turned to my co-pilot. "At your age, you can get away with anything. If you do any better than you're doing now, I'll have you teach my English classes as well."

"Not that," said Mari. "Take care of yourself and don't get sick. We can't do Emil's job and yours too."

I turned down the nanas' street. "Show the students one of your favorite movies."

"We could do that," Mari agreed. "We'd have to stop now and again to explain."

"The students would love it." I pulled into their drive.

"What are you doing this evening?" asked Mari. "Why not have dinner with us?"

Ordinarily I accepted their every invitation. "Thanks. I appreciate it. But I have a lot to do."

"Of course," Lula said as she got out of the car.

Mari patted my shoulder. "Call us tomorrow."

"I will."

I waited until they got inside, but then I sped off. I didn't want Lula to read my mind long enough to realize I was planning a trip to Seventh Street.

Chapter Twelve

At eleven I turned off the laptop and headed for Twinkle's. The house was dark when I arrived, so I sat in the car, listening to the hum of the streetlight and waiting for the timer to kick in. A lamp shone in the house east of Twinkle's, but I didn't detect any movement. The Livingstons' place was already dark; the couple probably retired early.

After the light went on in Twinkle's living room, I quietly went to the front door and tried the lock. The key didn't come close to fitting. Then I went around to the side door under the carport. Bingo. Trying to act as natural as possible, I let myself right in.

The kitchen was messy without being a disaster. A crooked soap dish. Dishes eternally drying on a rack. A highchair and a booster huddled around the table. Boxes of Captain Crunch and Fruit Loops on top of the fridge. A smudge of jam on the wall.

The ordinary room was a reminder of how quickly things could change. One moment you thought your life was all set—and then, snap, you died without seeing it coming. Or maybe Twinkle knew something was off and never warned Emil.

The kitchen opened to a study on one side and the living room on the other. I went to the latter, where a blue sofa that was losing its stuffing ruled over a coffee table piled with kids' books. A big TV stood between two chests of toys. Old-fashioned lamps governed end tables. One lamp was attached to the timer.

The kids' bedroom held additional sets of toys; the children hadn't wanted for anything tangible. I wondered if they were sleeping soundly at their grandparents,' and what Henrietta and Malcolm told them. *Mommy went on a trip. Mommy will be back soon. Mommy went to heaven.*

I stood at the door jamb to the master bedroom wondering how much Twinkle's parents had aged overnight. No one anticipated such tragedies, so no one besides card-carrying pessimists prepared for them. The rest of us were too busy going about our daily lives.

To an outsider, the room seemed innocent. The master bed was stripped down to the mattress, a well-worn model whose brand name was no longer visible. I rarely felt squeamish, but even in dim light, the thought of Twinkle's severed head was too vivid for me. I backed away without entering the room.

A faint glow of light reached the study, but I didn't want to risk turning on another lamp. I stood in the center of the room and let my eyes grow accustomed to the dark shapes. The only furniture was a sturdy wooden desk and a swivel chair that faced the backyard. Joachín and I had crouched on the other side of the wall the night before.

Along the adjacent wall, Emil's clothes and toiletries lay on the floor in piles. So did random newspapers and magazines. Emil's laundry bag perched on top. He reasoned that no one would steal a bag of dirty clothes, so he used the white canvas bag as camouflage. The trick evidently worked on the police; his laptop was still inside. Since I'd helped pay for it, I flung the bag over my back. The machine was coming with me.

I'd forgotten to bring gloves, so I used a Kleenex to pull the chair out from the desk. The Dell, dotted with the residue from a hundred sticky notes, looked old but not quite ancient. Evidently the police hadn't thought it worthwhile; perhaps they'd found a tablet or a laptop. I took out my cell phone and used the flashlight app to help me review the correspondence beside the computer. Most of the mail consisted of ordinary household bills: gas, electricity, water. The list of charges on the Visa and Discover cards were lengthy, so I snapped photos of them.

The desk drawers I checked one by one. The top one held a calendar with appointments that went through May. I took more pictures. The middle drawer held a stack of receipts for Beauty Is You Cosmetics, evidently a side job. The receipts ranged from twelve bucks to over a hundred dollars. They were in reverse order from the most recent to the oldest. The newest one was three weeks old.

I'd never been one for makeup. My light skin color was difficult to match, and I was too impatient to work at it. I owned a tube of lipstick for the occasional formal dinner, a bit of eye shadow for the same reason. I couldn't remember when I'd used either. They might have dried up. Other women, maybe even most women, took such products more seriously. If Twinkle sold makeup on the side, she would presumably have local customers: neighbors, friends, co-workers. Maybe I could identify some.

Nothing else in the desk held promise. Twinkle probably had secrets, but they didn't jump out at me. When I pulled open the door to the closet, however, Beauty Is You containers tumbled out as if they were attacking. I yelled as I jumped back. Stacks of small boxes flooded my feet. I picked up the nearest ones: lip gloss and eyebrow pencils. The usual items. I stuffed several back in the closet, but then I saw the stack of brochures. Stapled to the front of each was a business card with Twinkle's contact information.

Might I pose as she? I couldn't think why I would want to, but I added some brochures and cosmetics to the laundry bag. I shoved everything else back in the closet and shut the door.

For all my trouble of breaking and entering, I had little to show for myself. I bucked up and entered the master bedroom. Three steps in, I tripped over the shag throw rug and landed on the bed. I scrambled off as if a bee were attacking my back. Yuck.

Once I planted myself firmly on my feet, I realized that the queen bed claimed a full third of the space. Matching chests of drawers dominated one wall. The opposite wall included a door leading to the master bathroom. A patio door led outside.

A killer could have easily entered the backyard, let himself in, and reached Twinkle. I approached gingerly as if someone might jump out at me as well. The dust on the door handle, however, seemed undisturbed.

In that case, logic said the killer had entered the house the same way I had.

I turned to the drawers. Where did women keep private things? With their underwear. One drawer was dedicated to high-end C-cup bras, lots of pastels with dainty lace. Nothing more. The next drawer, panties in matching lace.

The third drawer held hosiery—who wore hose in Tucson?—and an assortment of precisely ordered socks. Behind the footwear lay a set of slim notepads with peach-colored pages. I used similar versions for grocery lists. I picked up the notepad on top. It was an abbreviated diary that started with January. Twinkle had written a dozen entries. Most were brief notes such as $135 Safeway, RoadHouse 8:15. A few were personal: *Great to spend time with B again. She hasn't changed since middle school.*

Some days contained nothing but a capital E. E for Emil. The letter couldn't have meant anything else. I perused carefully, but nothing was written for February. She'd died on the morning of the seventeenth. The rest of the notebook was blank.

I snatched up the tome that lay underneath and thumbed through it backwards. Entries for December and November held capital Es as well. So did October and September. Sometimes the capital E was underlined, and an arrow flew from the E's belly to a point below the line. Overnights. Cute.

I squeezed the notebook as if I could strangle paper. I flipped all the way through the pages. The Es had started the previous March. One here or there. More in May. A flock in June. Sprinkles throughout July and August. I clenched my fists, wishing Emil were there so I could punch him. How dare he? And why lie to me? We weren't married. I hadn't chained him to the house. He could have simply left.

I grabbed the next volume down, but I only needed a few moments with it. The single December entry, from a little over a year ago, told me everything: *I met exactly the rightest man. He's the man I've been waiting my whole darned life for.*

Rightest? That was bad enough, but the content was unbelievable. All the evidence I needed was right in front of me. I started to pull out the page, but I caught myself in time. I only ripped a small corner. I carefully realigned the tip of the page and put all the notebooks back where I found them.

If the diaries hadn't made me so angry, I would have stolen them. I needed to leave before I did any permanent damage to the pages or kicked at the drawers that held them.

I possessed a house key. I would come back when I damned well felt like it.

***

When I got home, I opened a Guinness. Then I paced. First around the kitchen. Then the living room. Then both combined. Emil and his overnights. Unbelievable. If he remained in jail, he couldn't rot too fast.

But he wouldn't have killed her. He wouldn't have had a reason to.

Given the circumstances, I had no moral obligation to help him. If he got out of jail, he'd screw somebody else, wouldn't he? Betray the next woman. Swear eternal love and then two-time her because he was too cowardly to come out and say, Oh, by the way, darling, I'm not happy.

The message machine kicked in again. This time it was Mari. The nanas had been alternating.

"Hello, angel! We were wondering if you're okay. Give us a call, all right?"

They didn't want to know if I were okay. They wanted to know if I'd made progress. Since they were night owls, they would keep calling. I could turn off the ringer, but they'd leave messages until the box was full.

I called my home phone with my cell phone, ignoring the five texts from Joachín, and left myself such a long blank message that I filled up the message box.

That would teach the nanas a thing or two.

Finally I was so tired of hearing myself complain that I took out Emil's laptop. It opened with our usual password, Emil17Dervla. He hadn't even bothered to change it.

I went straight to his Google cloud, and, once inside, checked his calendar. No big Ts, but his calendar was populated with Beauty Is You events. No doubt Twinkle had set it up for him.

The next event was in two days' time. Since the email was conveniently provided, I could contact the host, a Brenda Davidson, and explain that I was substituting for Twinkle. Who better to know about Twinkle's relationship

107

with Emil than a bunch of female customers? And who would pass up the chance to discuss their murdered representative?

I could gather ammunition, lots of it. When the time was right, I would aim it at Emil like firecrackers on the Fourth of July.

So what that I knew nothing about cosmetics? I'd faked my way through language lessons often enough. I could easily fake my way through a makeup session, yet I had no reason to work so hard when I could recruit Mari. She genuinely enjoyed using makeup.

I reviewed Emil's laptop haphazardly but found no mention of Twinkle. I still couldn't believe that I'd been too blind to see the big E of the vision test. Never mind the elephant in the room; I'd missed the whole herd.

I tried to think of an inciting incident, but nothing came to mind. Emil and I hadn't fought or had a significant disagreement. We worked hard to grow the school and went for vacations on the Santa Catalina Island. We had dinners with the nanas. Sunday picnics. What had changed, and when?

Twinkle was a different question. She'd evidently been satisfied being the other woman. Maybe she liked Emil best for short periods of time. Maybe her needs were physical. His too. She could go back to attending the children after a quick half hour. Maybe she and Emil only needed twenty minutes. Maybe he paid her.

I shut the laptop and went back to the kitchen. I took another Guinness from the refrigerator, but I put it back again. Numbing myself wasn't going to help anything, and I'd feel lousy in the morning if I didn't watch it. I sat at a barstool, wondering if I could find something to break.

I couldn't help myself. I took Emilito from his perch next to the dog-cat and got out the pins. Jab, jab, jab to the place where it would hurt the most. Not only had the big fat coward mistreated me, but if he had strung Twinkle along for nearly a year, he hadn't been fair to her either. Jab!

Maybe he'd brought her here. While I suffered through a visit with my parents, perhaps she'd sat where I was sitting now, at the bar, while Emil cooked something up for her.

If she'd been in the kitchen, then she'd been in the bedroom too. My bedroom.

I jabbed Emilito's drawn-on penis so hard that stuffing came out.

***

I finally settled down enough to get out of my sewing machine. I hadn't made anything for so long I was worried the machine wouldn't come to life, but it started right up. I was halfway through Joachín's vest when I realized I'd forgotten what kinds of buttons it was supposed to have.

"Joachín?"

"Where have you been? I stopped by after rehearsal."

"Out running errands. Now, about your vest — "

"Who runs errands that late? Sure, Safeway closes at ten, but Bookman's closes at eight."

"Joachín, if we could concentrate on your vest — "

"Where were you?" His voice was sharp.

"Checking up on me?" I tried to sound flirty, but I was out of practice. Also, he was considerably younger than I was.

"Might be." He sounded vaguely flirty too. What was the Vargas Llosa novel about the narrator dating an older family member?

In reality fewer than seven years separated us. Those weren't so many in the scheme of things. Not even the difference of a generation. Not enough for anyone to notice.

But no. Ever since I'd dated Emil, Joachín had been a pseudo-nephew. I wasn't the kind of woman to be attracted to him.

Or maybe I was.

"You don't need to worry," I said. "I'm self-sufficient." I pressed on the sewing machine pedal long enough that he could hear the *whir*.

"You went to Twinkle's, didn't you?"

How could he have guessed? I might have gone out for a walk. Had coffee with a neighbor. Taken a long bath.

"You might as well tell me," he said.

I liked that we'd gotten closer. Spent quality time together. This was too close.

"There's no reason for you to think—"

No. Enough of my life was a lie. I didn't need to add Joachín to that equation. Perhaps I didn't need to come completely clean. Seventy percent would be good enough.

"It was a last-minute decision."

"You didn't take me with you. You said you would."

Had I? I couldn't remember. Maybe he wasn't completely clean either. "I wanted to check on one little thing. I was only there for five minutes."

"That's not true since I waited outside your place for fifteen. Never mind. Did you break in? Find a loose window?"

"Nothing so dramatic. I found a key to her house in Emil's glove compartment."

"Oh." He drew the word out to two syllables.

"'Oh' is right. If he rots in jail, I don't mind."

Joachín didn't reply.

"Maybe he'll get two life sentences, one for being a terrible boyfriend and the other for being a murderer."

Nothing.

"Joachín?"

"The nanas still love him. Maybe I do too. I can't tell."

The vest slid from the machine to the floor.

"Out of respect for the nanas, I might still try to help, but my heart won't be in it. "

"Give Emilito a few more jabs?"

"Good idea."

I snatched up a thick sewing needle, went to the bar, and sawed through Emilito's penis six or seven times.

"Feel better?"

"Strangely enough, I feel terrific." And I did. Who knew a doll could be so therapeutic? Maybe I had more violence in me than I realized. Maybe I could make a fortune designing dolls for disappointed lovers. "I'm sorry I forgot to ask, but how was rehearsal?"

"So-so."

"What did Laney do tonight?"

"How did you guess she was the problem? We barely waded through the reading. She kept interrupting with one brilliant suggestion or another. Tommy's ready to kick himself for not hiring Isabel."

"He's that desperate?"

"One more rehearsal with Laney and he will be."

"You can't audition someone else?"

"We're opening a week from tomorrow. We don't have time."

"You'll work it out. Tommy always brings things together."

"I'm not so sure. At this rate, he might end up in jail alongside Emil. But speaking of Tommy, he asked if you would come to rehearsal tomorrow night. He had a few more ideas about the costumes, and he wanted to see what you had so far."

"You'll keep teaching Basic Spanish?"

"You drive a terrible bargain," said Joachín.

"It's not a bargain if I'm paying you."

"That's not what I mean."

"What do you mean?"

I heard the faint sound of his breathing. "I know he's been a dickhead, but it's the least I can do for Emil."

"He's not even your family."

"He sort of is."

Joachín was in the same position I was, stuck between family loyalties and a hard place. As we said our goodbyes, I carefully stuck three pins in Emilito's penis. I set the doll on its back so the pins couldn't fall out.

When I returned to my sewing machine, I realized I'd forgotten to ask about the buttons.

Chapter Thirteen

When I heard the nanas' footsteps the next morning, I looked up from the screen where I had been fruitlessly studying Emil's emails.

I closed the laptop and joined them at my back door. Three tricky steps led up to the small porch, and I wanted to make sure they didn't trip.

Lula panted as I offered her my hand. She gave the handrail a death grip with the other.

"Did you have car trouble?" I asked. "You know that vehicle needs to be serviced."

"It's Emil! He's in trouble!"

He was in jail on suspicion of murder and his cousin was no skilled criminal lawyer, so of course he was in trouble. "He was attacked by a fellow prisoner?"

"Worse than that." Lula flung open the door and charged inside.

I held out my hand for Mari, whose hands were ice cold despite the day's moderate sixty-five degrees.

"His thingee hurt so much last night that he woke up screaming," Mari said.

I loved the euphemism. "Isn't he young for prostate cancer?"

"So much pain they sedated him," she said as we followed Lula inside.

I couldn't resist. "Probably has an STD. Or two."

As soon as I heard myself, my expression vanished like water going down the drain. If he had something, I probably did too. Jerk! "They took him to the hospital?"

"The doctors found nothing!" Lula cried.

The thought of Emil being carted to the hospital by prison guards was a pleasant one. His being embarrassed by problems with his private parts doubled my amusement. Unfortunately, the murderer had made a big mistake. He should have gone for Emil's "thingee" instead of Twinkle's head.

Lula paced in the kitchen. "Where is he?"

Emil's having an extra lover didn't mean that I did. The nanas should have known better. I wasn't the type. Yet.

"Where?" She hurried up the stairs as a woman half her age.

"Go ahead," I told the retreating figure. Not even a bulldozer would have stopped her. I should have been incensed, but I admired her determination.

Mari paced past the dining room table to the living room and back again. "Or maybe he's down here?"

Despite the tag-teaming, I couldn't take their invasion seriously. Did they think I hid lovers under the couch? I wished they could see themselves. I'd never witnessed them flying off the handle at the same time. Had they been trapeze artists, they would have flown out of the circus tent and over to the next town.

"You want to check my closets? I don't have a basement, you know."

Mari was as wild as a drug addict looking for a fix. "He's going to die of the pain!"

"What are you talking about?"

Lula pounded back down the stairs. "Where?" She spotted my purse on the kitchen counter, overturned it, and shook everything out.

Had they seen some crazy documentary? "You guys are scaring me." I put my arm around Mari's shoulders. "You need to calm down, both of you." I walked Mari toward her sister. "Of course I'm not seeing anyone. Why would you think so?"

Mari shook loose. "Where's Emilito?"

They wanted the doll? I pointed to the bar. Although one of the pins had fallen out, the other two were still firmly embedded in the itty-bitty penis.

Lula ran to Emilito and pulled out the pins. "I told you!" she shouted at her sister. "You didn't believe me!"

"Not at first," Mari said.

"What is wrong with you two?" I asked.

Lula patted the doll's head. "At first we didn't believe it ourselves."

"Believe what?"

Mari sat me down at the bar and took hold of both my hands. "This will sound a bit strange, but it can't be helped."

"Are you feeling okay?"

"You won't believe us right away."

"What's going on?"

Mari stared straight into my eyes. "You've got the power."

I looked between them. Lula stroked the doll as if it were a baby, and Mari looked on with the concern of a godmother. Two grown women hysterical over the pins I'd stuck into a doll. *Do not laugh at them.*

I squeezed Mari's hands once before wiggling free. "Tell you what. I'll put on some coffee."

I slid over to the kitchen before she could stop me. I filled the carafe with water and poured it into the Ninja. I placed a filter in the cup and reached for the Melitta Colombian Extreme. Then I put it back and reached for the Folger's decaf instead. The nanas were wound up enough, and they needed to teach Emil's Spanish class within the hour. If they had any more caffeine, they'd scare the students.

"Sit," I said over my shoulder.

As I monitored the coffee, I watched my friends carry the doll to the dining room table.

Lula patted the doll's head. "You'll be all right."

Mari stroked its body. "You have nothing to worry about."

"Did one of you have a nightmare?" I asked.

Tears of relief dotted the corners of Mari's eyes, but none had run down her cheeks. "Emil called last night. He was frantic. He didn't know what to do. We assumed, you know, a male problem."

"We didn't think much of it at the time," Lula said. "He's always been a hypochondriac."

Absolutely. At the first sign of a cold, off he went to Urgent Care.

"The hospital called at five a.m.," Mari said. "The nurse wanted to know if he were allergic to any medicines. By then he was too delirious to explain things himself."

Lula cradled Emilito to her breast. "We are so stupid! We still didn't catch on."

The hot water gurgled its way to coffee. I looked to the bar, where Emilito had spent the night next to the dog-cat, and back to the nanas. I might have been in some kooky dream, the kind you had after binge-watching reruns of the world's worst horror movies.

"Whatever is wrong with Emil had nothing to do with that doll," I said quietly. "You know that, right?"

"*Te dije,*" Lula whispered to Mari.

"*Sería difícil para cualquiera.*"

I struggled to identify any of the syllables while they continued whispering in streaks, sometimes at the same time.

I poured them each a coffee before topping off my own. "Nanas, you'll be able to teach your ten o'clock?" My own class wasn't scheduled until eleven.

Lula set down the doll, gently tapped its stomach, and looked at me. "Honey, you have the power."

I cracked a smile, still hopeful they would wake up from their lunacy, but they were dead serious. What legends had they grown up with as children? I knew about La Llorona, a lady who cried about her drowned children, and the chupacabra, a dog-like goat-sucker, but the nanas had never talked about the supernatural, at least not to me. Now they seemed convinced I'd nearly killed Emil.

"Special power?" I stalled as I pondered how to reason with them.

Mari caressed the doll. "Emilito confirms it."

"Poor Emil," Lula said.

Mari patted her sister's arm. "He should feel better already."

I had two batty women in my kitchen, and I needed both of them to go teach. "There might be some other explanation," I said slowly, as if trying to convince myself.

They shook their heads. Lula gulped down half of her coffee. Mari blew on hers.

"You guys made the doll. You must be the ones with the power." I grinned as if someone were taking my photo, but their expressions didn't change.

"¡Si mamá pudiera vernos —"

" — nos regañaría!"

Lula fanned herself with her hands, but I fetched her a calendar from the bar.

"Try this."

"Thanks. Much better."

"We always knew you were special," Mari said.

"I didn't do anything."

"Try not to blame us," Lula said. "We never believed this could work. We're as surprised as you are."

I nodded. Class started in twenty-five minutes. "So now what?"

"Be kind to Emilito," said Mari. "I know Emil has been terrible, but let's not make him suffer while he's in jail."

"Right," I said.

"You can do that afterwards," said Lula. "All you want."

"You'll be tempted," Mari said. "You'll have to exercise your willpower."

I would use willpower to hide my true opinion from the nanas.

Lula fanned herself so vigorously that the calendar flew from her hands, hit the wall, and bounced off. "I'm sorry, honey."

I retrieved the makeshift fan. "No worries! He's your grandson. Of course you're concerned about him."

I tapped my wrist where my watch would have been had I put it on. "Cover Emil's advanced class?"

Lula popped right up from the chair. "Of course."

Mari copied her movements. "Now we can stop worrying about Emil."

I herded the pair to my back door. "I'll meet you at school in a few minutes. Are you sure you're all right?"

Lula squeezed me. "We'll be fine."

Mari hugged me as well. "Now everything's all right. Well, almost."

All right, my foot. Emil was in jail, and both his grandmother and great-aunt had flipped off the deep end. I helped them down the three steps and waved as they headed for their car.

At least they didn't trip.

The calendar had fallen open. I would have turned it back to March, but I noticed a faint asterisk next to July

14th, the day after I was scheduled to fly to Ireland for a family reunion.

The handwriting was not my own. I never made notations in pencil.

I stared at the marking. Emil would have noted the date for a reason. A special birthday he needed to remember? Flor handled most of the family events, and she always warned us about upcoming birthdays.

What other dates would he note so far ahead of time? A dental appointment, perhaps. Or a yearly checkup. But Emil always wrote those in big letters on the calendar he kept at his desk upstairs.

Ah. An income tax extension. Possible, since the paperwork was complicated. I'd filed on time the year before thanks to panic and lots of caffeine. I grabbed my phone and googled.

No, the extension date was in October.

The date signified something different. Something personal.

I didn't have time to worry about it. I hopped on my bike and pedaled as fast as I could so that I could open the school for the nanas.

Chapter Fourteen

I taught mechanically, but all my business students concentrated so feverishly that they didn't notice. My thoughts were back at my house straining to think of a context. Normally Emil would have used his own calendar unless he was downstairs and too lazy to go upstairs. Too lazy or too occupied? He might have been in the kitchen, cooking. He made soups during the colder months. He might have been frying an egg and suddenly thought about — what? — and noted the date.

He might have been on the phone, pressed for time during a conversation. Considering the dates for our summer school courses. Talking to one of his buddies. Maybe his friend Dave had finally set a wedding date? Alfie's wife had learned when her baby was due?

Not likely at all.

I didn't like the coincidence that I was leaving the day before. He wanted me out of the way for — redoing the lawn? I insisted it was fine the way it was, but he wanted to get rid of the cheap river rocks and put in something more decorative and more expensive. Painting the balcony railing? We talked about doing it ourselves, but I wouldn't put it past him to hire someone. But no one hired a handyman half a year in advance.

Once I returned home, I whipped out the sewing machine and started in on the green velvet. While playing with seams and hems, my thoughts strayed. Emil had planned a party celebrating my absence. Perhaps it was the day he had initially chosen to move out.

When I stood to stretch, I had a sudden inspiration. I opened Emil's laptop and pulled up his password page, which he'd edited three weeks earlier. I looked through the eighteen pages of passwords: credit cards, bank accounts, online shopping. I had all the information at my fingertips. A large charge might tell me something. A bill from Home Depot for something I didn't recognize.

As I scrolled through the pages, I pictured one of Monet's haystacks. One in earth colors I didn't like.

Frustrated, I scrolled to the bottom of the page. Since when did Emil have an account with Air France?

I scooted right into his account. How very lovely. A trip for two to Nice, scheduled for the day after I left for Ireland. Returning to Tucson from Paris the day before I would.

Second passenger? Twinkle Witherbottom.

Damned jerk. Had Emil been standing before me, I would have thrown the laptop at him to see if he were smart enough to catch it. We'd talked about a romantic vacation in France for at least five years. It was a trifecta. He'd kept a mistress, maintained a front, and planned a vacation. He probably hoped I would react just the way I had, by kicking him out. I played into his hand.

I slammed the computer shut and walked in circles. Promenading along the Mediterranean. Waving from the Eiffel Tower. Luxurious dinners. The only image that comforted me was that of putting my hands around Emil's neck and squeezing, which gave me a completely new reason for wanting to rescue him from jail.

From his niche between the sheep salt shaker and the dog-cat, Emilito taunted me. *I dare you. I double dare you.*

Right. Stick a pin in a doll and torture its real-life model. *Chicken?* the glossy eyes asked.

The idea was delicious. What if I did have power over my former lover, former business partner, former everything! And what if, any time I wanted to, I could make him suffer? I cackled so loudly the neighbors probably wondered what I was doing all by myself.

I wouldn't need to torment him once I had a fabulous new boyfriend and reclaimed the business in a definitive way. But what if, after that, whenever I felt like it, I could give him a little punch in the conscience? When he was too sure of himself, for example. When he spoke to his students as if he knew everything there was to know about the whole Spanish language. When I learned of any new lovers. Jab, jab, jab! A little indigestion never hurt anybody. Why should he be happy? The idea of the good life was to choose a right mate and stick with her. We were the perfect couple. Everybody knew it. Even Emil.

Had he given me the slightest warning, I would have smoothed things over between us. Given up the Thursday night soccer games, the movies with the nanas, the lunches with Janice, the coffees klatches, even the Sunday jam sessions with the folk singers. Well, maybe not that. And the soccer games were good for my health. They were seasonal anyway. Moral: I would have made time for Emil somehow. Poor ignored orphan. Maybe I would have even arisen for some of his early morning—

No. That was going way too far. He fell far short of godliness. He might have softened his appearance, for example. I'd mentioned my fondness for moustaches. Had he tried? No. In the beginning I'd complained about his monochromatic wardrobe. His solution? Bought an extra blue shirt. What about the disgusting used tissues he left all over the house? He had plenty of flaws. I should have received a prize for putting up with him.

The nanas understood. That's why they'd given me the doll.

I snatched up Emilito as if he were a flight risk. Between the lumps and the loose stuffing, the figure had the zany look of not being quite right and knowing it, like the comedian who wore baggie clown pants or the Halloween vampire with a nylon cape. Maybe that's how the doll taunted me, by recognizing its imperfections in a way that Emil never had.

I might have chosen a gentler approach. I might have considered the world from my ex-lover's point of view. Instead I grabbed three red pins and jabbed them into Emilito's stomach. One, two, three! Why stop? Four, five six! I was ready for a third round when the phone startled me from my spell of bad intentions.

"Swing by for you before rehearsal?" asked Joachín.

"Perfect. Just finishing one last hem."

Better get here fast. Otherwise, by the time you arrive, Emilito will be in tiny pieces all over the floor because I will have poked the stuffing right out of him.

***

I patted myself on the back as Holland and Désirée flitted around the stage. Although Holland's hem was uneven and one of Désirée's buttons was loose, the velvet dresses fit well enough to be flattering. The maroon and green provided a pleasing contrast to the plain beige sofa and the equally plain throw rug that dominated the main set, which was a living room.

When the actors took a break, I turned to Tommy, who sat beside me in the third row. "Joachín said you would have suggestions."

The man's smile complimented his angular jaw. "I usually do! But the dresses look fine as they are. Showy, but not too showy. Feminine, but not regal. I hope you'll design costumes for our next show as well?"

"Happy to."

He indicated the stage. "What do you think so far?"

Willard and Désirée had plenty of experience, and it showed through. They already had a sense of timing, made eye contact when they spoke, and easily moved around the set. Holland was not quite as polished, yet she had a handle on the material and paid close attention to details. I couldn't judge Joachín. I was too fond of him to be critical, but he seemed to hold his own even though he was younger than the others.

"So far so good," I said. "I'm not a drama critic."

"Joachín says you know a lot about theatre."

I wanted to kiss my top supporter. "I haven't been in many plays, but I've read and seen tons of them. All your productions have been top-notch."

"*Boeing, Boeing* was so-so."

"The night I came the audience laughed itself silly."

"Berthe remembered her lines that night?"

"Almost all of them." I'd caught two mistakes, but she'd covered them up quickly.

"That's the true joy of live theatre. There's always something unexpected." He patted his forehead. "That's also why I have a receding hairline."

I patted my own hair, which was too wavy to control. We all had our little problems. "Let's hope you don't lose any more hair over this play."

"You're the ultimate optimist, aren't you?"

"I try to be!" And why not? After all, I had Emilito.

The second act began well enough with quick dialogue between Willard and Désirée and then Joachín and Holland. There was a pause when the maid—who'd been summoned—didn't appear on stage.

"Shall I go wake her up?" Holland asked.

"Laney!" Tommy shouted. "You're on."

For a moment the others shuffled around, glancing toward Stage Right.

"Laney!" Tommy shouted so loudly I jumped.

"Want me to read the part?" Joachín asked. "After this scene I don't come in again until page sixty-two."

Tommy turned to me. "Mind doing us the honors?"

I scrambled to my feet. "Of course not." I always preferred doing to sitting.

Holland beckoned me. "You can read off my script."

"Perfect." For the next five minutes I strutted around as the nosiest maid ever.

"What are you doing?" Laney yelled as she rushed on stage in the dowdy maid's costume.

I lowered the script. "Helping out."

"While I try on this horrid costume, you steal my part!"

She could criticize my actions, but not my handiwork. "If you want to wear a sexy maid outfit, try out for a play that takes place in France. I was reading your part because —"

That was all I had time to say. Laney lunged for the script. Faster and nimbler, I jumped out of the way. She bellyflopped onto the rug with a thud so loud the janitor hurried in from the back room.

Tommy rushed to the stage. "Are you all right?"

Clearly unhurt, she propped her chin onto her elbows. "I nearly broke a tooth. Or my jaw."

"Think there's a swimming pool in the living room, do you?" asked Willard.

"You should work on technique," said Holland. "When diving, it's best to put your fingertips together to generate more forward movement."

Joachín offered his hand, but Laney frowned and struggled to her knees, then her feet, by herself. "I don't know why I moved here. Everyone's horrid."

We looked from one to the other hiding various levels of amusement. Actors were supposed to provide entertainment, right?

Laney checked her knees. "I might have rug burns."

She probably did.

"Next time you want to ambush someone, sign up for a soccer team," I said. "Tommy asked me to read for you. Good thing I didn't use the most expensive materials on the maid's costume." I indicated the other two dresses. "Velvet tears right away."

Laney pouted. "Maybe I should just quit.".

Tommy put his hand on her shoulder. "You're overreacting. You slipped. Luckily, you're all right. Now, please, let's continue. We open eight days from now, and we need to be ready. Dervla, thanks for standing in. Let's take it from the top of the scene."

As I left the stage, I would have sworn Laney snarled at me. I didn't care in the least. If she wanted to use acting skills to impersonate a rabid dog, why should I stop her? But I analyzed her performance for the rest of the rehearsal. The other actors navigated through their parts while Laney struggled to follow the script. When offstage, she sulked from the edge of the first row. Physical age, mid-thirties. Mental age, around eleven. Maybe it wasn't her fault. She didn't have this or that growing up or she had abusive parents or bad boyfriends. We all had something to overcome, but we could control how we reacted. Or not. I could hardly wait for Joachín to take me home so that I could invite him in for a drink. Then we could gossip about her.

We needed the comic relief. Then we could fortify ourselves for the real work of finding out who murdered Twinkle.

Chapter Fifteen

As soon as we reached my kitchen, I pointed Joachín to the bar and opened the creaky cupboard. "We might need something stronger than beer."

He smiled as he swung one leg over a barstool. "Because of Laney?"

"Choose your battleground. For me it's because of Emil. He was planning to take our dream vacation to France without me."

"How do you know?"

I handed Joachín a clear tumbler and my bottle of Jameson. "Found confirmation of his airline ticket."

"Ouch."

I sat on the other barstool and poured liberally for both of us. "I would have spent tonight swearing at the walls if you hadn't come for me."

"Why didn't you tell me earlier?"

"Wasn't ready to talk about it."

"I'm sorry. I wouldn't have expected it from him."

"As soon as he gets out of jail, I'm going to kill him."

Joachín winked. "So he might as well stay in?"

How had I never noticed the dimple on his left cheek? I held my hand as a gun and pretended to shoot Emilito. "Exactly."

Joachín leaned a few inches back. "You don't mean that."

I pointed to the area of the ceiling immediately below my bedroom. "We lay in bed musing about sailing down the Seine together. Visiting the Arc de Triomphe. The Sacré-Cœur. How's that for a betrayal?"

I took a huge swig, told myself to slow down, and took another. "I dreamt up the fantasy vacation, but Twinkle was going to take it." I set the glass down so hard it might have cracked.

"Maybe Emil was planning to surprise you by joining you in Europe somehow."

I held up my glass for a toast, and Joachín obliged me by clinking his glass with mine.

"He bought two tickets."

"Oh."

"He orchestrated the whole thing. Even convinced me that we should shut down the school for three weeks and suspend classes. 'Let's give the students a break,' he said. 'And us.' 'What do you want to do with the extra time?' I asked. 'Spend quality time hiking.' Hiking all the way into someone's bed. But never mind. You've heard me complain enough. Let's talk about Laney instead."

"I don't mind. Talking it out always helps."

How had this teen become a sensitive man without my noticing? He'd never had a serious girlfriend, yet he listened with the grace of a fiancé. Or what did I know? I'd never been engaged. Maybe it was the grace of simple kindness.

"I appreciate the offer," I said, "but Laney is more fun to talk about. At least everyone enjoyed her nosedive except for her."

When Joachín laughed, his eyes lit up. "If she can trip herself once a night, we might be able to tolerate her after all. We're fed up, but it's my fault. I insisted Tommy give Laney a try to avoid Isabel."

"Laney is probably an okay person," I said. "New town, no friends — what's her day job?"

"Something to do with health. Medical records or something."

"Yawn. I might be on edge too. I know! How about if I make a doll for her?"

"What?"

"You know. A nana doll." I dragged him over to my sewing machine, which was still lording over the dining room table. I handed Joachín some scraps. Pick one."

"You weren't kidding."

"You'll feel better. What more do you need? It'll only take a few minutes."

For a moment Joachín eyed me suspiciously as if I were challenging him to take the bait. Then he fingered through the material until he found a brown scrap. "This one will do for the head." He pulled out a strip from a white sheet. "Her body is kind of whiteish, so you could use this."

I handed over a packet of miscellaneous buttons from every torn shirt I'd thrown away. "Find her some eyes. And a nose, I guess. If you want, bring in some cotton balls from the bathroom and we'll give her some cleavage."

"Since you insist —"

"I do."

"You're right. We'll feel better."

"Not me, you. Laney doesn't affect me in the least. She's not my problem."

"She will be when she lists the changes she wants to her costume."

"Are you kidding? She's scared of me. She's the regular barking dog without a bite."

Using Emilito as a model, I cut the body pieces, sewed them together, and turned the result inside out. I'd misjudged the size, so I sewed on the feet separately.

"Let me do the eyes," Joachín said. He'd already threaded a needle.

We stuffed the figure with leftovers from a pillow. The doll was ugly, but I liked it.

I set the doll on its back and gave it a spin. "What should we call her? Laney-ita doesn't work."

"Let's go with Lanita instead." He pounded the doll's stomach with his fist.

"Don't break the furniture." I pushed the pincushion in his direction. "Be my guest. Stick a pin in her. You'll feel better."

"You're sure?"

"Go for it. She's not my problem. She's all yours."

Joachín slid a pin into her right breast and twirled it. He might have been a child with a new toy. "I love this!"

"See? You feel better already."

"Sure do."

"I forgot to tell you, but I have bad news."

He added a pin to her left breast. "What?"

"The nanas are losing it."

Next he applied a pin to Lanita's neck. "You mean they're forgetful? They are getting up there."

"They stopped by this morning in hysterics."

He added a pin to Lanita's shoulders. "They're usually rational. What happened? Bad news about Emil?"

"You'll never guess."

"Somebody else is sick?"

"The nanas might be."

He slid a pin into the doll's thighs. "Stop torturing me."

I nodded toward Emilito. "They said I have the power. Can you imagine?"

Joachín pierced Lanita's foot but pulled the pin out again. "The power."

"I know. Crazy, right? And they were so insistent. Evidently Emil woke up with terrible pain. Kept screaming that his penis hurt. At first they thought he was faking, but eventually the guards took him to emergency."

"You.... You put pins in his—"

I crossed to the bar and came back with Emilito. I pushed my finger into the doll's drawn-on penis. "You bet I did."

"He woke up screaming?"

"Funny coincidence, huh? You've got to love it."

Joachín stared into me as if he could stare through me. "They said you have the power," he said quietly.

"I know. Crazy, huh?"

"Emil had a headache."

"What?"

"A bad one. A couple of days ago."

"So?"

"After you put pins into his head."

"He gets headaches when he's stressed. So what?"

Joachín sat back as if I'd shared my darkest secret. He wasn't smiling.

"What's the matter?"

"Maybe they're right."

"Oh, come on."

He squeezed hands. "They would know."

I popped to my feet and put my hands on my waist. "Are you hearing yourself?"

He loosened Lanita's pins.

"What?"

He shook his head. "We don't want to overdo things."

"Come again?"

"We're not trying to kill her. We want her to quit the play." He jabbed the top of her head a couple of times and then set down the pin. "Give her a bad night. That's all."

Just my luck. I had an attractive younger man in my dining room, but he was as looney as the nanas. I held up

131

my freckled hands and shook them. "See here? No special powers."

"The nanas are never wrong."

"You're overreacting to a couple of coincidences."

"One coincidence? Fine. Two? There's a pattern."

"So I have magical powers."

"Deny it all you want to. That won't change a thing."

I crossed back to the bar and came back with Emilito. I picked up a pin. "You're wrong, and I'll prove it to you." I stuck the pin in the doll's ear.

"Stop!" Joachín snatched Emilito from my hand. "Not so deep. You don't want him to go deaf." He eased the pin to the edge of the fabric so that it barely stuck in.

I watched him more carefully than I would a cheating student. "Otherwise he'd lose his hearing?"

"You never know."

I poured myself another Jameson. "Another for you?"

"I need one. But then I might not be able to drive."

"So stay over. The couch pulls out into a bed." He'd slept at the Arellanos' so often they kept a pillow for him. His excuse was that he didn't like to drink and drive, but I always suspected he wanted the company.

He stared at me without speaking.

"What's wrong?"

"I've never met anyone with the power before," he said. "What does it feel like?"

"Joachín, there's no . . . power."

"You're not Mexican. You don't understand."

"I'm not trying to be disrespectful or anything."

"It's not your fault." He drained the glass. Now I had to my credit two crazy nanas and a beautiful but crazy man who was about to get drunk.

"Maybe we could play cards or something?"

"No." He pointed to the bottle. "May I?"

When I nodded, he filled both our shot glasses to the top.

I went to the cabinet and took out two water glasses. "You better hydrate. And how about something crunchy?" I pulled out the top bag of snacks, which were pretzels. I filled a bowl to the top.

Joachín watched me silently, a cat about to pounce on a shadow.

"What?"

"I need to tell you a story. You'll want to sit down."

"Long story?" I smiled, but he didn't smile back.

Instead, of one accord, we moved to the couch.

It was going to be another long night. I turned off the glaring overhead light and flipped on a soft lamp instead. I sank into the couch, kicked off my sandals, and put my feet on the coffee table. "I'm ready."

"You probably aren't," he said softly. "But I'll tell you anyway."

He was rarely serious. I told myself to settle down, but I struggled. This wasn't my normal almost-nephew, but someone I didn't recognize, someone wistful and sad. "I'm listening."

"You'll fight me, but promise not to tune out until you hear the whole thing."

"I never tune you out."

"You know what I mean."

I did. I bit into a pretzel so I wouldn't say anything else to irritate him. He was sad and adultlike at the same time. I wasn't used to it

He took a deep breath as if he needed the extra oxygen to get through the next sentence. "You might remember that my dad was born in the States, but my mom was born in Durango, Durango, Mexico. That's the capital of the state."

I didn't remember. If asked, I would have joked that Joachín sprang forth from the Arellano house without any parents at all.

"Do you know where Durango is?" he asked.

I envisioned a map of the country, but besides Nogales, I'd only been to the coastal town of Puerto Peñasco. I wasn't sure which state that was in. "Not exactly."

He stretched out his right hand. With his left, he pointed to a spot an inch below his ring finger. "It's more or less here. Even though Durango is in Northern Mexico, a lot of weird stuff goes on there."

"Things get weirder as you go south?"

"More traditions, legends, you know, that kind of thing. Durango is more Spanish than Native Indian, but it still has rich folklore."

Emil had recounted stories about a giant woman and some short guy with a big hat, but he never sounded serious about them. I assumed they were along the lines of Rip Van Winkle, tales meant to entertain that had a moral backbone on a secondary level.

"Your mom told you about that kind of stuff?"

"Always my nana. My cousin and I would be sent down to Mexico for a couple of weeks every summer, partly to learn about our heritage and partly to give our parents time to themselves."

I imagined two young kids running loose while elderly grandparents hobbled behind. "You liked going down there?"

"Loved it. We spent all day long playing with our counterparts. I came to appreciate the experiences even more when I was older."

"Your grandparents told you about folklore?"

"I don't remember my tata. He died when I was young. But Nanina, that's what we called her, was fierce and independent. It's not so much that she told me stories. It's that stuff came out."

I could only wish I knew anything similar. I hadn't met a single grandparent. My parents had gone over to the Old Country to visit, but that was before I was born. Their parents never made it over to the States. My mother said they weren't interested. My father said they'd never had the money. I assumed the truth was a bit of both.

"What kind of stuff came out?"

"Nanina would say things like 'Don't stay out late at night because of the chupacabras.'"

"Don't people say that to keep their kids out of trouble?"

"Maybe. Maybe she meant it. Never mind. One night this lady came over. Lupita. She and Nanina sat in the kitchen for hours. Lupita couldn't stop crying. More like wailing. Like a wounded animal you might hear out in the wild. I'd never seen an adult so upset outside a cemetery or a hospital."

"Your nana let you stay in the kitchen?"

"She shooed us out of the room, but the lady cried so hard and the house was so small that we could hear every sound. She was a big lady too, you know, round, so she had lung capacity. The neighbors probably heard her next door."

"She found out she was dying?"

"No. She was upset because her husband was cheating on her."

Emil shot to my mind. What had he been thinking? That he was still a Mexican macho from the 1920s who could get away with such crap?

"I can understand Lupita," I said. "But I want you to know that I didn't wail."

Joachín ignored my levity. "That was fifteen years ago. Women weren't so independent back then, and they

135

had fewer options. If they learned their husbands were cheating, they mostly put up with it."

"That's awful."

"You don't have to tell me. It's embarrassing. Men had total control in those days, and, frankly, a lot of them were bastards."

"Lupita's husband was a good example?"

"The epitome. His affairs had gone on for years."

When I cringed, Joachín patted my hand. "That was the reality at the time. Still is to an extent. I know it's hard to hear about."

"If women don't stand up for themselves, no one stands up for them. That's what I love about the nanas. Nobody gets in their way. They don't allow it."

"Exactly. And they don't live in Mexico, which makes it a little easier."

No matter where you lived, societal pressure was always right around the corner waiting to sneak in. You had to work to fight it off. They had.

"Lupita finally got tired of it?" I asked.

"She might have gone on like that forever, looking the other way and suffering. The real problem was that she couldn't concentrate because she was having these horrible headaches."

"She made herself sick?"

"She didn't know what was wrong. She saw some doctors, and they couldn't help her. They said her problems were in her imagination."

"She probably felt guilty that she hadn't satisfied her stupid husband. How did she know he was cheating?"

"I'm not sure. Probably the usual lipstick on the shirt, strange comings and goings, so-called friends who mentioned they'd seen him *veinteando* — that means driving through town on the main drag, a street called Veinte de Noviembre — with another woman."

At least Lupita figured it out. That's more than I had done. "Nanina convinced her to leave him?"

"Not exactly. Here's the deal. Every day, Lupita was in and out of bed all day long because she couldn't stand the pain. The house became a mess. She stopped cooking. She hired a maid to come in and do simple meals. Her husband accused her of being lazy."

"Not her fault!"

"Of course not. Remember, she was a victim of her times. Tack on that she was middle-aged, so she operated from an older mindset. I know it's wrong. But that's what happened."

Sure. Men got away with murder all the time. Society looked the other way, relatives looked the other way—at least the nanas had Emil's number and were mostly prepared to use it.

"Couldn't she have gone to a lawyer, one who would have fought to get her a divorce?"

"At the time she was in too much pain to do anything else, so she came to Nanina."

In Lupita's place, I would have made him suffer. After kicking him with strong soccer feet, I would have clobbered him over the head with a metal pan until his other head hurt too.

"What did Nanina advise her?"

"I don't know exactly. She finally sent Luís and me to bed. We fell asleep with the TV on and Lupita still crying." He nodded toward the kitchen. "Do you mind?"

"Of course not."

He fetched the bottle of Jameson and poured us both another shot. We sipped, Joachín remembering his eight-year-old self and me imagining a lady who had invested her whole life into a man and then her children, and probably none of them had paid any attention to her. They'd taken her for granted her whole life until the crisis was so big that she couldn't keep it inside anymore.

Joachin laid his head back against the cushion and closed his eyes as if carrying the weight of the world. When had he grown up? I hadn't paid attention. But I appreciated that he was here, with me, tapping into memories that were so far back or so far buried that he didn't revisit them very often. They weren't easy to visit, yet he'd chosen to trust me with them.

His lips quivered.

I hadn't noticed those before either, full lips that graced his mouth as they tapered at the sides. They were delicate lips, almost like women's.

What was I thinking? I attempted to snap a pretzel in two, but instead it burst into pieces, most of which landed on the floor.

Chapter Sixteen

Joachín halted his reverie, if that's what it was, long enough to help me retrieve the pretzel bits.

"That's one sad story," I said.

His eyes drifted to the bottle. This time I poured the shot. If he hadn't seemed so serious, I could have reveled in having an attractive young man bent on getting drunk in my living room. But this was too unlike Joachín for the evening to feel comfortable. It was as if he had to ease the story out of his system like a thorn out of a lion's paw. Retelling the memory helped, somehow, but the process was still painful.

"A couple of days went by," Joachín said. "It might have been a week. I don't remember. It was toward the end of the summer. One morning Lupita came over early. We drove to another part of town, a barrio north of Tierra Blanca."

"You and Nana and Lupita?"

"Luís was there too. Nanina said we were having a *día de campo,* a picnic. She packed a basket and told us to bring along our soccer ball, so we were all excited about it. But first we went to pick up this lady. She was a little old thing who lived in a hut. She was all thin and bony."

"Frail?"

"More like wiry. Like she'd never had enough to eat her whole life. I'd never seen anyone with such long hair. Her ponytail was white and gray, and it stretched down to her waist. I could barely understand a word she said because she only had a handful of teeth."

"She sounds like someone from a fairy tale."

"Yes, a fairy godmother! You could think of it that way. But actually she was a *curandera*."

"A witch doctor?"

"Of sorts."

"Scary?"

"Not at all. She said 'hi' to everybody, even me and Luís, and she seemed nice, like she was happy to go on an adventure with us."

The only old person I could remember as a child was a great-aunt who had come to visit, my dad's mother's youngest sister. She'd come over from Cork, and the whole week she stayed with us she wore the same tent-like dress. She made my younger siblings sit on her lap, but I was old enough to wiggle away. She entertained us with stories about Ireland, but I didn't retain any of them.

"You know how dogs act in the car?" Joachín asked. "How they stick their heads out the window to feel the breeze? The little old lady did that. Like she didn't get out much. Like it was a treat that we had come for her."

"Did you drive very far?"

"It seemed so at the time, but to a little kid, any drive seems long. All I remember is that we went way out of town. We stopped out in the sierra. We were the only ones around, so we had the area to ourselves. We sat at the one dilapidated picnic table and had our *lonches* and our Jarritos. We were surrounded by mountains. A stream gurgled in the distance. I remember the birds too, and they chirped at us, or maybe for us."

"Sounds like a nice day."

"Nanina made a game of it for us. She even brought our favorite *churritos*. After we ate, she handed me and Luís the soccer ball and pointed to a flat area. Off we went, yelling and chasing each other. We were alone in this beautiful place, and we had the whole day to do what we wanted."

"And then?"

"I don't remember how it started because Luís and I were playing, but finally we noticed that the little old lady was taking baby steps while she held a stick out in front of her, a makeshift divining rod. First we laughed, because she was intense as she walked, and she only went a few feet at a time, like she was listening to the desert."

"She walked in circles?"

"She followed a path that led into a deeper part of the sierra, slowly, slowly, with Nanina and Lupita a few feet behind. It looked funny, you know? This little old lady with a stick. Luís and I went back to our kicking. What did we care what the ladies were doing? We were having fun."

Joachín stopped and drained his glass. "Maybe you should make me some coffee. Otherwise I won't make it home."

A drunken man, my living room, and no early classes to worry about in the morning. Normally it would have been the perfect setup.

I patted the sofa cushions. "You can sleep here. I invited you already."

"You wouldn't mind?"

I answered by topping off his glass. He countered by staring into an imaginary TV screen.

"We stayed a long time," he finally said. "We were in a valley between trees, so the shadows came in faster than they would have in the city. By then Luís and I were tired, so we sat on a couple of boulders and tossed pebbles back and forth. That's when we notice the little old lady. She's jumping up and down and pointing at the ground. Nanina takes a couple of trowels out of her purse, and she and Lupita start digging.

"At first Luís and I laugh at them. What are they doing, searching for gold? But the little old lady looks even more excited, and Nanina and Lupita dig faster and faster. We head over there ourselves. We sense that what they're doing is grownup and secret, so we sneak over without saying anything. We stay far enough back that they don't notice us.

"Finally Nanina and Lupita hit something. They throw down their trowels and use their hands to remove more dirt. Luís and I can't help ourselves at that point, so we run forward to see what it is. We're sure it's treasure! But the little old lady reaches down and takes this glass jar out of the earth." He held outstretched fingers nine inches apart. "About this size. Crazy, huh?"

"What's inside?"

"A fat little doll with curly hair just like Lupita's. She's wearing a pink dress, and Lupita is too."

"Strange."

"That's not the crazy part. That doll had three pins sticking out of her head."

"Pins?"

"Right in her brain."

"Wow. That's some crazy coincidence."

"Not a coincidence. Say what you want, but I saw what I saw. The doll was a copy of Lupita, and the little old lady found it right there in the hole in the ground."

I shut my eyes to recreate the scene: three women, two young boys, one jar. "Then what?"

"The little old lady removed the pins and threw them on the ground."

"Anything else in the jar?"

"A kind of Tarot card. It might have been from Lotería. The card showed a box or maybe a chest against a yellow background. There might have been a number or a symbol, but I can't remember what it was. I might recognize it if I saw it."

The nanas might have an idea. There might be another type of playing card Joachín didn't know about.

"The old lady gave the jar back to Lupita?"

"Not right away. She puts the doll back in the jar. She moseys around and finds some wildflowers. Yellow and purple. She says they're for health and adds them to the jar. She takes some pesos out of her purse and adds those too. They're for wealth, she says. And she puts the lid back on the jar and hands it to Lupita. Then we all get in the car and head back to town."

Joachín fell silent. He turned toward the window as if looking out on that moment in time.

"Must have been the strangest day of your life," I said.

"So far, anyway. Nothing else has come close."

"But it's just a crazy coincidence."

"Is it?"

"Couldn't be anything else."

"I don't know. All these years I've tried to imagine what happened."

I gave him a few moments. He knew the story was wild, yet he hadn't been able to get past it. He squeezed my hand in a brief thanks.

"Crazy, huh?" he asked. "That anyone could be so hateful."

"No matter what happened, I can guess what I would have done. I would have kicked at the earth and thrown rocks at the jar until it exploded."

"Lupita nearly exploded herself. She yelled swear words until she was hoarse. Nanina didn't try to stop her."

"Given her terrible marriage, she'd probably never raised her voice before. Her throat wasn't used to it."

"Exactly. But guess what happened next. Lupita started to laugh. Nanina too. And the little old lady. They laughed until they doubled over. All the way home, they laughed until they cried. At one point Nanina pulled over because she couldn't see the road through her tears."

"Did you and Luís laugh too?"

"I don't remember. But Lupita's headaches?" He snapped his fingers. "Vanished. Like that."

Sure they did. It was the power of the mind to listen and obey orders. "Lupita left her rotten husband, I hope."

"I don't know what happened after that. Luís and I came back to the States to start the school year. By the time we returned to Durango the following summer, Lupita had the house and a lot of money."

"She divorced her husband?"

"I don't know. I never saw the little old lady again, but Lupita dropped by quite often. She felt a big debt to Nanina, so she always baked us cookies. That was my first experience with the supernatural."

I raised my palms to the sky. "You're saying this whole thing was voodoo of some kind?"

Joachín poured us both half a shot. "What else could it have been?"

"Joachín, great story and all. But it's no special coincidence. The little old lady? She was probably paid by the husband to prepare the jar in the first place. She got paid to put it in the ground and then paid to dig it back up."

"Even if that were so, and I'm not saying it is, how do you explain the headaches?"

"Lupita had a reason to believe they ended, so they did. Simple as that."

Joachín fell silent again, and I worried I'd offended him. But he was an adult by now. Certainly he could recognize a hoax, but I didn't have to be the messenger. I wanted him to like me.

"It's a lot to process," I said.

He took a sip. "Think about me. Years later, I'm still processing."

"But look at it rationally. Really? Pins in a doll's head?"

He tapped the edges of his eyes. "I saw it."

"This is why you believe in the dolls the nanas made."

He nodded. "If it hadn't been for that day with Lupita, I'd write the whole thing off as a clever story. But I can't."

"What does your cousin say about all this?"

"He won't talk about it. Too weird. He'd rather pretend it never happened."

The option would be tempting. "Back up a step. Why didn't Lupita's husband divorce her?"

"Maybe he was happy enough being married to her. I doubt that he had anything to do with any voodoo doll. It's much more likely —"

"The mistress."

"Right. She got tired of waiting for the guy to get divorced, so she tried other tactics."

"Nasty."

"Nanina always said women were meaner than men."

"The husband was such a catch?"

"Probably not after Lupita got the house and half their money, but who knows? Sometimes people set their sights on someone, and they won't stop until they get what they think they want."

"That's a terrible plan."

"Yes. But in Durango, it was common. There's a lot of weird stuff in Mexico if you look for it." He pointed at me. "Or if it comes to you."

Warning bells sounded. "The nanas told you about me?"

145

"Didn't have to. Let me explain. You didn't grow up in Mexico. They don't celebrate the Day of the Dead down there for nothing. Look at Mari and all those auras and stuff. There's another level. Some people can tap into it. How or why? You'd have to ask that little old lady. She was tapped in. So are you."

I polished off my shot. "The longer you talk, the more it all makes sense. That either means I've had too much whiskey or not enough." The whole idea was ludicrous and beautiful at the same time. Special powers. Hidden abilities. Another dimension.

Joachín tapped the bottle. "Don't they have magic in Ireland?"

"I guess? I don't know much about it."

Joachín stretched his legs next to mine. "You have four full-blooded Irish grandparents. There's a power in that somewhere. Your mom never told stories about leprechauns and all that?"

"She never dwelled on the past, so she wasn't much of a storyteller." With five kids, she didn't have time to be.

Joachín waved an imaginary wand. "Maybe you picked up some fairy dust in New Orleans. I hear it's a strange place too."

Lots of cultures, religions, traditions, and mysteries were wrapped up in the French Quarter. Why wouldn't they stay there?

Joachín took my hand. "You don't want to believe you're special because it's intimidating. I understand that. But when Emil has a terrible headache tomorrow—"

"He won't."

We sat a while in silence, but Joachín started to yawn again.

"I should leave," he said.

"Why risk driving?" After I stood and pointed to the cushions, he stretched out comfortably.

"I'll bring a pillow and a sheet," I said.

"Great."

I hadn't had an overnight guest for so long that I searched all three upstairs closets before I found supplies. By the time I returned to the living room, Joachín was sound asleep.

I covered him with a light blanket and placed another nearby. Before I hit the stairs, I jabbed Emilito's ears.

After I retreated to my bedroom, I lay awake staring into the dark. Voodoo dolls. Jars found in the desert. Pink dresses. Ridiculous.

Joachín the man.

That part wasn't ridiculous at all.

Chapter Seventeen

Even though I arrived a few minutes early, both nanas were waiting for me out on the porch with their traditional warm hugs.

"Are you sure you don't want me to come along?" Lula asked.

Extra support would have been fine, but I worried an entourage would seem suspicious. Slipping in one extra guest seemed easy enough, and Mari knew about makeup. Lula, however, knew about lies. "I'll take you next time."

Lula leaned against the railing. "Let's hope there isn't one. The situation makes me nervous."

"I'm sure it will be fine."

I herded Mari to the car. She was nearly as anxious as Lula, which is why it took her three tries to attach the seatbelt. "Do you mind stopping at the pharmacy on the way back?"

"You don't feel well?" I asked.

"It's Emil! He's going crazy in jail."

It served him right. Maybe he'd become someone's boyfriend. Meanwhile, the nanas already knew he was a total hypochondriac. "What's wrong this time?"

Mari checked her lipstick in the mirror. "He has an ear infection."

"What?"

"His ears hurt so much he started yelling in the middle of the night."

I couldn't help it. I laughed. "It's a weird world." I backed out of the driveway, hiding my smile by driving in reverse. An ear infection? No way. *Curanderas?* A figment of someone's imagination. Joachín's story? The fake witch doctor was smart enough to devise her own retirement plan.

At the first stop sign, I turned to Mari and pulled on my right earlobe. "I don't mean to make fun of Emil, but this is all in his head, you know. What could be wrong with his ears? He hasn't visited a pool in weeks."

"I know it's crazy, angel, but all I can tell you is what he told us. He was crying. Can you imagine? That's how bad the pain was."

I imagined him groaning on a prison cell bed, waking up the other inmates. They probably thought he was crazy. The guards too. Maybe they thought he was faking, which would be worse.

"Evidently the pain was horrible," said Mari. "Ear infections are dangerous, you know. If you don't find treatment, your hearing might be ruined permanently."

A scheming pretend *curandera* was one thing, but the nanas had no way of knowing what I'd done to the doll. How could anything have happened between Emil and me? Mental telepathy? That was as likely as a doll that transferred pain.

"What have you been doing today?" I wanted to ease into the topic. "Make any more of those little dolls?"

"We've been too busy preparing for Emil's classes. Thank goodness we won't have to teach again until Monday, if then."

"I've thought about your little dolls. What gave you the idea to create them?" I spoke lightly as if filling the air with small talk.

Mari clasped her purse more snugly. "We were having fun. Passing the time. We couldn't get the hang of Tarot cards, so we were reading wikiHow. We came across the—NO! You didn't!"

I focused on the four-way stop sign.

"You did, didn't you!" Mari exclaimed. "It's the only explanation. Why would you do that?"

"All I did was stick a pin in a doll."

Mari held her head as she bobbed up and down.

"I didn't mean to hurt Emil," I said. "Joachín and I were playing around."

She bobbed more quickly. "Tell me everything! I need every detail!"

I turned onto a side street, pulled over to the curb, and switched off the engine. "After rehearsal, Joachín came over for a chat. And I was mad. Really mad. Because of that trip Emil had planned to go to Paris with What's-Her-Name. So I—" I jabbed my fingers at my ears.

"You left the pins in the doll?"

"I don't remember. I might have." Lula wasn't around, so I could lie.

"Those pins have to come out right away!"

"They're barely attached to the surface."

"It doesn't matter!"

The scene was as bad as telling a graduate student that her dissertation topic was worthless and that all her research needed to be tossed aside. I would have stalled until I found a way to soften the message, but we were on a time schedule. I couldn't spend all day on silliness.

"Nana Mari, there's no way that you can hurt somebody by putting a steel pin through a piece of cloth." I used my teacher voice, the one I used for explaining gerunds. After hearing the explanation, my students looked at me as if I were the crazy one, as if I had invented the rules of English grammar simply to complicate their lives.

"I wondered why your aura was shaky! You feel both guilty and confused." She made a quick circle with her index finger. "Go on, turn around! We have to return to your house."

Guilty? No. Not given the circumstances. Confused? Maybe. My head was full of nonsense, including a dream in which a little old lady digging for jars in the sierra couldn't find any. But I addressed Mari from my rational side. "We'll be late for our makeup party."

She clutched her cheeks. "Makeup can wait!"

Ninety percent of the time Mari was the most rational woman I knew. She was calmer than Lula and took the normal catastrophes — kids needing stitches, adults losing their jobs, friends passing — in stride. Now I sat with a maniac.

I picked up my hand-drawn map. "We've almost reached Brenda's."

"Your house! Now!"

The nanas weren't superstitious. Halloween? They took all ghosts and goblins as a healthy joke. Day of the Dead? They might have said a quick prayer. Tucson's All Soul's Parade? They'd attended the parade when it was downtown. Now that it took place on the west side, they found it too much trouble.

I started up the engine. "This whole idea is crazy."

"It doesn't matter if it's crazy or not!"

I wasn't ready to give in. "The pain is all in Emil's head. Maybe he's reading my mind or something."

Mari closed her eyes as she shook her head. "It's the power locked inside the doll."

"You didn't create it with Emil in mind. We added the picture afterwards. The doll might have been for anybody."

"Your house! Please an old lady!"

"You're not old."

That was the most I could bring myself to say. I couldn't tell Mari to her face that she'd dived off the Cliffs of Moher into the deep end. She and her sister had been too kind to me.

"I'm old enough to have seen a lot of strange things in my time," Mari said. "Maybe too many. But I need you to trust me."

"About a doll."

She didn't answer, so after I performed an illegal U-turn, I looked over. Mari's hearing wasn't as sharp as it once was, and occasionally I forgot to speak loudly enough. But she stared straight ahead as if she were alone in the car.

Somehow she had lost herself in the past. Such a memory couldn't be taken lightly, so once again I pulled over to the curb. This time I put on the emergency brake rather than turning off the engine. "You remember something. Or you lived through something."

"It was a small thing."

"Tell me about it."

"Another time, angel."

I needed the whole story, but she was in too much pain, and we didn't have time for history. I unhooked the emergency brake and sped to my house.

I stopped so abruptly as I pulled into the driveway that I jostled us, but Mari didn't comment on my driving.

"I'll just be a minute, all right?"

"Go!"

What was locked in her past? What would I have to do to get it out? Maybe I could get at her through Lula instead, but I doubted that I were clever enough to play one sister against the other.

I rushed through my kitchen, removed the pins from Emil's head, and laid them on the counter. The whole idea was ludicrous. A stupid waste of time.

Yet the Laney doll called to me. I gave each of her pins a twirl. Maybe, by accident, I pushed them in a little deeper.

Just in case.

***

Brenda Davidson lived in an attractive, sprawling house a block east of Country Club. The tall entryway was imposing, and the curated garden with varieties of colored rocks proved the woman had an eye for detail. She opened the door as I stretched my index finger toward the doorbell.

"Thank goodness!" The tall woman was sixty-something or better, with hair that cascaded around her face. She wore a casual dress, the kind more appropriate for a grocery store than for a party. "We were afraid you wouldn't make it."

"I'm called Angel," I said. "And this is my aunt." We couldn't have looked less similar, but if Brenda noticed, she didn't say anything.

"Please forgive an old lady," Mari said. "I couldn't convince my ankle to work this morning, so I had to stop and soak it awhile. That's why we're late."

Nana Mari! She was even faster than I was.

"I have a trick ankle as well," said Brenda. "It's awful! I have to be so careful that when it rains, I don't go out at all. Come on in, but watch your step."

She led us into a living room that was a showcase for a greenhouse. Deep potted plants lined the walls and filled all four corners. They provided oxygen for an assortment of women. Three were squeezed onto a deep blue couch. The rest occupied chairs that made a rough circle around a coffee table topped by a pitcher of tea, extra glasses, and a plate of Oreos. The ladies had left me an easy chair, but I ushered Mari into it as if her ankle really hurt. Brenda slid a footstool in front of her before rustling up an extra chair.

The ladies greeted us enthusiastically. As they introduced themselves, I jotted down their names and thanked them cordially. Lisa and Susan were around Brenda's age. They seemed the most comfortable, as if they were all old friends. Wendy seemed a bit younger. She sat next to Eunice, who might have been her daughter, and Tammy, who was Eunice's friend.

"Tea?" Brenda asked.

When we nodded, she poured us full glasses.

"Thanks so much for having us," I said. "We're so sorry that Twinkle—"

The most I told Brenda was that Twinkle had passed. The women had probably all heard about the murder on the news by now, but I didn't want to disclose more than I needed to.

"Was she your friend?" Brenda asked gently.

I shook my head. "Sadly, I never had the pleasure to meet her. You see, she was going to give up the Beauty Is You business."

"But why?" The big red tulips on Lisa's blouse granted her automatic cheerfulness.

"Corporate didn't tell me," I said. "I assume she got more hours at her day job, so she didn't have time for this work too. You know how it is with two small children."

The women nodded. Tammy passed around the cookies, but nobody took any.

"She said her job was dry but that it paid well," said Wendy. "We could tell she was struggling with the kids. Her parents helped out a lot, but they couldn't babysit all the time."

"Except now I guess they'll have to," I said as somberly as possible.

The women nodded. We might have gotten bogged down in sad stories right there, but I had costumes to finish and a theatre to get to, so I needed to move things along. "I guess there wasn't a Mr. Twinkle?"

"Angel! That's the wrong question to ask," Mari said sharply. Her tone was according to plan; we'd decided I would ask indiscreet questions, she would shoot me down, and hopefully people would share juicy details.

"Right, right! I'm so sorry," I gushed. "I didn't mean to sound nosy. But it seems that a lot of times, the Beauty Is You representatives are single women, like me. Our schedules are more flexible because we don't work around as many factors."

"You're right," Lisa said. "There was no Mr. Twinkle. I felt bad for her because she seemed like a nice girl. She didn't give up! She always reminded us to keep an eye out for an appropriate partner for her."

Appropriate my foot. She had to come up with one who was living with another woman?

"I've tried computer dating," I said, "but I've never met anyone nice."

"Twinkle tried and failed," said Eunice. "We both met real losers that way. She would come down to Crave from time to time. When I took a break, we would have a coffee and compare notes."

Brenda shook her head. "She might have had bad luck online, but Twinkle lived up to her name, if you ask me. She wasn't solid. She was a nice enough woman. Don't get me wrong. But she was floating. As if she couldn't decide on a true direction. Although I suppose once you have children, you don't have much choice about things."

"I wasn't sure whether I liked her or not," said Susan, whose eyes matched her dainty sky-blue dress. "Do you remember when I hosted last summer? After my husband came into the room, she didn't take her eyes off him."

"Maybe she was jealous of a successful marriage," I said.

"Angel!" Mari played her part expertly. I made a mental note to introduce her to Tommy. He always needed qualified older actresses.

"Sorry." I might have tipped over a bookcase. The gossip streamed out of those women faster than water out of a broken faucet. They all had theories on women with roving eyes, husbands whose eyes roved back, what single women did to snag men, and the reason the women needed quality makeup products — to hang onto the men they had.

Unfortunately, they knew nothing concrete about Twinkle.

"I liked Twinkle," Wendy said. "She tried hard enough to make her way. But I always had the sense that her biggest problem was wanting what somebody else had."

Is that why she wanted Emil? Because I had him?

"It's like food envy," said Eunice. "You go to a restaurant, and everybody orders a dish tastier than yours. She was like that. Everyone else's partner looked good to her, but she didn't have one to share."

I laughed. "Surely she would have found the right man eventually."

"There was somebody," said Tammy. "I ran into her at Fry's a month ago and all she had in her basket was a bottle of wine, a fancy cheeseball, and some crackers."

"I buy those things too," Lisa said.

"I quizzed her! I said, 'Romantic dinner tonight?' And she says, yes, she has this new guy, and he's wonderful."

A wonderful new guy. Ha.

"A businessman?" I asked.

"I couldn't tell you that much. A teacher, I think."

Twinkle had bragged about her new teacher boyfriend. As if! For a moment I wanted to kill her all over again.

I giggled, playing the role. "She didn't share details about this mystery man!"

"She didn't want to jinx things, I think," Tammy said. "You know? You're not sure if something will work out, so you don't say too much."

"Or there was something about him she didn't want to disclose," Susan said. "Like maybe he was married."

Married. Or something.

Lisa smoothed her tulips. "Bless her heart. Evidently she didn't have much taste. After all, the boyfriend murdered her, right?"

"They don't know that for sure." I spoke quickly without realizing what I was saying. Then I promised myself to keep my mouth shut.

"I heard it was an open and shut case," Brenda said. "They have the man in custody."

"I heard the same thing," said Lisa. "But maybe the guy was a hook up."

Eunice nodded slowly. "While I wouldn't say she was the sharpest pencil in the box, I don't think her taste in men could have been that bad."

"She had two children with different men," said Mari. "At least that's what I heard." I silently applauded Mari. She hadn't heard a thing, but she lied so smoothly she didn't blink.

"Bless her heart," Lisa said again. I didn't hear a twang, but she must have had at least one parent from the South. "Maybe the guy was married, but she didn't know it. They don't always tell you."

The conversation turned to terrible, lying men. I bit my tongue to refrain from chiming in because I was afraid I might trap myself by saying too much. I dived into my bag and pulled out lipstick and rouge, which I passed around. "As I explained to Brenda, I'm not fully trained. I can't take any new orders. But I can sell the products I have with me and leave you with free samples."

The gossip stopped like an on/off switch. The women scrambled for the lipstick tubes and eye shadow. Mari jumped into the act, eagerly giving advice according to skin tone.

Twinkle might have passed, but skin care kept right on going.

Chapter Eighteen

I poured myself a cup of vanilla-flavored coffee before taking a seat on the porch. I wafted the steam toward my nose. Mari did the same with a cup of her own.

Lula brought out a tray of *polvorones,* tri-colored Mexican cookies that she bought from La Estrella. "You were gone a long time."

I snapped up the nearest cookie. Lula knew I couldn't resist them.

"Dervla did an expert job," Mari said. "She wheedled out more information than a star journalist interviewing a spy."

"That's why we need her so much." Lula pointed to her ears. "Emil was clueless when I talked to him. All he could think about was how much pain he was in."

Mari rocked in her chair. "He's all right now."

"How would you know that?" Lula abruptly looked at her sister, who in turn nodded toward me.

Lula shook her head. "She didn't!"

Mari rocked harder. "Don't blame her too much. It's a lot to take in."

Lula imitated jabbing pins into a doll. "You . . . ?"

"Joachín and I were playing around. I thought it would make me feel better.'

The nanas fell silent. For the second time that week I assumed I'd be banished from the family.

Lula pulled up her skirt a bit to allow for ventilation. "It's a common mistake. Sometimes even fatal." She caught her sister's eyes. A flicker of understanding passed between them. They'd had over seventy years to build a close bond around all their secrets.

"I wasn't trying to hurt him," I said. "Not seriously, at least. You have to believe me on that."

"Of course you weren't, honey," Lula said. "This isn't anything you would know about. You're too young."

"And you're not Hispanic," added Mari.

I was saved by sincerity. Had I been lying, Lula would have known it anyway, and Mari would have been alerted by my aura.

"There must be an Irish equivalent," Lula said to Mari. "Otherwise, how did she activate it?"

Mari picked up a *polvorón*. "I've asked myself the same thing all afternoon."

I felt more confused than ever. "How could I activate something? I didn't do anything special. You saw me! I was right here when I put in the first pin."

Mordy chose this moment to saunter onto the porch and lie next to my feet.

Mari nodded. So did Lula.

"No," I said. "You're not telling me that the cat knows something about me that I don't."

Lula topped off her coffee. "Mordy is never wrong. He can sense things about people. That's why we never reprimand him if he bites. He only punishes someone for a good reason."

"That's why he never bites you, angel," said Mari. "He knows you're good-hearted."

I had superpowers, and the nanas knew my true nature because of a cat. The world had gone crazy. It had chewed me into bits and swallowed me up.

"Now what?" I asked glumly. "Emil will kill me when he finds out about this."

"Why would we tell him, angel?" Mari asked.

"He wouldn't believe us even if we did," added Lula.

I was having cookies and coffee with two Cheshire cats and one who bit bad people.

Mari refilled my cup. "When you do have special powers, it's best if people don't know about them."

"But I know you see auras." I turned to Lula. "And you see through lies."

Lula nodded. "You didn't know that when you first met us. Know a person long enough and naturally you find out. Until then, it's a secret weapon."

"How so?"

"Remember the first time Emil brought you to meet us?"

Of course I did. It was a birthday party for Flor. At first the crowd intimidated me, but by the end of the evening, I felt strangely comfortable.

"We were vetting you," Lula said. "It's natural. Any relative would do the same. But Mari and I could tell right away that your intentions with Emil were simple and straightforward."

"I could see your peaceful aura," said Mari. "It was clear that you cared about Emil in a loving way, which was the only thing we cared about."

"That's why you accepted me right away," I said. "Even that first night."

"Having gifts is an advantage," Lula said. "You want to use them in the right way, of course, such as by protecting your family. That's one reason we disliked Isabel. She was too self-centered to care about anyone besides herself. She would drag poor little Joachín behind her because she couldn't get out of it. That's why we took him in so quickly, so to speak. He was a wonderful boy, and we were glad that he and Orlando enjoyed spending time together."

It all made perfect sense. At the time I wondered why the nanas accepted me so easily. In truth they had extra insights to read the situation.

"Enough about that," Lula said. "Since you left me alone most of the afternoon, at least share what you learned."

"Eunice's aura had a red tinge, but I saw nothing major," said Mari.

"She hid information about Twinkle?" I asked.

"Not necessarily." Mari turned to her sister. "The women generally liked her, but Susan thought Twinkle was flirting with her husband."

"It's as we thought," Lula said. "She was the type to get around."

"In which case a whole string of jealous women would have been thrilled to see her six feet under," continued Mari. "Jealousy is the strongest emotion of all, you know. At least among women."

"Stronger than grief? Or motherhood?" I asked.

"From what we've seen, motherhood comes close," Lula said. "Grief does not. But a jealous woman will do anything."

"Even commit murder?" I asked. "That's crazy."

"Why not?" asked Lula. "I've seen such things happen."

Mari leaned toward me. "You've never witnessed jealousy, have you?"

My parents weren't jealous of one another; I wasn't always sure they liked one another. They got along in a distant way, doing their own thing. My sister Tully had already married and divorced. Jan was still married, but I wasn't sure how much she cared for her husband. "I don't come from a family of romantics or anything like that."

"You don't come from people who show passion," Lula said. "So you wouldn't know."

"But we would," Mari said softly. "It's rougher than you imagine."

I thought about the crazy story Joachín told me about Lupita and her husband. "I guess jealous women can be pretty incredible," I said.

"Men can be jealous too," said Mari. "They're not immune."

No, but they seemed slightly more rational. "What I don't understand is why they didn't kill Emil instead of Twinkle."

Lula fingered the necklace on her chest. Today she wore a string of violets. "Don't try to understand it logically. Do you kill your partner or frame him to make him suffer? It doesn't matter. You get revenge either way."

"So Emil is lucky I'm not Hispanic?" I asked.

Mari laughed. "That's one way to think of it!"

"We should look into Twinkle's former lovers," I said. "That might tell us something. Emil ought to know at least a name or two."

Mari's gaze followed a college woman who strolled past wearing short shorts and a sweatshirt. "Smart women keep quiet about such things."

It was hard to tell one way or another about Twinkle. To be polite, I stayed awhile as the nanas batted back and forth possibilities, but my mind drifted. When dusk fell, I texted Joachín. *Going to Twinkle's if you want to join.* Within seconds he wrote back *On my way now.* I felt bad for excluding him on the previous occasion, and two heads were better than one.

There had to be useful clues at the house. We had to find them.

Chapter Nineteen

I parked several houses away, covered the rest of the distance on foot, and sailed through the carport as if Twinkle's house were mine. The first sound I heard was dripping water. I followed the hose out to the backyard. Since the police tape was gone, maybe Henrietta and Malcolm had come over to do some watering. Given Tucson's temperatures, it wasn't unusual for people to leave water dripping, but the hose no longer had a nozzle. It rested on a pile of rocks where it watered nothing but dust.

I went back to the side of the house, stretched my shirt to use as a glove, and turned off the water. Who was petty enough to steal a five-dollar nozzle? A random thief or a calculating neighbor who knew that Twinkle wouldn't notice?

Perhaps I shouldn't berate a thief at the exact moment I was breaking and entering. Not breaking, actually. I had the key. Merely entering.

The timer hadn't kicked on yet, so the house was dark. I used my cellphone as a flashlight, pointing it at the ground so it wouldn't give off too much light.

The kitchen was newly organized. It hadn't been a disaster before, but I assumed it was Henrietta who had put away the dishes and replaced the sponge. She and

Malcolm would have come over several times by now, for clothing, toys, paperwork. But I wasn't worried they would come at this time of the day. At the moment they'd be focused on getting the children to bed or keeping them there.

I meandered through the other rooms, but only the quiet seemed unusual. I imagined the laughter from two kids chasing each other and a happy mother fondly playing with them. Now there was nothing.

At the edge of the bedroom, I paused for a breath. The bed had been remade, but my mind shouted *crime scene*. Twinkle had died here, violently, and not by her own hand. Who had enemies that were so angry? Lovers so jealous? I felt my throat close as I imagined the saw. How much warning did she have? Five seconds? None?

I made my way to the dresser, dug beneath the undies, and took out the bottom notebook. The first line announced that she was a high school senior. Then she got down to business: *J. is a dreamboat and he doesn't even know it. If only he would look at me instead of that silly M.L.* I could understand the gist of things. My own high school experience had been one disappointment after the other. The boys I liked didn't like me, the ones I dated were duds, etc. It hadn't been until Emil that I found, at least temporarily, someone I considered a soulmate. So much for that.

I heard a door softly close. "Joachín?" I went through to the kitchen, but I'd missed him. "Joachín," I whispered as I walked down the hall. "Where are you?"

When I heard a step beside me, I turned. Then somebody conked me on the head so hard I didn't hear anything else.

***

"Dervla! Dervla!"

When I came to, Joachín was kneeling at my side in the hallway. He'd put a cold cloth on my forehead.

I struggled to sit up.

"Take it easy," he said. "Don't move yet. Make sure you can feel your hands and your feet."

One by one, I wiggled my fingers and toes. Then I laughed. Joachín was no doctor, and he had no idea whether he was telling me the right thing to do or not.

I sat up, slowly, but didn't notice that anything was particularly wrong with me. The diary, however, was nowhere in sight. "Help me stand up."

I struggled to my feet, using Joachín to balance.

"How do you feel?"

"Bad headache," I said. "Very bad. And that's not because of some voodoo doll or because I feel stupid. Do you know what happened?"

"I was waiting a few houses away when you arrived, but I was on the phone with Tommy. I walked toward the house, but somebody pulled up on one of those electric scooters. He, I'm pretty sure a 'he,' drove up under the carport, parked, and darted inside. I didn't have a chance to warn you, and I didn't want to call 9-1-1 either."

"Good thinking." I was the idiot who hadn't locked the door behind me.

"I dashed right up to the living room window. I pretended I was shouting to a friend, 'Someone entered the house! Call the police right now! Hurry up!'"

"And then?"

"I ran around to the back. Meanwhile your attacker sneaked out the side door, hopped back on the scooter, and took off. I'm sorry. I didn't catch the license plate."

If Joachín hadn't been such a quick thinker, I wouldn't have gotten off so lightly. Why hadn't I noticed his car? I should have waited for him, but I'd been too focused on getting inside the house.

I rubbed my head. "Wonder what they hit me with. Not that it matters."

Joachín looked around. "I don't see anything out of place."

"No. But some things are definitely missing." I opened the dresser drawer that now held undies and nothing more. "Twinkle's notebooks about wonderful men. That's what they came for. They were probably going to break in themselves, but I did the trick for them. Very nice of me." Worse, I'd let the best clues yet slip through my hands. I chided myself for not stealing all the evidence in the first place.

"You can't blame yourself," Joachín said weakly. We both knew he sounded lame. "You couldn't expect that anyone was watching the house."

"Hold it," I said. "Hear that?"

In the distance was a siren. It might have been a firetruck or any other emergency vehicle, but why find out the hard way?

"Time to leave," I said. "Leave your fingerprints anywhere?"

"Not that I know of. You?"

"On the notebooks, which probably won't matter." I handed Joachín my key. "Lock the side door. Hurry!"

I hobbled to the master bedroom and opened the door to the backyard. As the sirens neared, I forced myself to wait three seconds for Joachín. Together we slid outside.

Joachín escorted me to the back wall, a stone partition about five feet high. After he held his hands together as a personal steppingstone, I hoisted myself over. He nimbly scaled the wall right behind me.

Safe. Now we were two people in an alley, not two thugs at a crime scene.

For a moment we stood panting. We'd escaped. Maybe we hadn't deserved to. Technically, our antics probably made us criminals.

The sirens stopped in front of Twinkle's house.

Joachín patted the concrete. "Now what?"

On a different day, I would have suggested we watch the action from the alley, but my head hurt so much I thought I might faint again. "See if you can get to your car without raising suspicion. If you can, come pick me up. We'll deal with my car later."

"If the police are watching?"

I sank to the ground. "Wait until they're gone. I'll sit right here and rest. If anyone happens to see me, they'll think I'm homeless or drunk."

While Joachín headed down the alley, I leaned against the wall and ordered myself to stay awake. At any moment I expected a rude voice to shout at me or rough hands to drag me to my feet while shining a flashlight in my eyes.

As soon as the siren blasted again, I lay down.

I must have dozed off for a minute. Or ten. By the time Joachín picked me up, my head was murky.

The coast, however, was perfectly clear.

Chapter Twenty

Joachín held open the door and we entered the theatre. The evening's bustle had already begun. Down on the stage, Holland and Désirée milled about, consulting their scripts. Tommy reviewed his notes from the couch.

Joachín noticed that I latched onto the handrail.

"You don't have to be here tonight."

"I'm fine." I was too shaky to be "fine," but I was a practiced liar.

"I'll explain you're not feeling well. They won't ask questions."

They were too kind to be picky, and they realized I was doing them a favor. But I always hated giving in. "I promised to shorten Laney's dress."

"There's no real rush."

"No, but I might as well do it tonight. By tomorrow we might have some new crisis." I was almost certain we would. I turned to the carpeted stairs that led to the stage.

Joachín hovered as if afraid I would fall at any moment. He might have been right. "The dress was perfect the way you designed it."

"Yes, but she hated it. So what if she shows a few more inches of leg? I don't care, and Tommy doesn't either. It's a small battle." It was also an example of an inexperienced actor grasping at shreds of authority she didn't deserve. Luckily, Tommy and I were practical enough to be on the same page about it.

"You could take the dress home and work on it there."

"Tommy said you had a sewing machine in the rehearsal room."

"Might be crap."

"I'll give it a try."

"You won't be bored sitting all alone?"

I appreciated his concern, but what I wanted more than anything was just that: time alone. I needed to process the evening's adventures, meaning the adventures so far. "I'll be quite all right. I'll turn on the speakers so I can hear the whole rehearsal." The fact that I wouldn't listen was a different matter.

"You can text me if you need something."

Did he have to worry so much? "When I'm working, I don't usually answer my phone unless I'm expecting a call."

"May I see your phone?"

I handed it over.

"I'm adding in a ring tone for me, okay? That way you'll know to answer it if it's important."

"What tone are you choosing?"

He pressed a button, and a donkey brayed.

"Ow," I said. "Not that one."

"What's your preference?"

He reminded me of the nanas, which reminded me of Mordy. Also, if anyone was a cat's meow, it was Joachín.

"Put in a cat sound."

"At your command." He punched more buttons as we headed down to the stage.

Tommy hurried over to us. "Dervla! Glad you could make it. Joachín wasn't sure if he could track you down."

I patted his arm. "Usually he can find me when he has a mind to."

Tommy pointed to a vague area behind the curtains. "Listen, your original costume was fine. Don't change Laney's dress by much, but we'll all tell her how much sexier she looks afterwards."

I didn't mean to laugh, but I did.

"I know, I know," he said. "It's ridiculous to treat her with double thick kid gloves, but since Joachín talked us out of using his sister—"

"Half-sister," Joachín shot out.

"Yes. Right. Anyway, we'd best give Laney one more chance. The reviews from her previous work were positive, so I'm trusting she can pull things together on stage."

"Her acting might pass," Joachín said. "It's the rapport with colleagues that needs work."

"We don't have time for behavioral miracles," I said, "but give me a few minutes to set up. Then send her over with her dress, and I'll make a show of doctoring it. Any other costume issues?"

"One or two small things. A sleeve that came loose, a seam that, well, Willard is a little heftier than you thought. Nothing major."

I retreated to the rehearsal room, which testified that action was well under way, By now the mirror over the sink was splattered, the makeup tables were crowded with supplies, and the cushions from the two ratty couches were disheveled.

I'd barely taken the dusty cover off the sewing machine and moved it to a central table when I heard loud stomping. I didn't have to look to guess that Laney was the one bulldozing through the door.

In her hands she held the dress I'd made for her, but she wore a skintight maid's outfit that might have been a Halloween costume. The bodice barely covered her breasts and was topped with itchy, frilly lace. The hem was so short that it barely covered her crotch. Classy.

171

She tossed the dress in my direction, but it landed on the floor a few feet away. Then she slid her hands from her chest to her waist. "This is what my dress should look like!"

"The play takes place in England. In the 1950s."

"I don't care. While I'm on stage, I need to shine. My character holds the whole play together. Don't you realize that?"

The last difficult person I remembered working with was a sincere but misguided Korean student who insisted that English spelling was so stupid that we needed to petition to change it.

"Are you trying to ruin my career?" Laney asked.

As with my student, I feigned close listening. What had made her so needy? Bad family? Possibly, but I had gotten past mine, and that had been a feat. Bad boyfriends? Didn't everybody have those? I should have been angry at her reaction, but it was too childish to take seriously. She was too damaged. Many people were. I avoided such lost souls as often as possible. When I absolutely had to confront them, I did so as quickly as possible.

"I'll work on the dress right away," I said. "I'm sure I can make it more flattering."

"It better be! Do you know who's coming to this play?"

I had lots of guesses. The mayor? Theatre professors from the U of A? Laney's grandparents? "You tell me." I cocked my head as if that would help me hear her better.

"My agent!"

An agent? To help her audition for jobs in Tucson? "You have an agent."

"I hired him yesterday."

Now I felt worse for her. What she needed was a reality check.

"Another thing," she said, "I'll need a slip. And lining for the sleeves."

The black material was not see-through, and it was sturdy enough to have some shape to it. "Why?"

"Because this cheap material you chose gave me a rash."

Clothing dermatitis was nearly always caused by polyesters, not cottons, which is what I'd used for the dress. "Did you eat any unusual foods yesterday?"

"Are you saying I'm fat?"

"Food allergies often cause rashes."

"I do not have a food allergy!"

Now that I was paying attention, I noticed red marks on her arms from where she'd been scratching.

"New soap?"

"It's the material! If you can't fix it, start over and get it right."

Ah, the downside of working with theatre people. Most were reasonable enough to consider advice. Then there were the others. But not everybody could alleviate their irritations by sticking pins through helpless dolls.

"Laney!" Tommy shouted. "On stage, please."

Rescued by default, I smiled a saccharine smile. "I'll work on the dress."

"You do that." She patted her bodice. "Even though this outfit is much, much better."

Yes. For a French farce set in the sixties, it was perfect.

As soon as she left, I picked her costume up from the floor and brought it over to the machine. While I took up the hem a full quarter of an inch, I listened to the action on stage. By now the actors had discovered some direction within their parts. The first scenes sailed right along with occasional comments from Tommy or a few words about staging.

"Laney!" Tommy shouted. "I've told you before. You don't burst into the room. You're the maid. You enter the room. Daintily, if possible."

"All I did was walk through the door."

"You're the servant. Be more subtle."

"Yes, sir!"

I pressed down on the lever, and the Singer buzzed across the seams.

I didn't bother to measure. Just to be ornery, I made the seams uneven. Laney would be too concentrated on her bust to notice.

While I manhandled the material, I considered the bigger picture. I had to find a way to learn more about Twinkle.

***

Two hours later, Joachín supervised while I "cooked." After pouring a bag of chips into a bowl, I opened a jar of salsa.

"Why not make Laney's hem so lopsided that the whole audience notices?"

On a whim, I also dug out some cheese spread. "Good plan, but people would assume I'm a bad seamstress. It would hurt my reputation. This is my new career, you know."

"Your reputation could be built on helping the rest of the cast stay sane. We need a good joke, you know." As he winked, his eyes lit up.

I bent a chip until it snapped. "Maybe Tommy will fire her after all. Or do you think he likes her somehow?"

"He generally dates men."

"Yes, yes, I know that." I'd guessed his orientation right away, something about the lithe way he moved. "I mean, Tommy seems to have a soft spot for her. Maybe she reminds him of some old relative or an old friend or something."

"He's giving her the benefit of the doubt. Aside from her messing up every entrance, how did the play sound?"

What did I know? I usually read plays. "Coming along, I would say. People stumbled over words here and there, but that's normal."

"I have some memorizing to do. Mind running through the lines with me?"

"Right now?"

"Tomorrow sometime. Tonight I need a rest. You do too. I'm so sorry I got to Twinkle's late. How's your head?"

I massaged a bump. "Thanks to you, my head is still here. That might have been a close call."

"Do you think someone followed you?"

"From the nanas'? Maybe. I don't think it had to do with me."

"A woman from the makeup party?"

I scooped salsa on my chip. "Several made catty remarks about Twinkle, but none were cutthroat. If anything, the women were generous toward her."

"Maybe someone was watching Twinkle's house?"

"Then why pull up on a scooter?"

"They might have been watching from down the block. Or maybe someone gave them a high sign."

I scooped up even more salsa. It was a food, right? "Possible. It wasn't a random burglary gone wrong. It had to do with Twinkle."

Joachín crunched a chip. "With the diaries."

"As if someone knew about them. Now we'll have to work backwards by thinking about her friends instead. And colleagues." I reached over and poked Emilito in the belly. "Even Emil."

"Whoa. Remind me to be nice to you."

"You're always nice to me."

He stared into the bowl as if the formation of the chips meant something. "I'd have been nicer if I hadn't met you as my friend's brother's girlfriend."

He smiled slyly at the chips.

This made me blink. Even though I'd briefly pondered my reaction to him before—

No. We were fond of each other. That was all. Anything else would be nearly incestuous. Besides, there was an age difference. "You're telling me you go for older women now?"

"Not that much older, my friend!" He rotated the bowl.

I was flattered and encouraged. Breakups always kicked the old self-esteem.

Distracted, I bit into a chip so awkwardly that it crunched into pieces that landed on the floor. We both scrambled to pick up the crumbs, butting heads in the process.

"Ow!" I cried.

Joachín took my arm and helped me back on the stool. "I'm so sorry!"

"Risking my life to keep the floor clean," I said. "There should be something poetic in that."

"You find poetics in everything."

"Life's more fun that way."

"Speaking of which—" He leaned past me to grab Lanita. "Don't you think she deserves a few jabs?"

"Very funny."

"You have the power."

Headaches, one sore little penis, and two bad ears. "Coincidence."

"You can't be sure." Joachín took a few steps back. "Come on. Have some fun." He tossed Lanita to me.

"We can be almost sure." I tossed her back.

"How did so many crazy women come into our orbit anyway?" Joachín tossed high, and Lanita bounced off the ceiling.

"She's like Twinkle in her own crazy way."

Toss, toss.

"She might have been Twinkle, except that Emil never met her."

Toss, toss, toss.

When Joachín's toss went a little wide, I stretched to catch the doll. I grabbed ahold of the foot, which ripped off.

"Oh, no!" Joachín shouted.

I bent under the table to retrieve the rest of her body. "Call a doctor!" I returned her to the spot on the bar next to Emilito.

Joachín pet her head. "Poor Lanita."

"Poor, poor Lanita!" I placed the ripped foot nearby.

"Got any Scotch tape?"

"Aren't you getting carried away?" I asked.

"Not me. Seriously. Humor me. Tape her together. We want the show to go on."

I fished some tape out of a kitchen drawer and handed it to Joachín. "Be my guest. I wouldn't bother."

As he carefully wound her foot to her leg, I checked my watch. "We're both teaching classes in the morning."

"I wanted to talk to you about that. Why schedule classes on Saturday?"

"Because so many people sign up for them. But we can revisit that once the business is totally mine."

Joachín punched Lanita in the stomach. "Forgive me for arriving late to Twinkle's."

"You already apologized."

"I care about you, you know."

There was something extra in his voice, a special lilt, a hint. I wondered if he'd ever seen *Tune in Tomorrow*. I'd looked it up; the film was adapted from Mario Vargas

Llosa's seventh novel, which was *Aunt Julia and the Scriptwriter*. In the American version, set in my favorite party town of New Orleans, a young Keanu Reeves fell for Barbara Hershey, his sexy, sophisticated political aunt.

For a moment I imagined their first clandestine kiss. Then the image vanished.

I saw Joachín to the door, but when he hugged me good night, I felt a tingle.

Imagination? Wishful thinking? When I'd come into the family, Joachín was a kid. He'd done a lot of growing up since then.

Maybe, so had I.

Chapter Twenty-One

After class the next morning, I drove to Farmwell Insurance. I parked in the shade and turned off the engine. What kind of insurance company had Saturday hours? One that was like a language school, stubborn enough to go after dollars any way possible. I'd planned to march in and ask about Twinkle with the excuse that she'd promised to explain an insurance policy to me. I was dressed nicely enough—heeled shoes, dress pants, pale yellow Foxcroft blouse, white Chrisitina sweater—that any decent agent would be happy to speak to me long enough to answer a few pesky questions. But my head hurt so much I couldn't talk the rest of me into it.

Yet we didn't have time to wait. As soon as we found a reasonable suspect, we could liberate Emil from jail and get on with our lives. The nanas and Joachín could leave the Spanish teaching to Emil, and Emil could catch up on the accounting. No, I was the one who would do that from now on. But we needed Emil. Shmuck though he was, he did know how to teach Spanish.

My head was a vibrant reminder of the close call. Why had I been so headstrong to sneak into Twinkle's in the first place? I could have called the police station and reported what I'd heard. But then I might have to explain how I'd come to be at the Beauty Is You circle. How I'd given away free samples that weren't mine. How I'd investigated on my own.

Scooching all thoughts of Emil aside, had Joachín and I flirted the night before? It wasn't my imagination. I'd felt a vibe. We both had. An undercurrent that pulsated between us. Not just compassion. Joachín felt bad for the terrible way Emil had dumped me and let me go, but now that Emil was off my emotional plate . . . .

What would the nanas say if I dated Joachín? Would we be ex-family-cated? Best not to think of it. I had work to do. But my head hurt worse than ever, and I didn't want to enter the building, engage in conversation with a colleague of Twinkle's, and then blow a lead because I couldn't concentrate.

I took the last two dusty Ibuprofen I had in my purse and reviewed my notes as I stalled. Farmwell seemed run-of-the-mill; it offered the usual policies for auto, life, and home. A quick comparison showed that the prices were competitive. The company was small, which was probably both good and bad: good because it was local, and bad because the policies wouldn't transfer as easily if the owner left town. I wondered how well Twinkle had fit in.

Go inside and find out, my mature self said. Or maybe it was my immature self. Since I'd gone to the trouble of dressing up and finding the place, I couldn't turn around and leave.

The front door opened onto a hallway with a bulletin board on the left side. In the center was a notice with Twinkle's picture: Memorial Celebration for Twinkle Whitherbottom, announced in the kind of cursive letters used for wedding invitations. Poor woman. Even in death she'd been mistreated; they'd misspelled her last name.

I read on. Memorial Celebration Saturday, 4-6. All of Twinkle's colleagues and customers were invited. The address was 5860 E. North Street, which was a few blocks away. At the bottom a note had been added in pen: Please invite anyone who might not have heard.

I hadn't heard, so I considered myself invited. Now I had plans for the afternoon.

"May I help you?"

"Oh!"

The man who had ventured out of the office was so quiet that he startled me, or perhaps my hearing was off thanks to my aching head.

"I'm sorry. Didn't mean to frighten you." He wore a brown suit whose shoulders were made for a bigger man, and his white shirt collar was limp. Too many washings.

"That's all right. I'm just so upset. About Twinkle." I pointed to the announcement, which gave me a few seconds' lead time. "I can't believe that she's gone."

The man hung his head as if he'd been practicing the gesture. "We're all beside ourselves about what happened to such a nice colleague."

He sounded too upbeat to be sincere.

"She was nice, wasn't she! She was so helpful when I was trying to set up some policies."

"I have all her files! If you want to go over something, I can give you the details. Just let me get your name." His grin was almost wolf-like if baby wolves had a sweet side. I could image all the agents swooping in, ready to fight over her clients.

"I can't think business right now. I came because I wanted to see if there was anything I could do. For Twinkle's family, I mean." I gestured at the flyer. "Thanks for setting something up for her."

The man hung his head again, and this time he managed to do it more deeply. Maybe he liked neck exercises. "Please stop by. Now, your last name—"

I've almost always been immune to a hard sell. The harder the sell, the better my immunity. Today was no exception. Had I been a real customer, or even a potentially real customer, I would have been appalled. "I should go get my husband," I said. "He was the one who spoke to Twinkle initially, and he'll want to pay his respects." I pointed to the flyer. "You'll be there, won't you?"

"I'll definitely try, but if you'd give me your name—"

"See you then." I scooted off before he had a chance to get out another word. I would go to the reception, all right. I'd be armed with a husband one way or another.

***

As I pulled into the drive, the nanas looked so serious that I knew they were speaking to Emil. That was exactly what I wanted. They were each on the landline with separate phones, uh-humming, but I couldn't afford to miss the opportunity.

"Mari, please!" I indicated the phone.

She held her hand over the speaker. "Emil says the food is inedible," she whispered.

"Please! Now!" I must have looked distraught. She handed me her phone. "Emil, Dervla here. Tell me more about Twinkle. Right now."

"Nice to talk to you too," he said. "And why worry about my health? Do you know how tightly we're packed together in here? Do you know what they're serving us as an excuse for dinner? Do you have any idea—"

"Shut up. I'm trying to save your butt. Just ask Joachín."

"Don't tell me you've shared my problems with—"

"Tell me about Twinkle's former boyfriends. Every detail you know. And details about her workplace."

"I don't see how her boyfriends—"

"She might have dated some co-workers. Tell me about any she ever mentioned. If I'm going to show up at her memorial, I have to sound credible."

There was a pause.

"Well?" I asked.

"What she shared with me is private. I don't need you prying into her sex life so you can gloat about it."

I handed the phone to Mari, sat, and closed my eyes. If I counted to a hundred, I might resist exploding.

Luckily, I didn't need to. The nanas laid into Emil with a stream of Spanish that must have been so profane the angels in heaven heard it at the same time. Even Mordy bothered to raise his head and look up, vaguely concerned. Lula and Mari yelled so vigorously that they might have been CEOs in charge of a failing bank.

I stood against the porch railing, ready to bolt.

Lula handed me her phone. "His Highness will talk to you now. I'm going to make more coffee."

"The first words out of your mouth better be an apology," I said.

"Dervla, I'm freaking out in here! Do you realize that —"

"Doesn't sound like an apology to me."

Silence. Incredibly, he still had to think about what to say. How had I dated him for so long without recognizing such flagrant character flaws?

"Okay, I apologize, but only because you're there with the nanas and I know your own family is so messed up that —"

"That's it." I set the phone down next to the coffee cups. "I'm sorry. I can't help a guy like that. I've had it."

I walked out toward my car even though Mari hurried after me. "Angel, he needs you! If we can't find out what happened, he'll stay in jail!"

After I swirled around, I placed my hands on her shoulders. "He'll wiggle out of it. Or he'll be so annoying they'll kick him out because they can't stand him anymore."

I continued to my car. Of all the ridiculous, stupid things to say. Of all the ridiculous, stupid attitudes that one man could have. Of all —

"Dervla, wait!" Mari reached for my arm, but I was too quick for her.

I turned the ignition switch so far the motor made a scratchy, clanking sound. I started the engine on the third try. "You better think twice about whether you want him back or not."

Ramming the accelerator, I backed out of the driveway so sloppily that I clunked my poor vehicle on the curb. Apologies! Messed up families! Emil was so messed up himself he couldn't distinguish fantasy from reality. His precarious condition hadn't sunk in. He still thought he had a leg to stand on and that I would care one way or another.

He was completely wrong. I hadn't cared since the moment he'd dumped me. He made his snap judgment; now I made mine. I had better things to do with my time than listen to him insult me. Way better. I wasn't sure what those things were yet, but I didn't need to.

Actually, I could think of one thing I needed to do without losing a moment: push a few dozen more pins into Emilito. By the time I got done, maybe he wouldn't have an itty bitty penis at all.

***

Despite two more Ibuprofen, I poured myself a Jameson. Whoever claimed you couldn't mix alcohol with pain relievers was probably wrong. I didn't care either way. There was no place I needed to go, so I wouldn't be drunk driving. I went out to my balcony and put my feet up on the other chair. I was prepared to sit there the rest of the day and maybe half of Sunday. I purposely left the phone in my purse, where I wouldn't notice it vibrating.

Then I practiced sulking. I wasn't as upset with Emil as I was with myself. How had I spent six years with the man without realizing how awful he was? Had I been so in love that I'd ignored every neon sign flashing in my face? A different thought was scarier. Had I been as selfish as he? Maybe that was how we had gotten along so well together. We'd been partners in selfish crimes. That meant we'd both been awful, maybe to everyone.

I recalled our first days in grad school. When he finally suggested going for coffee, I assumed ours was a meeting of the minds. We had similar interests in literature, we liked one another's writing—why wouldn't dating be a natural outcome? We started slowly, ostensibly because we were both busy, with a couple of coffee dates, finally dinner, and eventually a sleepover. I assumed the process was caused by the nature of the situation, not because he was extricating himself from someone else. Why wouldn't we have a good relationship? We were suited to one another. We saw eye to eye on playwriting, on literary criticism, even on politics.

I'd never seen through the veneer. Emil didn't deserve me or anyone else. I gave my poor head more mental kicks than a footballer gives a soccer ball. The relationships I'd had from childhood with any of my siblings ought to have taught me that much—don't trust another person. Don't give in. Don't—

"Dervla?"

I leaned over the railing. Joachín stood in my driveway next to his car. I hadn't heard him pull up. I was that out of it.

"Can we talk?" he asked.

Why should I trust him either? By now he was part Arellano. "About Emil, no."

"Not about Emil, then."

"Are you sure you're not here about Emil?"

"Why wouldn't I be here about something else?"

Joachín was around my height, five-eight, or perhaps a bit shorter. He worked out enough to be well toned, but his muscles didn't bulge out of his clothing. If I had to, I could push him out of my house the hard way — even if it were over the balcony.

"The back door's open. Come on up."

He glided to the back door and bounded up the steps. He strode onto the balcony looking as handsome as he had the night before. He wore a T-shirt I'd picked out for him a couple of years earlier when I'd gone to Cabo San Lucas with Emil. Against a light green background, a smiling marlin swam alongside a fishing boat taunting a thwarted tourist.

"The nanas said you were upset." He gave me a brief hug and took the other chair.

"A little."

"Emil was a *pendejo* again."

I nodded. "Why should I care if he ever gets out of jail or not? Better if he stays in. Then I won't be forced to see him. Ever."

"But you need a Spanish teacher. The nanas are getting worn out, and my Spanish, as I warned you, isn't that good. The students need Emil."

I faked an angry look. It wasn't Joachín's fault that Emil was on our minds. "You promised not to talk about him."

"Forget about Emil. But he's a good teacher, don't you think?"

"You don't think I can find a better Spanish teacher in Tucson? I could find five tonight without trying!" Inadvertently, I'd raised my voice.

Joachín nodded, humoring me.

"I could find twenty within a week and that's without asking the nanas for help. Spanish teachers in this town are such a penny a dozen that — "

Joachín placed his hand on the top of my head, slid it around my ear, and ran it down my shoulders. "Shhh."

We had a three-second stare down before Joachín smiled. "Better?"

"Sorry," I said more calmly. "Usually I don't get upset. In the last week, I've been angrier than I've been in the last few years altogether."

"I understand that. But I was wondering—"

"I say 'no' to all of you! Where's Emil's mother? Why hasn't she come back from San Francisco to deal with this? She should be down here rooting for him like a real mom. Of course, maybe she thinks he's guilty. And jail is actually good for him. At some point he'll stop complaining about his treatment and start pondering how he got there. He might finally realize that the few people who are trying to help him—"

"Dervla."

"He deserves to rot behind bars! Jerk! But that's okay. Let him choose jail over a little common courtesy. God knows that—"

Joachín gently put two fingers on my lips. "I came to ask if you'd go to rehearsal with me. You didn't answer my text."

Finally I shut my big mouth long enough to realize that Joachín hadn't been sent by the family to ask for another favor for Emil.

So why had he come? I'd finished all the costumes. Tommy had asked me to give them a hand with the sets, but they hadn't started working on them yet. Nobody would possibly need me at the theatre.

True, we'd flirted the night before. Joachín would be spending the night at rehearsal, so was this a seemingly innocuous way to extend our flirtation? Maybe it was an invitation of another kind. Nearly married woman, suddenly alone. Probably lonely. Needy.

An easy target. Somebody who might be willing to listen to a kind of family member pretending to act on her behalf.

Yet the invitation wasn't unattractive. There were lots worse things than being the subject of a handsome younger man's attention. So why not?

Clearly I needed time to sort things out. I couldn't do so on the spot, especially not with such a bad headache. Maybe somewhere someone had made a doll of me and put fifty pins in it.

Joachín lightly patted my arm. "Tommy asked me to bring you with me."

Oh. My flicker of excitement trickled out. I didn't mind that Tommy wanted something; maybe there was another costume mishap. But he could have called me and asked me himself. Oh. Maybe not. He might have tried.

"I gave Tommy your number. I hope you don't mind, but since you didn't answer, he asked if I would reach out. Since I had to come right by your place anyway, I promised to stop."

Of course. Tommy had asked for a simple favor, and Joachín had complied. My pseudo-relative's actions were perfectly reasonable. I'd jumped to conclusions about everything. Luckily, I hadn't lodged my foot any farther down my throat. In an act of charity, I also granted myself a get-out-of-jail-free card. The last twenty-hour hours had provided more drama than the plays I'd read in college. Funny how they hadn't prepared me one bit for real life.

"I hope Laney doesn't expect another alteration," I said.

"Tommy didn't tell me. But would you mind coming? Or if you'd rather drive yourself, you could stop by for a few minutes whenever it's convenient."

On my own I might not have gathered the energy to leave the house. The alternative to accompanying a charming escort to the theatre was to spend the evening on Netflix, perhaps with multiple bowls of popcorn.

"For Emil, not even a spitball. For you and Tommy, anything."

Joachín tapped his watch without looking at the time. "Maybe we could get going?"

I glanced at the bedroom clock: 6:53. We had seven minutes to get to rehearsal on time.

"Of course!"

We traipsed downstairs. As I marched past the bar, I paused, thinking that Emilito could use a few pins.

I didn't need to. Joachín had stuck two pins on the edge of the doll's throat. They weren't deep enough to do any damage, but they made me grin.

At least one person was unequivocally on my side.

Chapter Twenty-Two

We'd barely walked through the door when we were applauded.

"Joachín! Dervla!" Tommy, Willard, Holland, and Désirée clapped from the stage. A shaggy white terrier ran out to greet us.

"Havie!" Joachín bent down, and the dog leapt into his arms. "His real name is Haversham, but that's too long."

I knew the reference: the family from *The Play That Goes Wrong* had been inspiration for anyone who wanted to have a good laugh at the theatre.

"Cute, isn't he?" asked Joachín.

The shaggy darling let me pet him as well, and for a few moments we were too enthralled with pet love to think about anything else. I'd grown up with dogs, and I'd always enjoyed being with them a lot more than spending time with my siblings. It was Emil who hadn't wanted us to be tied down with an animal.

When I motioned for Joachín to pass him off, Havie jumped into my arms and licked my nose. That's what I liked about dogs. They were uncomplicated. They didn't judge. They made friends with you immediately. "Are we having a party instead of rehearsal?" I asked.

Tommy grinned. "With any luck, we'll have a bit of both despite what you might call a setback. But in the theatre, you learn to be flexible, don't you?" The others nodded. "You never know what will happen." More nods. "Catastrophes are common."

The cast grinned as if they'd planned a successful surprise party.

"Do you notice who's not here?" Tommy asked.

Joachín and I looked at each other. *You don't think--?* I asked silently.

He shook his head half an inch.

"Come!" Willard said.

As we joined the others on stage, Willard poured us sloshes of red wine in small plastic cups. "Sorry," he said. "I thought to bring wine, but we don't have any glasses."

"We also don't have Laney," Désirée said.

Joachín's face was blank. I hoped mine didn't read "stunned."

"You'll never guess what happened!" Tommy said gleefully.

"Oh, we can guess," said Joachín.

"Not in a million years!" Holland patted her poofy hair.

Désirée twisted the big silver loops of her necklace. "We wouldn't wish her harm. Really, we wouldn't."

"Come on!" Tommy said. "Guess!"

Joachín looked at me, his eyes twice as wide as usual. Then he turned to the crowd. "She came down with pneumonia?"

"No!" they cried.

I had no energy for diplomacy. "She fell and broke her foot in about a million pieces."

"Wow!" Tommy said. "She texted you?"

"No."

"You've got it a bit wrong," Willard said. "Only three places. But bad breaks, all three of them."

"She fell down the stairs?" asked Joachín.

The others laughed. I credited Joachín with sounding sincere, but after all, he had trained as an actor.

"Let me guess," I said. "She slipped and fell while walking around her own living room."

"Exactly!" cried Tommy. "She went straight home after rehearsal, but when she got up to fetch a snack, she tripped on a little hiccup in the rug. Can you believe it? To fall that hard? The doctors said she won't walk properly for months."

Oh, I believed it. I was still stunned, but I believed it. Four coincidences were three too many. The magic wasn't locked up in the nanas. It was locked up in me, and I didn't know whether to celebrate or fear myself.

Willard settled into the stage couch. "Drat. There's no way Laney can do the play. I practically cried when she informed us. I've put up with a lot of young actors in my time. They're often difficult! It comes with the profession. And her acting is passable. But she came in so sure she was the star of the show that no one wanted to interact with her. Get it?"

We got it. Everyone else was in the best of moods, but I was at the crossroads between triumph and remorse. I hadn't meant to harm her, not that much. It wasn't my fault Joachín couldn't throw.

Maybe I was supposed to be thankful. The doll might have landed on its head, in which case Laney would be dead, and we would be wondering why she hadn't shown up for rehearsal.

"Now we have a little problem," Tommy said.

I nodded. "You'll need Isabel. Is she close to the same size, or will I need to start over?"

Holland scrunched her mouth. Désirée checked her nails. Willard looked over at Tommy.

"We could contact Isabel," the director said. "But you know a lot about theatre, right? Joachín said your dissertation was on Martin McDonagh?"

"Yes, but writing three hundred pages about an Irish playwright—"

"You were in several undergraduate productions?"

"Yes, but it wasn't hard to get a part. And that was years ago."

Tommy waved both arms. "Why not help us out? We open next Friday!"

"I'm seriously out of practice."

"You're a teacher," said Tommy. "You act non-stop."

True. I acted cheerful when the students couldn't understand a thing. I acted compassionate when they offered lame excuses for not studying. And yes, I'd studied Irish drama every which way. I'd had small parts in undergraduate productions. That didn't mean I could fill in for a bona fide actress.

I faced the roomful of blind optimists.

"You'll be fine," said Willard. "And if truth be told, it's not that big a part."

"That's not what Laney said."

"Won't you help us?" Tommy asked.

I was so fond of the group that I wanted to tell them what they wanted to hear, but I didn't trust myself. "I'm afraid I would ruin it for the rest of you. I might have stage fright and panic and forget all the lines."

Tommy tapped his forehead. "Stage fright is imaginary. It's an excuse, not a reason."

"We don't want to have to deal with Isabel," said Holland. "Sorry, Joachín."

"Trust me," he said, "I'm with you guys."

"I'm sure you can find someone else who will be appropriate," I said.

They frowned, milling around. Willard refilled our glasses; after all, they were small.

"Think about it for an hour or two?" Tommy asked. "We have to make a quick decision."

"I'll think about it." I silently promised myself to do nothing of the kind. The troop liked to complain, but working with Isabel couldn't be all that bad.

In truth it wasn't my acting I was worried about. I was afraid I might hurt somebody. It was as if someone I didn't know had sneaked inside my body to create havoc. Laney's foot was broken in three places? I was lucky it hadn't ripped off altogether.

Holland raised her glass. "I realize we can't spring something on Dervla and expect her to instantly solve our problems. But tonight I was hoping for a run-through. Dervla, even if you don't want to perform with us, would you mind reading through the part tonight? Tommy could do it, but it's better if he can watch."

A nice, safe favor. My favorite kind. "I'd be delighted to help. Just loan me a script."

Joachín handed me his before I finished the sentence. "You'll be great. Trust me. And cue me in? I'm not sure I remember every line."

"Happy to."

Despite the wine, or perhaps because of it, the actors swung into gear. Laney's absence elated them despite the trouble it caused. They darted around the stage with extra energy and focused as if the play were opening the next day.

It was a pleasure to watch the first scenes. I had to cue Joachín now and again, but despite what he'd told me, he knew the script well. The problem was that my head continued to throb, and I'd run right out of expired painkillers.

"Dervla?" Tommy asked.

Whoops! I'd missed my first cue. "Sorry!" I dashed on stage, stumbling around worse than Laney had the night before.

"'There you are, dear,'" said Holland, following the script.

We launched into the scene, a mild setup for later in the play. I felt awkward at first, but the longer I read, the more I fell into character. Willard was right, of course, about teachers being actors. I constantly pantomimed to help students recall words. I exaggerated my expressions as I coaxed them to say "sad" or "embarrassed" or any other human emotion. Learning a foreign language was like being in a play anyway, the play of your own life as you took on different identities. It was always a lark impersonating someone else, and for a brief second I thought of myself in Laney's sexy French maid outfit, nearly missing my next cue.

I sat down for the next scenes, delighting in the cast's progress. Havie kept me company by sitting at my feet. But when I stood to deliver my lines, I felt shaky. I climbed the short set of stairs up to the stage wondering what was wrong with me. I read through a couple of pages, strangely drained. I was mid-scene with Holland when I lost my place in the script. Before I could find it again, the script fell from my hands.

I cursed myself right before I slumped to the floor.

***

I was out for a minute. By the time I came to, Joachín knelt by my side. Désirée fanned me while Havie barked. The actors spurted out questions until I held up my hand. "Could you all speak more softly?" I put my hands over my eyes and rested them on my temples.

Then they whispered so softly I couldn't hear them. That was all right too. I half heard their questions as well as Joachín's half-true answers: Had I been doing all right? I'd been under stress. Did I need a doctor? No. I would be fine. Joachín would stay with me to make sure.

Then I felt Joachín gently touching my cheek. "What can I do for you?"

"Help me sit up."

He guided me while the others watched in silence. Holland handed me a paper cup filled with sugar water while Tommy bent down beside me. "I apologize for what I said about stage fright. Some people do have it. For the same reason, some people can't give speeches. I'm so sorry that being on stage—"

"I'm okay. I haven't been sleeping well."

"That's no excuse. We shouldn't have sprung such a crazy idea on you. We made assumptions that were unfair. You'll have to forgive us. We were so excited about ridding ourselves of Laney that we didn't bother to think of anyone but ourselves."

I drank the water in a swift gulp. "I don't know what got into me. It's nothing. I'm sorry I messed up your read-through. Please carry on, won't you?"

The actors shuffled their feet.

"I think we've done enough for one night," said Willard. "Tom, what do you think?"

He nodded, presumably relieved they'd rehearsed at all. "I'll contact Isabel when I get home. Joachín, do you know if she has any other current engagements?"

"We're not exactly on speaking terms. I mean, we speak if we have to."

"Right. But you can work with her for the purposes of the play?"

"I can."

"What about the rest of you?" Tommy asked.

They nodded unenthusiastically. I registered their feelings, but I couldn't help them. I wasn't sure I could even stand up.

"I wish we had a better solution," Tommy said. "But it's only a three-week run, so we don't have to put up with her forever."

"No," said Holland. "It will only seem like that."

Joachín, who was hovering, read my silence as pain. "I should get you home."

The others mumbled approval.

"Need any help?" asked Tommy.

"Maybe to get out to the car," Joachín said.

I let Joachín pull me to my feet.

"I'm fine," I lied. Then I let Tommy and Joachín half-carry, half-walk me outside and stuff me into the car. I waved feebly as we drove off.

When we arrived at my place, I let Joachín carry me up to my room. When he offered to sleep downstairs in case I needed anything, I nodded because that was easier than thinking things through. I said goodnight and crawled under the sheet. I'd probably fallen asleep before Joachín made it downstairs.

I slept so soundly that I didn't wake up all night long. If I had any dreams, I didn't remember them.

Chapter Twenty-Three

I woke to rays of sun streaming onto my floor as they welcomed a new day. I was pleased that my head didn't hurt. I was less pleased to hear voices in my kitchen. Although they spoke too softly for me to hear whole sentences, I knew the intruders at once. Lula and Mari were interrogating Joachín.

I dressed quickly, not because I worried the nanas would invade the bedroom, but because I wanted to eavesdrop. It's always useful to hear what people say about you when they don't think you're listening.

I sat at the top of my stairs.

"There's no way," Joachín said.

"There has to be," said Lula.

I smelled coffee. French Vanilla. I was glad that someone—Joachín?—had the sense to make some.

"She won't go for it," Joachín said.

"You're not sure about that," Mari said.

"I am."

It was a strange sensation hearing someone speak on my behalf. Normally I preferred to speak for myself, but since the nanas had gone to the trouble of making a personal appearance, in the morning no less, they probably wanted me to do something else for Emil. In that case, I particularly appreciated Joachín coming to my defense.

"You won't know until you ask," Mari said.

"Which you need to do for us right away," Lula continued.

The nanas were completely in character. Lula made demands and people did as she asked. Mari swam in optimism until she floated to the surface, triumphant. They had missed their calling. They worked so well together that they might have been a comedy act, but they were so persuasive they should have gone into law or maybe politics.

"Just this one last thing," Lula said. "Then we promise to leave her alone. You too. Time is precious for Emil, you know. The poor boy is wasting away in jail."

Coffee was poured. The top of the sugar dish was set on the counter. Spoons clanged.

"Please?" Mari asked. "You know how very much it means to us."

"You don't have to convince me," Joachín said. "I'm not the one Emil insulted."

"He didn't mean to," said Lula.

"He's under lots of stress," said Mari. "None of us has been in that situation, so we can't properly imagine it."

"You realize that Dervla is even-tempered," Joachín said. "Emil pushed her too far."

That was for darned sure.

"Yes," said Mari. "She's remarkable."

"Yesterday she was so mad at Emil that she wouldn't talk about him," Joachín said. "She blew up when I mentioned his name. Wouldn't tell me what happened."

For a moment, even the nanas were silent. I savored the thought of their squirming.

"Do you know what that tells me?" Joachín asked. "He was a regular *cabrón* when he talked to her. It's risky to insult people—maybe the only people—who can help you."

"Emil didn't make the best choices," Lula said, "but think of his stress level!"

His stress level would have been worse if we'd been speaking in person because I would have punched him. Maybe twice. Maybe low.

"Dervla feels stressed too," said Mari. "That's why she doesn't recognize his desperation."

Really? Mari was giving me the benefit of the doubt too. They both were. But I didn't need to spend the rest of the day listening to the nanas stuff their feet into their mouths. I made extra noise as I walked down the stairs, relishing my theatrical entrance.

"What was that were you saying?" I asked. "Did I hear something about desperation?"

The nanas were in full swing making themselves at home in my kitchen. Lula juggled silverware and plates as she prepared to set the table. Mari fiddled with a burner. She hadn't been able to find an apron—in fact, I didn't own one—but she'd wrapped a bath towel around her waist and wore a dishtowel down her blouse.

"How would you like your eggs?" Mari asked from behind the stove. "You need protein. Joachín explained about your fall."

I appealed to Joachín, who held up his hands as if to say he was helpless. He was probably right. I looked over to the couch where his blankets were askew; the nanas had managed to wake him too. At least it would have been clear that he'd slept downstairs. They would have noticed that much right away. If they'd had questions, they would have asked. Or assumed.

"I don't have any eggs," I said. Or much of anything. Grocery shopping was on the To Do List, but that's where it had stayed.

"We brought a few things," Lula said. "We weren't sure what you would want."

"Pancakes, then," I said, testing them.

Mari extracted a pan from my bottom shelf. "We can do that."

I sat at my dining room table, wondering whether or not I was in my own house. The two had come in like tornadoes. No, Tasmanian devils. Joachín didn't stand a chance against them. Neither did I. It was best to stay out of their way.

"Where's your pancake mix, angel?" Mari called out.

Of course I didn't have any. "Eggs will be fine."

"She'll want chorizo too," said Lula as she set out four napkins. Then she looked at me. "Best stuff when you need extra strength." She joined her sister at the sink.

"Joachín?" *What the heck did you tell them?*

He handed me a favorite cup, one with a frowning cat that said, "I'm silently correcting your grammar."

I raised my eyebrows at him. *Well?*

He indicated the whirlwind helpers. "They showed up a little while ago. I explained why you needed to sleep in."

"They came to cook me breakfast?"

Lula came over to the table. "We knew you weren't well yesterday. We worried you would get worse, and we were right."

At the stove, Mari cracked eggs over a skillet.

"You've never come here on a Sunday before," I pointed out.

"When you were here with Emil we didn't want to intrude," Lula said. "Young people need their privacy."

"But you came today because—"

Mari turned around as she stirred. "What Lula said. We sensed you didn't feel a hundred percent, so we wanted to help out."

People often act uncharacteristically. They read books you never expect them to pick up, attend the type of movies you know they don't like, buy silly shoes they won't wear more than once a year. These are normal inconsistencies. No one is "normal" all the time. But this was different. It was unimaginable. I didn't need any magic to figure that out.

"What do you need?" I asked.

Lula poured glasses of orange juice all around, which meant I would have none for Monday morning. "Why would we need anything?"

The only time I'd seen the nanas on a Sunday morning was for Easter egg hunts, which usually started at the crack of eleven o'clock. They didn't believe in going to church or getting up early. I smelled not one big rat, but two.

"You need something," I said. "Something big."

Lula stopped fussing with the silverware. "Dervla, you know that we love you. We want you to be healthy."

Mari momentarily left the stove and hovered around me. "But we want you to consider investing in an insurance policy."

"To be on the safe side?"

"Exactly," said Lula.

Finally the pieces fell into place. "You went to Twinkle's memorial celebration yesterday, didn't you?"

"What?" Lula asked, smiling.

Mari shook her head, but I knew better.

"You both went," I said. "Good work. You might expect me to be thankful except that I'm done helping Emil. But all right. I'll play along. What did you find out?"

As the chorizo sizzled, Mari stepped away from the stove. "Twinkle had a lot of satisfied customers. It seems that she did a decent job."

"So?"

"We thought you might help us go through her client list."

"Why would I do that? And how could I anyway?"

Lula unfolded a paper napkin and placed it on her lap. "Not you. All of us."

The chorizo was so rich in chili peppers that for a moment I didn't care. Then I woke up as if the coffee had kicked in suddenly. "You found a list. And you stole it."

"It's not stealing if it's out there in the open," Lula said as if explaining the benefits of vegetables to a small child. Then she addressed her sister. "See there. I told you she'd figure it out."

"Yes, yes," Mari said as she brought over the skillet. "I owe you a dollar. Now let's eat."

Occasionally Emil had prepared brunch for me. More occasionally I'd done the same for him. Mari's cooking was far superior. Even though I wasn't hungry, I polished off a full plate of scrambled eggs and chorizo before I realized what I was doing.

The nanas recounted their experiences at Twinkle's event, which mostly consisted of agents angling to pick up new clients. We also shared a good laugh over Laney and her poor foot.

"Cinnamon bun?" Mari asked.

"Way too full," I said.

She placed one on my plate anyway. "Eat what you want."

The dough smelled wonderful and fresh. Maybe I could eat half.

Mari slid a bun on Joachín's plate as well. "There was something we were hoping you could do for us today."

"I can't help you with that little list," I said. "Insurance agents don't work on Sundays no matter how diligent or desperate they are."

"That's true." Mari went to the bar counter and retrieved Emilito. The doll no longer had pins at his throat; Joachín must have removed them before admitting the nanas. "You know, you can use your powers for good as well as for evil."

"I hate to say this, but the whole power thing—"

"Look what happened to Laney!" said Joachín. "You broke her foot!"

I gave him the angriest look I could muster on such a full stomach.

In return he awarded me a pathetic half smile. "Deny it if you want to, but I know what I saw."

Lula brought over my dog-cat. "If you do need something to blame, it would be New Orleans. If you hadn't gone to visit your cousin, you wouldn't have come back with a trigger."

My dog-cat a trigger. Couldn't wait to call Keevah. She's the one I could blame.

Mari propped up Emilito against the saltshaker. "The power is strong in you. I know that's hard to understand. It's not something you asked for. But if you have a gift, don't you think you should use it?"

I didn't want to seem ungrateful to—whom, the universe? But why should I do anything I didn't want to? If I had a special power, certainly a lot of other people did too. Did they feel obliged? They probably kept it to themselves, which was right where it belonged.

While I formulated a response, I made the mistake of looking Mari in the eye. She smiled so tenderly that all I could think of was how much she wanted to help her nephew. Then I looked at Lula, who smiled in the exact same way.

Joachín wasn't any better. He looked at me as if I were the only possible savior for the lot of them.

I wanted to send them away, go back to bed, and forget the whole thing. Of course I wouldn't be able to. Even without the breakfast bribe, I couldn't ignore the nanas' plight. Over the years they'd done one nice thing for me after the other. Granted me instant membership into the family. Encouraged Emil and me to start a business. Loaned us money. Listened to problems. Cheered successes.

They hadn't been obliged where I was concerned. They might have written me off as the *güera* or the "next one." They'd come to my defense every time, even at Emil's expense. No matter what they wanted, I wouldn't be able to turn them down. Raise bail money? Even if I had to go bankrupt. Lie to the police about Emil's whereabouts the night before Twinkle was killed? Risky. Stupid. But if asked, I would. For family, you did such actions even if they were wrong or illegal or ill-advised.

I wiped my mouth on a leftover napkin from Emil's thirtieth birthday party. "What exactly did you want me to do?"

Lula petted Emilito's head. "If you take him out, it would be like getting him out of jail."

"What?"

"He's been stuck in the house, but if you go over to the park—"

I blinked a few times, sure that dust had fallen into my ears, causing me to hear nonsense. "You want me to take the doll for a walk?"

Lula nodded. "That would mimic releasing Emil from jail. Symbolically speaking, of course."

I'd no doubt heard crazier things, but I couldn't think when. "Should I strap him to my headband and go for a jog?"

If they noticed any sarcasm, they ignored it.

"It wouldn't matter," Mari said softly. "Simply go around to happy places you and Emil liked to visit together."

"This will help because—"

"Maybe the police will find a technicality and release Emil."

"He's been accused of murder," I said slowly. "They won't back down on something as serious as that."

Mari took my hand. "Maybe the police will find new evidence. I know it sounds unusual. But promise you'll try? It might not help, but it won't hurt anything. We'll all feel better. When we talk to Emil, we can tell him we're doing as much as we can."

I looked from Lula to Mari. They beamed like cats sure they were about to be fed tuna fish. "I can't just loan you the doll?"

Lula shook her head as if I'd asked whether the sky were green.

"You have to do it yourself," said Mari. "You're the one with the power."

"Only me."

"That's right," Mari said. "You're the lucky one."

Lucky? I was caught. Trapped by two little old ladies who were a lot spunkier than they looked.

And determined. I waited for them to remind me how much they'd helped me the previous week. Make me feel indebted for the years of family dinners. Discuss family values. Mention hardships they had faced during their marriages, their move to the States, their struggles to go forward with their lives. Instead they twinkled smiles.

Joachín was no help. He copied them.

"Emil and I often went to Himmel Park on Sundays," I said. "It wouldn't hurt me to go without him for once."

Mari raised her hand in triumph. "That's the spirit!"

Lula high-fived her sister. "We knew we could count on you!"

"She fainted last night," Joachin said as if I weren't in the room. "That might happen again. She's pretty weak."

Didn't they notice how much I'd eaten?

"Can we count on you to go with her?" Mari asked.

He addressed me. "You don't mind, right? A stroll through the park."

"With a doll."

"Yes."

"Three's usually a crowd," I said.

Lula clasped her hands together. "A crowd is a party!"

"I reserve Sundays for the Irish singalong." After we sang for an hour, we gossiped for another two. I wasn't sure which part I liked the best.

"Today you'll make an exception, right?" asked Lula. "For us?"

I had plenty of time to do both, but I didn't need to disclose every detail. "Just this once."

"All settled!" Mari stood and gathered dirty plates. "Time to clean up and get out of here. These kids have better things to do than talk to us all day."

Kids? What kids?

I picked up additional dirty plates. "I can do that."

Lula took the plates and sat me back down. "Rest now. Save your strength."

I wanted to get up, but under the table, Joachín put his foot on mine. *Let them fuss.*

Though it seemed wrong, I let two old women wash and dry plates. They cleaned the table better than it had ever been cleaned since Emil and I owned it. I might have hired them.

Instead I reconciled myself to perambulating Himmel Park with a doll. I would do one round. Then little Emilito could find his own way.

Chapter Twenty-Four

Since it wasn't far away, I let Joachín escort me to Himmel Park on foot. We started around the perimeter from the east side. As would be expected on a lovely Sunday afternoon, families picnicked on the grass while children ran around shouting. Middle schoolers kicked at a soccer ball. Spring would give way to summer soon enough, and at that point most of the natives would hibernate indoors. For now everyone wanted to take advantage of a 75-degree day.

"Are you doing all right?" Joachín asked.

"Worried I'll faint again and you'll have to carry me home?"

"Not worried. I'll let you lie down until you feel better."

I swatted his arm but missed. "What I'd like to do is join in on the soccer game."

"No way."

"They need a better goalie."

The goalie dove for a ball, missed, and clunked into another player.

"Don't even think of it," Joachín said. "Tomorrow, maybe."

"It's more fun to play than to watch."

"Tomorrow," Joachín said sternly. "Emilito?"

I patted my bag. "Inside my purse doesn't count?"

He shrugged casually. As long as I'd come this far into craziness, I might as well go all the way. I dug Emilito out from the bottom.

"Careful," Joachín said.

"Be careful with this doll? You're kidding."

"Don't break off one of its limbs or anything."

"I won't." I didn't have a handy pocket, so I stuck Emilito half in and half out of the purse and closed the zipper so that he would stay put. I couldn't have felt more foolish, but now the doll had a perfect view. "I don't know how I got myself into this."

"By trying to help Emil," Joachín said simply. "You're right to be mad. He messed up in a stupid way. But he's not a monster down deep. There's a reason you spent so many years with him."

Maybe six and a half years weren't a lot in the scheme of things, but they represented twenty percent of my life. How could I have wasted so much effort? I kicked myself for being nonchalant and naïve.

In the beginning, I wondered why this gorgeous Hispanic man would bother to talk to me. He was a comfortable height without being too tall, muscular without being a body builder. His smile invited me to keep talking.

For our first date, he invited me to the Loft, the local art cinema. I silently thanked him for choosing a German film because I was forced to read subtitles. Otherwise I wouldn't have kept my eyes on the screen. I would have been too distracted to pay attention. Then we couldn't have had the all-night discussion after the film.

Maybe we'd fallen into a relationship too easily. We hadn't spent time pining for one another. One date led to steady dating led to living together. The progression was so natural that I never questioned it.

Unfortunately, I hadn't cultivated it either. Emil slipped out from under me because I hadn't paid enough attention to our relationship. Wasn't there such a thing as fair warning? Evidently not. I'd been too blind, too complacent. I assumed Emil and I were in it for the long haul. I jumped to conclusions about the strength of our relationship.

I wouldn't make the mistake a second time.

Joachín and I climbed the sharp incline to the top of the hill. The park covered about six blocks, and from the apex we had a complete view: the large grassy areas to the south, the swimming complex to the west, the tennis and pickleball courts to the north, the jungle gym and Himmel Park Library to the east.

"There's a stray ball," Joachín said.

He fetched an orange ball that a kid had left behind. "Play catch?"

"If you won't let me play soccer, catch will do."

We tossed the ball gently, from ten feet away. Then we moved farther and farther apart so it would be more difficult. Joachín had a smooth pitch, but the way he stretched his graceful limbs was remarkable. The only balls he missed were the ones I threw crookedly.

"You're good at this," he called out.

"I had a lot of siblings and no money. We played catch a lot."

"Me too."

We played more vigorously, aiming for sky-high shots, when I crashed into a hole—maybe a rodent's?—and tumbled to the grass.

Joachín ran over instantly and knelt beside me. "I should have known better," he said. "You're not well."

I rubbed my ankle. "That's not it, and my ankle is fine. I didn't notice the hole until I fell in it."

"Are you okay?"

"I have a bit of a trick ankle after all those years in soccer. I need to baby it from time to time."

I led him to a shady patch of grass, and we plopped down.

"Are you sure you're okay?" he asked.

"Just pausing. If you walk too fast, you don't see anything."

My second date with Emil had been right here, a walk through the park. After we discussed all our favorite plays and their authors, we turned personal. While I'd avoided the topic of my own family, Emil had told me all about his: the nanas, his parents, his brother, aunts, uncles, cousins, nephews, nieces. He told me about so many relatives that I couldn't remember a single name afterwards. I was envious of the way he spoke about them because they sounded like friends, not obligations.

Joachín pulled on the sleeves of the light sweater he wore around his shoulders. "This is the first decent day we've had."

The temperature was mild and the breeze was gentle, so the park became even more crowded. A family walked right in front of us: two little girls dressed up for a party, a contented mom chasing after them, a panting father carrying a heavy backpack. A young dogwalker followed: a teen of about fifteen trailing an exuberant Greyhound. He stopped to talk to the young woman with a pair of terriers who was coming from the opposite direction.

It was a perfect Sunday at the park. Peaceful, serene. The space was a healthy reminder of the importance of acknowledging the beauty of everyday life, the gift of nature, the freedom to live your life the way you wanted to.

Oh. Freedom. Emil. Any happy thoughts vanished.

"We should start on that list of clients tomorrow," I said. "I'm not convinced we'll find anything, but we'll feel proactive."

"Do we know if Twinkle had any siblings?"

"No idea. We can ask the nanas to doublecheck with Emil tomorrow." I rubbed against Joachín's shoulder. "Maybe she has an evil step-sibling like Isabel."

Joachín pinched a bit of dirt. "Sorry you're stuck sewing for her."

"I can hardly wait to sew a dress for my former boyfriend's former girlfriend, but never mind. A job is a job." I didn't really mind. The situation was ridiculous, but she wasn't my problem.

Joachín watched the dirt fall from his hand.

He saw the best in everyone except Isabel, so it finally dawned on me that he was still in pain. "Want to talk about it? Your relationship with Isabel, I mean."

"No."

Time didn't heal everything.

"You still think about it."

"I try not to."

For a moment I concentrated on the gentle breeze, the teen still flirting with the woman with the terriers, the family party decorated with balloons.

"Isabel had to take care of you and didn't want to," I said slowly. "It happens to older siblings all over the world."

I would have sworn that in my family, it happened to me the most. By the time I was twelve, my older sisters successfully argued that I should be taking care of Roisin and Mickey while they went out screwing around. Literally. So I got practice with kids while Tully got pregnant and Jan made friends with all the boys in the neighborhood.

Joachín inhaled with his eyes shut. He'd never much spoken about his family that I could remember. He saw his dad on required holidays, but by evening he was back with the Arellanos. I never questioned his actions because the Arellanos were always more fun.

He pulled out a blade of grass and tossed it, but the green strand only traveled a few inches. "There are bad feelings all around. Isabel was six or seven when Dad met my mom."

Ugh. Family histories were always complicated. "That's when your dad left Isabel's mother."

"Yes. But I'm told they never got along. Isabel remembers them always shouting at one another."

"It's not like your mother interrupted something."

"I don't know. No one has ever told me about it. But at any rate, they'd been married about a year when I came along. When Isabel was so much older that she had to help take care of me."

"Which she resented."

"She resented me generally. Probably from the moment I was conceived. Sometimes she'd break something on purpose so that I'd get a spanking."

Sibling rivalry. I knew it so well. "I'm sorry to hear it. That's so unfair."

"Isabel wasn't trying to be fair. She wanted all the positive attention for herself. How's that for a memorable upbringing?"

"Not so great."

"It backfired on her because one day Dad caught her. She got the spanking. Triple force, because the more she protested, the more Dad realized how many times she'd lied to him where I was concerned. She's resented me royally every day since then."

"It was her own fault."

"Of course it was."

With some siblings, that's what happened. They lied, they cheated, and they dodged responsibility. Mine were perfect examples.

"Imagine how happy Isabel was to take me with her to see Emil."

"Was your dad punishing her?"

"No. He thought I could keep her out of Emil's pants."

"Parents! They have the craziest ideas. I'm sure that worked."

"Right, if you mean not at all. They were sixteen, so naturally they were curious."

"At least you wound up in a safe space."

"That's just it. The first time Isabel dragged me to the Arellanos, I was put off by them. So many relatives at once and all that. But the nanas saw through Isabel right away, how she shuffled me around every chance she got."

"The nanas adopted you."

"Absolutely. Isabel and Emil would slip off on their own, usually to Emil's room, but Orlando and I became friends straight away. The nanas would give us pocket money for the movies or treats or whatever we wanted. They welcomed me from the beginning."

For me they'd provided a definition of family. Back home it had always been a contest over who was better, who was right, who forgot to do a chore. The Arellanos had their issues too. The nanas didn't approve of Emil's mom moving to San Francisco. They were short with younger relatives who left dirt on the floor or forgot to clean their plates. But they also listened. They paid attention to everyone in their sphere and helped out however they could. In return, the relatives were loyal to them. And the pseudo-relatives too.

"When Emil broke up with Isabel, things were even better." Joachín smiled, and for a moment I imagined him the teen I'd first met. "By then I was driving, so I could come on my own and spend as much time as I wanted. I can't count how many nights I've spent over there. Sometimes it was me and Orlando and the nanas. We'd watch Pedro Infante movies or play poker. The nanas would quiz us about the girls we were meeting, and we would giggle and deny everything. Then we'd break down and tell them everything they wanted to know."

I could imagine the foursome squashed onto the couch, watching old Mexican film stars in black and white, laughing as they passed around a bowl of popcorn.

"That's why I'm always there for them," I said.

"Me too."

Joachín picked up a twig and tossed it. "They like you way better than Emil, you know."

I laughed so loudly it came out more like a big sneeze. "They do not."

"I spend more time there than you do. Orlando and I help them clean up while they're puttering around the kitchen. 'I like that Dervla,' Lula always says. 'Emil better make sure he's good to her.' Mari chimes in with the same message."

"Good to know." It was. Although they accepted relatives without question, they didn't like everybody.

"They're livid about Twinkle," Joachín continued. "The day you went over because you thought you needed to say goodbye? They were so mad they couldn't eat that night. Had Orlando and me pick up some Chinese, but they skipped dinner, went straight to their bedroom with a bottle of Brandy Presidente, and swore a blue streak."

I stretched my toes into the sun. "I assumed that if Emil were dumping me, the nanas would do the same."

"They're loyal to family, but they're loyal to friends, too."

"Emil didn't see that coming."

"He was stunned. Orlando and I laughed about it for hours."

"Somehow he thought the nanas would be delighted he was sleeping around on me. Imagine that."

"He's an idiot. That's the only explanation."

We greeted a man walking by with two collies. The dogs were identical as far as I could tell, but they were so excited to be out for a walk that they could hardly hold back from running.

Joachín kept his eyes on the dogs. "Speaking of which, I think the nanas think I'm sleeping with you."

I couldn't read his response. Embarrassed? Worried? Amused? "They didn't see the blankets on the couch?"

"They did."

"If you were sleeping with me, why wouldn't you have been upstairs?" I asked.

"To keep up appearances? Because I snore. Or you do." He watched the dogs until they disappeared down the hill.

The nanas didn't miss an innuendo, intentional or otherwise. They were smart about people.

"Worried about your reputation?" I asked.

He lay back on the grass. "Too late. For you too."

I lay back as well. "Surely they don't think I'd jump right into bed with somebody else?"

"Maybe they thought you wanted to make Emil jealous."

"They should know that we're through. Completely."

Joachín turned on his side. "Never say never."

"You watch too many James Bond movies."

"Know what that means?"

I felt Joachín's gaze, but I concentrated on the sky. "What?"

"I need a faster car."

We both laughed. That was the key. Keeping things lighthearted. Accepting bad news and moving on. Making new alliances. Fighting different battles.

Or, in this case, allowing yourself feelings for a teen turned man.

While focusing on the clouds, I stretched my pinky to find his.

Silently, he wrapped it around mine.

Chapter Twenty-Five

After I finished with the twentieth name on the list, I closed the computer. Nothing so far. Not a single person seemed of interest. The clients were regular people who held jobs around town. They represented a range of ages and ethnic groups. On the surface, they had zero personal ties to Twinkle. She wasn't their friends on social media pages. A few were close to her age, so I gave those names an asterisk. Perhaps she'd known them from school, so they might have been friends for a long time.

But so far, nothing. I imagined possible angles, but reconstructing someone's life was harder than I imagined. Who kept records anymore? Most data was stored online and then lost due to the introduction of new technologies or the failure of old ones.

I took out my calendar and reviewed the days I'd been out of town. Five days to go back east at Christmas. Three to visit friends in Phoenix over Thanksgiving. Two in October for a teachers' conference.

I couldn't bare to look at more specifics. My schedule was set in advance with plane tickets and other travel arrangements, so Emil could have capitalized on my planning. I kicked myself for making things so easy. He was flattered by her, bored by me, whatever. There must have been a trigger.

I dug further back. Studying Twinkle's Facebook homepage for the twentieth time. I coordinated her posts with times I'd been out of town over the past year. Nothing conclusive. She was social. She had a lot of friends. Evidently she had parents who didn't mind babysitting.

Too bummed out to think straight, I draped my body over the couch. On another occasion I would have indulged in a power nap, but I wasn't tired. I was depressed. My lover had been two-timing me, probably for a while, and I hadn't noticed.

Even though I heard the buzz from across the room, I ignored the first two texts that came in. At the third buzz, I troubled myself to get up, cross to the counter, and check the number. Joachín. "Yes?"

"We're taking a break pretty soon if you still have time to swing by. If you don't, they'll all understand."

"They think I'm recovering from yesterday."

"Yes. They don't want you to hurt yourself."

"They're sweet. But as you know, I'm fine. I'll come over soon."

"No rush. Whatever's best for you."

What was best for me was to get out of the house and stop moping. I ran a comb through my hair, turned on a light to discourage intruders, and slipped outside.

***

The atmosphere at Tucson Theatre was nowhere as cheerful as it had been the night before, but it wasn't morose, either. The players were working through the script in a straightforward manner. They were so concentrated that the first creature to notice me was Havie. Joyously, he barked at my side.

While the actors plowed through their lines, I swooped up the pup and joined Tommy in the fifth row.

"Thanks for coming down," he whispered. "We will pay you eventually, you know."

"Luckily for you, I'm not in a hurry."

"I'm sorry about last night."

Havie licked my nose.

"To be honest, it wasn't stage fright. I've had a lot going on. I'm not sure what all Joachín has told you."

"Your innocent boyfriend is in jail."

"Ex-boyfriend. Way, way, way ex-boyfriend. But yes, that's the gist of the story."

Tommy scratched Havie's ears even though the bundle of slobber was in my lap instead of his. "A jury won't convict an innocent man."

"The trial might not be for months. Never mind. I came here to get away from my life. How is everything working out tonight?"

He indicated the side stage, where Isabel tapped her foot. Her face was buried in the script.

"Isabel is delighted to join us. Told me so nine million times."

I could hardly wait for the chance to sew for Isabel. I didn't like her one bit better than the nanas did. "Think she'll work out all right?"

"She'll have to. You don't mind taking her when we reach a stopping point?"

"Not at all. I'll be fast."

As soon as Isabel strode across the stage, I knew her measurements. The outfit I'd made for Laney wouldn't work at all, so I'd have to start all over. Isabel wasn't much overweight, but she was taller than her counterpart and bigger boned. Hopefully she wouldn't be as picky.

As Isabel read her first lines, I understood why Tommy hired her. She had stage presence. She had a clear voice and enunciated carefully. However, she was awkward, as if her limbs were too long for her body. She miscalculated the steps she needed to reach the dining room table and banged into it. On her way out of the scene, she hit the edge of a chair so hard it fell over backwards.

As long as she stood still, she was perfect.

Chapter Twenty-Six

As soon as her scene ended, I led Isabel to the rehearsal room to make a show of taking her measurements. She took off her jeans and T-shirt and placed them over a chair. Her plain golden cross sparkled against her chest, but as far as I knew, Emil never attended church with her.

"Thanks for making a special trip," Isabel said. "I realize you'd already made the costume for that other woman."

"No worries." As I took the tape measure from my purse, Emilito nearly sprang out. I violently shoved him back in. What would Isabel make of a doll with Emil's picture on it?

"I'm sorry I didn't have time to talk to you the other night," she said. "I was in a rush to meet a friend."

I draped the tape measure around her bust. "No worries. I was running late myself."

Isabel stood straighter as if posture would give her a bigger bustline. "It's always interesting to see who your husband chooses next, don't you think?"

Whom. Bust, 43. "Emil was your husband?"

"He promised to marry me."

Small, but a dig nonetheless. Maybe I didn't blame her. Waist, 39. "How old was he at the time, twenty?"

"A promise should be a promise. But human nature, right? I hear Emil dumped you from one day to the next."

More of a mean streak. Hips, 46. How would she have known that detail unless Emil told her himself?

"It would have happened sooner or later," Isabel continued. Big mean streak. Kick a dog when it's down.

I tapped Isabel's leg below the knee eight times harder than I needed to. "Think this is about the right length?"

"You're the seamstress. You should know."

I measured down from the waist. "I do know, but Laney bit my head off when she thought the skirt was too long. We're running out of time, so I thought I'd skip that step."

"I can't believe they offered her the part," Isabel said. "Was she any good?"

A redirect. Presumably so I could stew over her poignant digs. I busied myself by jotting down numbers I'd never look at again. "I can't judge about her acting, but Tommy was thankful you could step in so quickly."

"He's lucky I didn't have another engagement."

He was one lucky man, all right. "I'm sure it's hard to learn lines so quickly. You must have a gift for memory."

"I can manage that. But with a heads up I would have eaten differently last week." She stuck her fingers inside the elastic of her panties. "I'll lose two pounds by the time we do the show. Can you account for that?"

People always told me they were going to lose a couple of pounds, and, rightfully, I never believed them. Make the costume so tight she couldn't breathe? No problem. I made an illegible notation. "The dress isn't meant to be too close-fitting. You'll want to be comfortable when you're moving around onstage." Or falling around.

"That set is too narrow. How am I supposed to dodge all the furniture? Tommy is a nice guy, but as a director, he's basically an idiot."

An idiot who rightfully didn't want to hire Isabel if he didn't have to.

"He went through the pages so fast I didn't have a chance to take good notes," Isabel continued. "Joachín will have to help me. At least he didn't turn out to be a jerk the way Emil did."

I scraped her arm with the tape measure. "Sorry." Next I measured from shoulder to sleeve. "Emil does have his faults."

"We both know about that."

I put the pencil in my mouth as I measured across her back. Of course. Just as Emil started seeing Twinkle while still living with me, he probably started with me before breaking up with Isabel. He'd operated according to his maximum sexual convenience. Why give up one thing until being absolutely sure of another? Why not eat a plate of brownies and a pound cake at the same time?

Because your ex-lover is going to pin you until it really, really hurts. That's why.

"But now Emil is in big trouble," Isabel continued.

"Yes, he is." Why did people with the gift for the obvious insist on flaunting it?

"Not that he doesn't deserve it. Sleeping around like that."

By now I wasn't sure who deserved what. Isabel hadn't deserved Emil, either, but he'd put up with her. That part was on him. Certainly I hadn't been as hard to put up with? I was fun. I was flexible. I tried new things.

Isabel turned around. "You have to keep in mind that it's a Latino thing. I don't mean that as an excuse but as a reason. We're hotter than Anglos. We just are. Our men have to have sex, lots of it. And most of us feel the same way. So if two people aren't heated to the same degree—"

D. R. Ransdell

Enough was enough. "Who cooled off—you or Emil?"

"Just because I don't read books all day long doesn't mean I'm not as smart as you are," Isabel said.

Of course it didn't. But I loved that Isabel worried it did. Sure, Emil and I had spent nights discussing Godard and Truffaut, but intellectual discussions weren't the cornerstone of our relationship.

Twinkle didn't even read. I'd been through her house twice without detecting a single book without pictures.

To look official, I reviewed my measurements.

"I have to wonder what he talked about with that Twisty person. Or whatever her name was," Isabel said.

Maybe Emil and Twinkle didn't bother to talk.

I made a final notation. "Thanks. I've have everything I need."

She stared me straight on. "You don't think Emil did it, do you?"

"Of course not. Do you?"

"Honestly? No. But I sure don't know who did."

The murderer was no random thug. He had known when to come that morning. I patted the bump on my head. He'd known when to come for me. He'd been watching the house because he lived nearby.

That meant I'd have to keep looking.

***

When we reached my place after rehearsal, Joachín and I both assumed he'd be coming in. I had a moment of doubt when he put his arm around my shoulder as we walked up the drive, but I shelved any worries. It was comforting to have him sitting at the bar keeping me company while I milled around the kitchen scraping together a few snacks.

After I poured the man a shot of Jameson, he smelled it appreciatively.

"Sorry you had to put up with the great Isabel," he said. "And I'm doubly sorry she was such a bitch."

"Maybe not that bad. As soon as she started in with little digs, I put on my armor so they'd bounce off."

"She's lucky you took the right measurements."

"That doesn't mean I'll make a comfortable dress for her! But despite her posturing, deep down, I can understand her."

"In what sense?"

"She still cares about Emil."

"She had plenty of time to get over him."

"She doesn't want to. That's different." I poured myself a little bigger shot than I'd given Joachín. After all, I wouldn't be driving home afterwards.

"She's a bully," Joachín said. "When she doesn't get her way, she goes ballistic."

I crunched a carrot. "Maybe. Or maybe you're overreacting."

"'You're a pelican around my neck,' she used to say. She didn't even quote Coleridge right."

She hadn't been much of a role model. She'd been a terrible older sister. But she'd also probably been a little girl who was ignored by the most important adults in her life. I knew that feeling backwards and forwards. It left you with a sense of doubt. I hadn't brushed it off until college, when professors praised me for work I hadn't even spent time on.

Thanks to Emil that doubt had resurfaced, multiplied itself, clobbered me over the head, and left me with a handsome man in my kitchen. Could have been worse.

"Maybe Isabel thought she was being clever. And that was years ago."

"So?"

I deliberated over broccoli spears. "It might be time to get over it."

"The way you've gotten over your family by running away from them?"

My face heated up. Alcohol didn't throw me half as fast as truths. Joachín had hit the nail so squarely on the head he'd plastered it right in. I'd been accepted into all five graduate school programs I'd applied to. I took the offer from the school that was the farthest away. I got along with my family better from a distance. That way we had less opportunity to fight.

"I think of it more as self-preservation," I said.

"I've got the Arellanos, and I've been too lazy to leave town," Joachín said. "We're both guilty of avoidance."

"That's easier than facing up to the fact that your siblings dislike you."

Joachín pushed around the carrots without picking any up. "You never talk about them."

I tried not to think about them. Five siblings who competed for our parents' attention but had to act out to get it. I'd probably trained harder than any of the actors on the stage. But my relationship with my parents had eventually improved as long as I saw them for controlled periods of time, never mentioned politics, and agreed with every uneducated opinion they offered.

"I'll tell you more some night when we don't have to worry about Emil," I said.

"Fair enough. And tomorrow I'll help with that list of clients."

"No good," I said. "We need to be in the field."

"You mean visit Twinkle's street?"

"Right. The whole block."

"Sounds dangerous," he said, unconcerned.

"Scared?"

"For you."

"I'll be fine."

He chose a broccoli head. "I'll help you on one condition."

"No, you won't."

He cocked his head sideways. "Oh?"

I smiled. "You'll help me anyway."

"You're sure about that?"

"Quite sure."

He picked up a pin and held it above Emilito's stomach. "How sure?"

"Go ahead. I was ready to kill him tonight all over again."

Joachín gave Emilito a little stab and then put the pin back in the pincushion. "I need a favor. That's all. Just one." He winked.

Why had I invited him inside when now all I wanted him to do was leave? It had been too long a day. I'd been through too many emotions. If he asked me to kiss him, I'd be too embarrassed to know how to react, and by then the moment would have passed, never to return.

He put his hand over mine. "Promise me."

I leaned so far back I nearly fell from the stool. "Give me a hint."

"You're in or you're out."

"I'm not a gambler."

"In or out."

Worse, maybe he wanted to take me upstairs.

Doubly worse, maybe I wanted him to. He was gorgeous, he was lithe, he was gentle. The right color. Right height. Right weight. He was more concerned about me as a friend than Emil had been as a partner.

But I wasn't ready to consider a relationship. I was still reeling from betrayal. Surely Joachín knew that.

"I can't promise," I said loudly.

"I'll leave then."

"Okay." I pointed to the leprechauns. "I have to teach ten hours from now. I should get some sleep."

"One favor. Promise."

"I don't agree to blind promises. Tell me what you want."

Was it me, or did his eyes shimmer? I was glad I didn't have more substantial snacks. If he got hungry enough, he'd leave.

"You drive a hard bargain," he said,

I shrugged. Why couldn't my phone ring now and interrupt the moment?

He folded his hands together. "All right, you win."

I braced myself. Could he sense that I was nervous?

He tapped Emilito. "Make me a doll."

All these theatrics about a sewing project? I was thankful not to be dodging a kiss, but maybe I wanted one after all. "What kind of doll?"

"Like the others. One for Isabel."

Was I the only sane person in the room? "You're kidding."

"You've got the power, so why not use it? You saw what happened to Laney."

"Isabel didn't do anything to me."

"Tonight she went easy on you because she wanted a decent dress. You'll need a doll for her sooner or later."

"I won't be dealing with her later. She'll be all yours."

"It would make me feel better. What does it cost you?"

If a few minutes' work would make Joachín feel better, I would deal with silly. "First thing tomorrow."

"You won't forget?"

"You'll remind me."

Joachín smiled. "If that's what it takes."

I pointed to the clock with a pinky. "That, and a good night's rest."

"I should leave."

I wasn't sure. I suspected he wanted another favor. Maybe I did too. Maybe we wanted exactly the same one.

"I'll see you tomorrow afternoon when we canvas Twinkle's block. All right?"

He nodded as he stood. "All right."

I gave him a casual goodnight hug at the door before either of us could say or do anything we regretted. No matter how we felt about one another, we had to find out more about Twinkle's neighbors.

And be careful while we were doing it.

Chapter Twenty-Seven

When I walked into class, a bouquet of Johnny Jump-ups greeted me. The bobs of yellow, white, and violet sprouted from a makeshift vase fashioned from a wine bottle.

Beautiful, but my birthday wasn't until the very end of April, so what were they thinking?

They knew Emil was still in jail. They probably knew more about him than I did.

"Thank you so much." I rotated the vase to view every wildflower.

"We know hard for you, Mr. Emil still at police," Nayela said.

I'd guessed correctly. The students knew everything. No wonder they watched me patiently. They may have wanted more information, but I had less than anybody else. "You guys are the best. I mean it. Thank you."

"What we can do for you?" Antonio asked. "How we help?"

Yessica raised her hand. "We do something. Yes?"

What I needed helpers for I couldn't ask my students to do for me. That would be against some teacher code somewhere. Probably.

"We like help you," said Julio. "No problem."

Ginger and Lily nodded solemnly.

My school wasn't like regular ones. It was private and I catered to adults. Ostensibly I made my own rules. But how could a teacher contemplate putting her students in danger for her own cause? But it wasn't my cause, they wouldn't be in danger, and it was only right to accept help when it was freely offered and you genuinely needed it.

Also, if they could help me, I could continue teaching them, whereas if the school went under, I wouldn't be able to help anybody.

"I'm not sure it's proper for you to help me."

"What is proper?" asked Ahmed.

"Maybe it's not right."

"Is right!" Yessica stood. "Say us what we do."

Nayela shuffled to her feet as well. "We do now!"

My right hand flew up to my heart. My left hand motioned the students to sit, which they did. I had a sudden brainstorm. If the students could help me while practicing a genuine use of English, I was still doing my job. Kind of.

"Okay, here's my idea. Let me explain, and you can help if you want."

I went to the board and drew a facsimile of Twinkle's neighborhood: her street, the streets on either side, and the approximate number of houses.

I pointed. "A bad person lives around here. I need to find someone suspicious."

"Suspicious?" Ginger asked.

I gave them a few moments to consult their cell phone dictionaries. At least we had a new word for the day.

"One of these neighbors killed Twinkle, Emil's friend." I made a violent motion of cutting off someone's head.

"But you Emil's friend," said Lily.

"Emil's other friend," I said.

Lydia lit up. "Twinkle, twinkle, like the stars," she sang.

I clapped in delight. "Yes! That's the name of the woman who died. One of the neighbors"—I pantomimed for added emphasis—" was watching the house. He waited for the right moment, and he—" I pantomimed the murder a second time.

"Still can't believe is happen," said Nayela. "Tucson dangerous."

"No. This was personal." I pointed to the board. "But I don't know where this person lives. Close by. Maybe Twinkle's age."

"How we help?" Lydia sounded as enthusiastic as if we'd been preparing for a picnic.

"You go to the houses and see if the people act normal."

"Normal?" asked Ahmed.

"Right. See if they seem nervous or worried."

"Why we go the houses?" Antonio asked.

Nayela clasped her hands. "We act like we from the religion!"

"No religion," I said firmly. What did that leave? Political brochures were too unpopular. What we needed were Girl Scout cookies.

I envisioned the block. The neighbors needed lawn services. Fresh paint on their houses. A bit of landscaping. Dog poop pick-up.

"I've got it!" I cried. "Lost dog!"

Moments later they scoured the Internet for the kind of dog they wanted to lose. After they decided on a Golden Retriever, they wrote questions and imagined possible responses. With a gusto I'd never seen before, they practiced in teams.

I circulated, assisting with pronunciation. If they were determined to help, this was the perfect opportunity.

***

From the barstool at my kitchen counter, I was carefully diagraming a three-block radius when Michael O'Donnell called. I knew why. He checked up on me whenever I missed a singalong. He was a few years younger than my dad but quite ready to step in as a more uplifting surrogate.

"So I guess last Sunday you were on the lash," boomed the rich voice.

"I wasn't drunk at all."

"In that case?"

I'd met Michael and his wife at the Live Theatre Workshop production of *The Cripple of Inishmaan* when I was in grad school. When he learned I was Irish, he begged me to join the Sunday singalong. At the time, I was too busy. The Sunday after I graduated, I stopped by. Michael was delighted to learn that even though I couldn't play a note on any instrument, I usually sang in tune. By the end of the evening he'd dubbed me a natural craic-lover, meaning that I had a healthy respect for having a fun time.

"If you're wondering why I skipped singing, it was a cross between Emil breaking up with me one day and his being arrested on a murder charge the next."

"Yes. Well, the misses and I had a few questions about that dryshite. We were hoping you would explain all about it."

I paused. It was hard to discuss important personal details over the phone. "It's quite a long story, but I've been trying to get Emil out of jail."

"Dervla, don't be mad at me for asking. Are you sure he didn't do anything wrong?"

Did pretty sure count? "Emil is a creep, but he's no killer."

"He never came to singing with you."

Not true. He'd come once, decided he hated Irish music, and never come back. "He used Sundays to catch up on work."

"That's what they all say when they're off doing something else. Are you sure you really know him?"

No, but I wasn't ready to admit it. "Emil could never murder anyone."

"That's what I told the missus. That young Dervla wouldn't be hanging out with any ruffian. But that's why I'm calling. Ciara wanted to send you over a casserole, and I said, that might not be what she needs right now. So, tell me, what do you need?"

I leaned back and rested my feet on the wastepaper basket. My love life might have gone to hell, but I could hardly believe my fortune. Not only had my students offered to kick in, but my friends had as well. "Michael, it's funny you ask. Are you busy this afternoon?"

He wasn't. When I explained why I wanted him to meet at Seventh Street and Norris at three o'clock, he swore he would look forward to it.

By the time we hung up, my eyes were moist. I would have expected the nanas to come to Emil's rescue. Orlando. Joachín. Michael's offer was a reminder that life was simple when you thought about it: friends and family. What more did you need?

I turned on the desktop and printed out fliers of our "lost dog." I didn't include a phone number. Instead I opened a new Gmail account. The username I chose was Twonkle.

***

As I dismounted my bicycle near the community benches at Seventh and Norris, the nanas honked. Lula pulled up beside me. "Don't think you're getting away with doing any detective work on your own! Why didn't you tell us?"

"You're teaching Emil's classes. That's enough."

"Nonsense," Mari said.

As far as I knew, they weren't mind readers, at least not yet. "How did you know I would be here?"

Lula turned off the engine. "Your Nayela is dating our Lawrence, although I suspect he's studying Spanish to have the excuse to give her a ride to school."

Mari got out of the car. "He's a terrible student, but he'll be here any minute to walk around with Nayela."

Lula locked the car with a key — that's how old it was. "But let's get back to the important point. You were going to investigate without us."

I might have protested, but they saw through me too easily. "I didn't want to put you in a bad position."

"Emil's the one in the bad position," said Mari. "Don't you worry about us."

"What if Twinkle's parents show up and get suspicious?"

Mari shook her head so hard that her wavy hair danced. "Unlikely."

"It could happen."

"Honey, we could get run over as we cross the street," Lula said. "Nobody promises you tomorrow. But Emil needs our help. You know what happens to people in jail. They get beaten up and worse."

"We need to get him out of there by the end of the week," Mari continued. "And we'll do anything. So give us Twinkle's block. We're old. We might not have that much time anyway. We don't care if it's dangerous."

"Dangerous?" Michael asked as he pulled up. He gallantly introduced himself.

"How should we organize, angel?" asked Mari.

I prayed there was strength in numbers. "Since Twinkle's block is the most important, would you like to canvas it together?" I handed them a flier of our fake lost dog.

"With two lovely ladies as my escort, I can't get in trouble," Michael said.

They were plenty capable of getting into trouble together, but that was a possibility I would have to live with. I might have thought things through more carefully except that, with unusual punctuality, all the students arrived around the same time. As soon as they paired themselves up, I handed out fliers and assigned them a specific side of a specific block.

Lula pointed to my clipboard. "What are you going to do?"

"I'll keep track of everything. If no one answers the first time around, we can try again a little later."

"The criminal might have a day job, you know," Michael said.

"The best we can do is narrow things down."

While my students accosted neighbors, I rode my bike in slow loops. I wore exercise clothes and a helmet to look inconspicuous, but when Lydia and Yessica approached an elderly lady sitting on her front porch, I dismounted and pretended to be checking my bicycle tire. I didn't want to miss a single word.

Lydia held up the picture while Yessica explained about the poor lost dog.

"I haven't seen any strays around here," the lady said. "Are you sure this is where it got lost?"

"We used to lived on Eighth Street," Lydia said, messing up her past tense. "We think the dog come back."

She spoke so convincingly a lawyer would have believed her. Why hadn't I thought to use role plays in class? They were a great way to exercise language skills.

"I've heard of lost animals finding their way home," the woman said. "Sometimes I think our pets are smarter than we are."

"Our dog so smart," Yessica said. "Usually he run home. But this is so nice neighborhood, somebody feed him and he like new family."

The woman beamed. "You're right! This is a very friendly neighborhood!"

Friendly indeed. I mounted my bicycle and headed back to Seventh and Norris, where Joachín and Orlando waited for me on the benches.

Joachín winked. I wasn't sure if he were being nice or flirting.

"Good job," Orlando said. "Let everybody else do the hard stuff while you pedal around supervising." Nearly as handsome as his uncle Emil, Orlando could get away with saying almost anything. His black hair perched on his head like a pom-pom, and bushy eyebrows crowned deep brown eyes.

"It's called delegating. It's an art."

By the time I parked my bike under the tree, Orlando waited to hug me. "I'm sorry about my uncle being such a jerk."

"Thanks."

"I still can't believe he broke up with you like that."

"I'm not sure I believe it myself."

"He did this before, you know," Orlando said. "Ran out on a girlfriend. Blindsided her, too. If he were here right now, I'd punch him for you."

"If he were here, I'd punch him myself. But never mind. For right now, we have to concentrate."

"I hope you saved something for us," said Joachín.

"I was going to assign you the hardest part—returning to the houses of anyone who seems odd or off."

"Anyone like that so far?" Joachín asked.

"Not that the students have told me about."

"Give it time," Orlando said. "They might come up with something."

Joachin pointed across the street to a row of duplexes. "Do you know if any of the buildings are empty? You can't discount the snowbird factor."

Lots of people spent summers back in the Midwest or up north. Depending on the bitterness of the winter, many didn't leave Tucson until after Easter.

"I thought of that. I'm keeping track." I took out my drawing of the houses in the area. I'd X'd through a couple that seemed empty.

Joachín's cell buzzed. He frowned as he read the text. He nudged Orlando. "We have to go. Now."

"What happened?" I asked.

"I don't know. Isabel says it's urgent. I have to get home right away."

"Your dad?" I asked.

"What else could be urgent?" They headed back to Orlando's car. "I'm sorry."

"Let me know what's going on as soon as you can."

"I will," Joachín said. "Luckily, the house is close by."

I crossed my fingers that the alarm was false. Joachín and I had enough going on. We didn't need a sick parent on top of everything else.

Chapter Twenty-Eight

Two hours later I was treating the students to Rocco's, the best place in the neighborhood for drinks and breaded mushrooms, where Emil, though he didn't know it, was buying. We ordered drinks and commandeered the outdoor tables to share results about our "lost dog."

Although a couple of students had run into unfriendly neighbors, overall they were psyched that they'd communicated effectively. Yessica learned where she might get a job as a stylist. Julio learned he could make a mint as a vet if he would agree to make house calls. Meanwhile, Michael had a lovely time swapping stories while he escorted the nanas.

In terms of learning useful information about the identity of Twinkle's murderer, the afternoon was a bust. The students had nothing to report. None of the neighbors seemed strange or suspicious. Any mention of Twinkle was met with the same response: that poor, poor lady and her poor, poor children. How could she have met up with a madman?

Had the neighbors been the jury, Emil would have already been in the electric chair. They blamed him completely because, after all, who else would have been entering Twinkle's house so early in the morning?

I butterflied among groups on the pleasant patio before taking a place next to Michael. "Thanks for pitching in."

He dripped ranch sauce over the tablecloth. "I didn't learn a single thing to help you. Any chance Emil will be released due to a technicality?"

"I'm working on it."

He gave my shoulders a fatherly squeeze. "I'm glad you're all right. I hope to God he was never violent to you."

"Not at all."

"If you're hot-tempered, it doesn't take too much to grab a knife and go at it."

"Emil wasn't like that, but he did take me by surprise. I thought ours was a meeting of minds and all that."

Michael speared a breaded mushroom. "Minds might meet, but something else meets first!"

"Right." I speared a mushroom myself; I'd ordered three baskets, hoping I'd wind up with leftovers. "I thought we were set for life and all that. Never mind. Here's a question: Can you tell me anything about Irish magic?"

"Magic? What do you mean?"

"You know, special powers? Stuff like that."

He forked another mushroom. "Little lady, we Irish are a great people. And we love to tell stories. That's why we made up leprechauns. But magic? Why would you be thinking about that?"

"I don't know. The idea popped into my head."

"Very interesting, young lady, but I'd tell it to pop back out."

Special powers had to be associated with my heritage country somehow. Maybe Irish and Cajun traditions had crossed inside me somehow? No. Ridiculous. "What about writing a curse or an oath?"

Michael set down his fork. "I've never witnessed anything along those lines, but I do remember my granny talking about 'the dark prayers.' That was like a spell, I guess. Harming your enemies from a distance."

That was me. Remote pain was my specialty. "You don't believe it."

"They're only stories, but I could ask the missus. She knows more about the history." He leaned back while the waitress filled his water glass. "But if you're wanting to put a spell on that boyfriend of yours, I'm all for it. That feckin' eejit is lucky you didn't push him off a balcony. You know the saying about being in heaven a half an hour—"

"—before the devil knows you're dead. It was one of my great-aunt's favorites."

"I hope your boyfriend takes it to heart."

Why waste time? I knew how to use a shotgun. "Michael, thanks for the advice. And for walking around with the nanas this afternoon. Are you sure you didn't learn anything important?"

"Twinkle's neighbors on the west?"

"The Livingstons."

"Right. The man says he and his wife heard strange noises the morning Twinkle was killed. Debated calling the police. Finally did. Now they kick themselves for not acting quickly, but he claims the whole damned block has gone to ruin. They bought the house in the 80s, and the neighborhood has slid downhill every day since. They're so mad they're thinking about moving."

"A murder could change your view about a place."

"He knows that's a special case. He's tired of the daily thievery."

"Gangs? Kids?"

Michael subtly nodded at Yessica, who was talking Ginger's ear off. "According to him, it's all about the Mexicans."

Tucson was an hour north of the border. People who crossed over illegally often made it to the southern edge of the city, where they scrounged around for water or portable items to hawk. I hadn't heard stories of their reaching midtown.

"Has he lost a lot of stuff?"

"A flowerpot once. A nice doggie dish. Last week, a power cord and a reciprocating saw."

A saw! Just the thing to cut somebody's neck with.

"How does a saw reciprocate?" I asked.

"It's an electric tool for cutting branches and such."

The "such" being necks. The murder weapon itself might well have belonged to Mr. Livingston. Surely he wouldn't— but what motive could he have had? I needed to learn more about him too.

"The police haven't helped him with the robberies?" I asked.

"He never reports anything. Not worth the time, he said. He doesn't like the police, but he's still mad about the saw. It only happened a few days ago. If I had one myself, I'd loan it to him."

Michael was always complaining about computer technology, so it was my turn to give him a hard time. "Too new-fangled for you?"

"An electrical saw is too sophisticated. When I have too many branches, I wrestle with them myself. Gives me a bit of exercise."

Michael's point was well taken. To kill someone with a saw would take strong arms along with iron will. But now we had another complication. The murder might have been premeditated. It also might have been a last-moment inspiration because an elderly neighbor left a power saw where anybody could snatch it up. Thanks to Emil, anyone could open Twinkle's door and walk right in.

***

Even though I was expecting him, Joachín rang the bell four times before I turned on a light in the kitchen and reached the door. Out of breath and disheveled, he practically fell into the house.

"What's wrong?"

"Kitchen. Drink."

I stood back. He went straight to the bar and sat on one of the high stools.

"Beer good enough?" I asked.

When he nodded, I handed him a can of Guinness. I took out another for myself.

"Do you have thick walls?" he asked.

"Fairly good. Why?"

"Argh!" He yelled so loudly that any sleeping neighbors would have wakened. My walls weren't *that* good.

"Difficult rehearsal?"

"She thinks she owns me!" He put down the can before taking a sip. "No sense of privacy. None!"

"Is your dad all right?"

"Do you know what Isabel considered 'urgent'?"

"You can't fault her for a false alarm when it comes to someone as old as your dad." At least Isabel was watching out for him even if she didn't do that much.

"Her emergency had nothing to do with Dad. She wanted my staging notes! I raced over to the house ready to chase an ambulance, and she says, 'Well, where is your script?' I could have killed her. I didn't even have the script with me. I had to go back home and get it."

I barely kept a straight face. "Very annoying."

"I assumed Dad had another heart attack. While I'm risking a dozen speeding tickets, I'm texting Tommy that I might miss rehearsal. I run into the house, and guess what? Dad is watching an old Western, and Isabel wants to know where to put her big feet!"

I could imagine both Isabel's desperation and Joachín's annoyance. He didn't know how lucky he was to have only one sister.

"She is a little clumsy," I admitted. "Fetal alcohol syndrome, maybe?"

"Or big feet."

I opened the beer can for him, and he took a swig.

"But you helped her with the script?" I asked. "Gave her a sense of where to come in and all that?"

"We worked out a few details."

I clinked my can against his. "Cut her some slack. She's had the script for two days."

"If she thinks she's professional, she needs to learn faster than that."

Such an expectation wasn't reasonable. Even Joachín knew it wasn't reasonable. "At least she's trying."

"Don't make excuses for her. She's not your relative."

Joachín's memories had been simmering in a pot over the stove, but they'd finally come to a boil. I slid onto the stool beside him. "Don't you think you'd better save the overreacting for the stage?"

"I'm sorry." He took hold of my arms. "You're the last person I want to yell at."

A current bubbled between us. I hadn't expected it.

He hadn't either. He unhanded me and sat back. "I didn't mean to get carried away."

"No worries," I said automatically.

Isabel had gone straight out of our heads. For a moment we stared at one another, but I didn't trust myself to decipher my feelings. I needed to weigh them first. Think things through. Have time to panic.

"Don't let your sister play mind games with you," I finally said.

"Half-sister," he answered slowly. "No. I won't."

More staring. We might have been in high school.

"Did you— Do you—" he started.

Neither one of could get out a sentence. I reached over and took his hands, studying them as if they held answers.

"Is it possible that you feel something about me the way I feel something about you?" he asked quietly.

"I might." I most certainly did. But how could I when Emil was barely out of the house?

The leprechaun clock ticked. I took the sound as a cue. "As I told you before, I'm shelving personal thoughts for right now. Until we get through this thing with Emil. And you get through opening night."

"Right."

His gaze didn't leave my face, but his eyes glistened in the light. He might have leaned in to kiss me. I might have leaned in to kiss him. Instead, we resisted long enough for the moment to pass.

"How was Isabel at rehearsal?"

He blinked, back to normal. "She was a hot mess. Stumbling around the stage. Missing entrances. Zero concentration."

"Nerves?"

"Maybe worried about learning her lines."

I took a swig and let the cool liquid drip down my throat. "Who cares? I honestly wouldn't spend time thinking about her."

"I try not to."

"I made you a present to help get her out of your system."

He looked to the sewing machine across the room. "Really?"

"I didn't do a great job, but I suppose that's not the point."

He ran to the table and fetched the doll I made in honor of Isabel. It was cruder than the one I'd made for Laney, but I'd been in more of a rush.

"This is perfect!" Joachín shouted. "I dub her Isabelita!"

The black yarn made adequate hair. The dress was a navy blue, which was unexciting, but for color I'd decorated it with random buttons. Using snips from a paper clip, I'd made a cross and glued it to her neck.

Joachín fingered the doll gently, then not as gently, and then he squeezed it. He reached for the pincushion. "You don't mind? I'm not the magic one anyway."

"Why wait? I made her for you. You know you'll feel better—"

" —if I stick a pin in her."

"Exactly."

Joachín gave Isabelita several sharp jabs. "This is for pretending it was urgent." Jab. "This is for making me worry!" Jab, jab, jab.

I sat back and let Joachín have at it. If poking pins into a doll could change your mood, why not go for it? If the language school failed, maybe I could make a new career by designing what I would label "comfort dolls." Solid customers might need three or four apiece.

In the meantime, Joachín needed to regain his equilibrium. I was glad to help him find it. I took out an extra box of pins.

Chapter Twenty-Nine

The next afternoon I was on the front porch with the nanas when their house phone rang. Lula nodded in my direction; I was the closest to the phone. I checked the I.D., pressed "speaker phone," and answered before the second ring. "Emil?"

"You again? If you're bothering my aunts . . . . "

Lula dashed up and snatched the extension. "Young man, not only did we ask her to come, but she has a standing invitation."

"She's meddling. What happened to me is none of her business."

"Emil!" Lula shouted so loudly that Mordy got up, moved two feet farther away, and plopped down into an instant sleep again. "Get over yourself and answer her questions as best you can."

"But—"

"No buts, young man. You're not in charge."

Two thoughts competed in my brain: first, that I loved Lula now more than ever, and second, if Emil wound up in jail for a few years, it would do him good.

"Are you ready to listen or not?" I asked.

"Dervla—"

"I'm doing the talking here. I'm going to read a list of names, and I want to know if any ring bells. Twinkle would have mentioned clients who were important to her, and I want to reach out to them."

"I don't think I can help."

"Crabby, Craddock, Cragg, Crankshaw—"

"Crankshaw. I remember something about him."

"That's progress." I made a notation and kept reading.

All in all, Emil flagged three names, Crankshaw, Machado, and McLoughlin.

"Good job," I said. "Now tell me everything you remember about her customers for Beauty Is You."

"They were all women. I didn't pay attention."

"Brenda, Lisa, Eunice—"

Emil sighed as if speaking were an effort. "She liked Brenda. She went barhopping with Eunice a few times, or sometimes they went for coffee."

"That's all you've got?"

"What should I have? She didn't like to talk about herself."

Sure, she did. Emil just didn't like to listen.

He took a deep breath as if demonstrating his lungs still worked. "If you could let me talk to Lula now," he said softly.

Oh, yes. Another list of requests. I wanted to make a list of the most privileged prisoners in history to see if his name were on it. "Tell me everything you remember about your run that morning."

"Dervla!"

"You must have seen something, noticed something, anything!"

Say it. Say that you remember seeing the saw in the neighbors' carport.

"You know how I am in the morning. I roll out of bed and out the door. I don't wake up until I'm halfway through my run."

"People notice more than they think they do."

"What?"

I'd read it somewhere. Couldn't remember where. "There must be something."

"I already told the police—"

"Tell me. The police want a conviction. I want a business partner."

"Hey, I meant to ask. How are the students doing?"

"What did you notice on the run!"

Mordy moved another foot away.

"Stop yelling, Dervla. You don't have to lose your temper."

I wasn't one bit sure about that.

Mari picked up the extension. "Tell us your whole story all over again. Maybe you left something out."

"All right, all right. The first thing is that the alarm didn't wake me up because I was already awake."

"You heard something?"

"No. I woke up. I turned off the alarm and slipped into the guest bathroom."

"Why not the master bedroom?" I asked.

"I didn't want to wake Twinkle."

Unbelievable. He'd never once made a special effort not to wake me. As soon as he left jail, he'd be fairer game than a turkey on a turkey farm in mid-November. "Continue."

"The morning was cool, so I put on a sweatsuit, socks, and a jacket. I put on a scarf but took it off and left it behind."

Leave it to Emil to concentrate fully on himself. "Details on the surroundings, please."

"There's nothing."

"I'll start then. Why did you park across the street instead of in the driveway?"

"By the time Twinkle leaves for work, she's in a big rush. Was in a big rush. I stayed out of her way."

Which was why he'd been given a key. Convenient. "What else?"

"There was a guy out with his dog."

Finally a hint of something useful. "On Seventh Street?"

"Yes. But he was walking toward Twinkle's house, not away from it."

"What kind of guy? What kind of dog?"

"A little one."

"Like a Shi Zhu?"

"A who?"

"Never mind. Describe the dog."

"A brown hairy thing. I was already cranking up the speed by then."

"The man?"

"Our parents' age, give or take. He wore a bulky coat."

"Color?"

"Tan, maybe. Beige. A cap covered his ears. I noticed because it was overkill. Oh. Sorry."

I overlooked his word choice. "What kind of cap?"

"Black or gray. With flaps."

"You spoke to him?"

"You don't talk to people when you're running!"

Fair enough. Especially if you were an unfriendly son of a gun. "You were on Twinkle's side of the street?"

"Yes. The south."

"All right. Continue."

"Continue what?"

For God's sake, I was talking to an absolute idiot. How had I never noticed? "Who else did you see? What cars did you notice? I'm trying to help you here, but if you're too shallow to think of anything, there's not much I can do."

"I was concentrating on breathing! If you'd ever run with me, you'd know that."

Ah, there it was, the not-so-subtle insult waiting on the tip of his tongue every day since he moved in. Wouldn't I run with him? I ran several times in the beginning, but he made it a point to fault me for slowing him down. I'd allowed myself to be dragged out of a comfortable bed at a stupidly early time only to go a block or so before he berated me for inconveniencing him.

"It takes two people to make a relationship," he continued. "If only one person is willing to bend —"

Enough. I threw off the seatbelt. "If Twinkle had been out running with you, she'd still be alive."

Silence, finally, which was preferable to listening to Emil. The nanas circled me, nodding vigorously.

I might have been careening downhill, but I was still on a roll. "Guess what it takes to have an affair? One asshole live-in lover."

"That's not fair."

It was more than fair. It was ultra-fair. I handed the phone to Lula. "He's all yours."

Mari held her hand over the receiver. "Stay and have coffee with us?"

I gave them each a hug. "Not today. I have a costume to finish."

"Let us know if there's something we can do," Lula said.

"Where did everybody go?" Emil shouted.

I'd suffered the man for six years. What was wrong with me? It might take a team of therapists, who would charge more money than I'd ever seen in my life, to explain that I was an idiot.

But for the time being, the idiot still had to help the two little old ladies who were caught in between me and Emil. It wasn't much go on, but my only lead was to find the man who had been out walking his dog while Twinkle was busy letting someone cut her head off.

251

For that, I needed a dog. More precisely, I needed to call Tommy so that I could borrow one.

***

After Tommy startled me by tapping at the window, I waved him and Havie in through the kitchen. Excited by new surroundings, Havie barked as he squirmed.

"Are you sure you don't mind walking him this afternoon?" Tommy asked.

I'd successfully insisted that "Is there anything I can do for you?" included premium dog sitting. "I don't mind."

"I haven't had time to take him on decent walks lately."

"I need an excuse to get out." I held out my arms, and Havie jumped into them. "Walk around with a dog, and you always feel legitimate." Especially when traipsing through the neighborhood of a killer.

"Did you have a chance—" His eyes traveled to the Singer.

"Almost done." I herded him to the dining room table where Isabel's maid costume was about to receive its sleeves.

Tommy toyed with the fabric. "She ought to love it."

"If she doesn't hate it, we'll still be doing well," I said. "I'll bring it by tonight to doublecheck the size."

"Keep your fingers crossed that we survive the rehearsal."

I was glad for the umpteenth time that I wasn't a director. "Isabel seemed all right when I measured her."

Tommy brushed dog hair off his shirt. "She was cooperative the first day. Now she's back to normal. She's not horrible, mind you. I've dealt with a lot worse, but she's still a challenge."

Havie jumped from my arms to the counter, sniffed at the dolls, and bit into Emil.

"Havie, no," Tommy said.

"It's all right."

"He tears things up." He picked up the dog. "Give the toy to me."

Havie relinquished Emilito, whose stomach now had a puncture wound.

Tommy set Havie on the floor and returned Emilito to its spot on the counter. "Are these voodoo dolls?" He gave Isabelita a squeeze.

I didn't need Tommy thinking I was the silliest woman he'd ever met. "There's no such thing as voodoo," I said firmly.

"Of course not. But it's fun to consider. Way fun." He pulled on the blond doll's hair. "This almost looks like Laney."

"Coincidence. I was messing around."

Tommy closed one eye and squinted. "From this angle, it still reminds me of Laney." He set the doll down. "Wishful thinking. See you in a bit?"

"Absolutely."

I carefully placed Isabelita and Lanita in their spots. Then I finished the dress. Every few minutes, my new assistant, Havie, came over for a pat on the head. As long as he approached every dog-loving stranger on Twinkle's block with the same energy, we'd be all set.

***

After we passed Twinkle's house for the fifth time, I led Havie back to my car. Once again the chasm between theory and practice dropped me in its pit. The one lady who was out walking her dog disappeared into her house before I managed to park. After that, Havie and I walked for ninety minutes without spotting another dog-lover, much less a dog. Were all the lazy neighbors taking naps at the same time? Or, just our luck, the dog-walker Emil had spotted the morning of Twinkle's murder lived several blocks away or was just visiting.

Maybe the nanas and I couldn't help Emil after all. Lula and Mari would be stuck teaching advanced Spanish while Joachín refreshed his memory about formulating past tense. I would feel mild guilt if Emil were convicted, but given the circumstantial nature of the evidence, he should have a chance at getting off. So what if all his hard-earned money went to a decent lawyer? That would help Emil keep his priorities in mind: have girlfriend, don't cheat.

Above all, learn from your mistakes. When it came to men, I could only pray I'd learned from mine.

Chapter Thirty

When Havie and I reached the theatre, the actors were assembled on the play's living room. By now the beige sofa was matched by an equally beige loveseat. The coffee table contained a vase where Isabel would hide the keys so that Désirée assumed her husband were sleeping with Holland. To the right, a short staircase led up to the bedroom.

With one exception, the actors milled around, studying their notes. Isabel stood behind the loveseat as if it would protect her.

"Try it again, Isabel," Tommy said. His voice had never sounded so tired.

"I don't understand what's wrong."

"You have to walk behind the coffee table, not in front of it. We want the audience to concentrate on that vase. We want to focus their attention."

"I'm only blocking their view for a second. Why is that a big deal?"

Tommy paced in a small circle as he ran his hands through his hair. Joachín left the stage and plopped into a seat in the first row of the audience. Willard approached Isabel but changed his mind and went the other way. Désirée and Holland glared.

"Try it again, please," Tommy said. "If you'll remember, we open three days from now."

"It doesn't do us any good to keep trying it if she won't walk the way she's supposed to," Holland snapped.

"It doesn't make any difference," Isabel said. "Why can't I do it the easiest way?"

I imagined the directive from her point of view; maybe Tommy's request did seem arbitrary, at least on the surface.

I went up to the stage. "I can demonstrate. I'll walk through the scene both ways. Isabel can see what it looks like from a distance."

"Excellent!" Tommy said. "Isabel, give Dervla your script and come watch with me."

Isabel gave me a hateful glance as I passed her on stage. Instead of handing over the script, she tossed it. I snatched it like a Frisbee and winked as if I were in on the game.

"Yes," Tommy said. "Now, when you enter the room—do you see the line, Dervla? You say, 'I'm afraid we may have a visit from the police.' Then you cross into the room, pass between the loveseat and the couch, walk behind the coffee table, and climb the stairs to the second floor."

I read the line and did as asked. While it took a moment's concentration to clear the table, there was plenty of room.

"Fine," Tommy said. "Now pass in front of the table."

I did that as well.

"Do you see the difference?" Tommy asked Isabel softly. "When Dervla walked behind the vase, we could still see it. We could focus on the fact that the key inside the vase opens the lover's door. Right?"

"If the audience is so stupid that they forget where the key is—"

Tommy's jaw tightened. "Let's look at this another way. I'm the director. You are not. Do what I ask you to do. It's that simple. All right. Thanks, Dervla. Now if you wouldn't mind changing places with Isabel again, we can try it from the top of the scene."

Isabel sulked as she passed me, but when I held out the script, she took it. I sat next to Tommy in the third row.

"From the top," Tommy said.

To her credit, Isabel started out all right. I never once thought she was trying to mess things up. When she got to the phrase "from the police," she looked at Willard. Instead of clearing the legs of the coffee table, she caught one leg with her heel. The vase tottered, fell, and shattered. The unexpected noise was so loud that Isabel darted, fell against the end table, sputtered across the floor, and knocked into the handrail so hard that the stairs collapsed into themselves. Then she tripped on the rug, landing on her butt with a thud that shook the stage.

Willard and Holland moved away. Désirée hurried over to Isabel. Havie joined the fray.

Tommy buried his face in his hands while Joachín sat next to me. "Aren't you glad you came?"

We didn't mean to, but we giggled. Then we couldn't stop. We buckled over, trying to conceal ourselves.

Isabel struggled to her feet. "You people are awful! I can't stay here another minute! I'm going home, and you can't stop me." She limped off the stage and headed for the lobby.

"Any bright ideas?" Tommy asked the company after the door closed behind her. "I've had all I can take for one night."

"I have plenty of liquor and I live nearby," I said. "Would you like to adjourn to my place?"

They did indeed.

***

By the time the gang left, it was after midnight. Joachín had ostensibly stayed behind to help me clean up, but we both knew it was an excuse to snicker over Isabel.

Joachín gathered dirty wine glasses. "I still don't understand why Isabel was so flummoxed by the stage directions."

I stacked paper plates. "She couldn't visualize them. Maybe she was honestly afraid she would trip. There's not much room between the sofa and the coffee table."

"It's a small stage, but you learn to work with it. You have to."

"Couldn't Tommy spread the living room out a few feet?"

"Maybe. But the last thing we want is for someone — Isabel — to fall into the audience."

"Is she always so clumsy?"

"No. Claims she hasn't been sleeping well. So? I don't sleep well either."

I took a sponge and wiped off the table. "Maybe something's going on in her personal life?"

"I should know?"

"She's living with your dad. That doesn't say much for her love life."

"She's seeing someone from Mexico or maybe Honduras. I don't keep up."

People went through bad spells, sometimes without knowing it. "Maybe she's depressed?"

Joachín wiped off the counter. "Maybe she should see a therapist. I don't know. I've never asked her about anything like that."

"Okay job?"

"She files documents at the Breast Cancer Center. Routine, but steady."

"She could be in debt."

Joachín plopped down at the bar. "I guess, but she doesn't have any expenses. Remember? She's sponging off Dad."

I sat next to Joachín and polished off the one shot of Jameson I'd poured for myself. "I felt bad for Tommy tonight."

"I did too. Reviewers blame the director." He placed Isabelita on the bar and nudged the doll in my direction. "Please?"

"She didn't mean to trip."

He set a pin next to the doll. "Something small. Make her butt hurt! Poke her ankle!"

"You know this is all imaginary."

"Please. For me." He grabbed my hand and kissed his way to up my shoulder as if he were the worst French lover ever. I laughed as I broke away from him.

He picked up the pin. "Just one. Please. Otherwise I won't sleep. No! Otherwise I won't leave!"

I immediately thought of dragging him upstairs, laying him on my bed, and slowly removing his clothing. Maybe not slowly. "A threat or a promise?"

He poked Isabelita in the chest. "Both." He handed me the pin.

Well, why not? "Elbow? Hip? Chin?"

"Just do it!"

I jabbed Isabelita in the stomach.

"That's it! More!" yelled Joachín.

I took a second pin, made several small jabs, and stuck the pin just below the surface of the fabric.

"Deeper! This is going to kill her!"

"Don't be silly."

"You said it's nonsense, so what's the difference?"

"Then will you leave so that I can get some sleep?" I wasn't concerned about sleeping, exactly. I needed to clear the fog of emotions in my head.

"Scout's honor."

"You were not a scout."

"I thought about being one." He tapped on the doll.

"All right, already." I pushed the pins in so hard that they nearly went through to the other side. "Satisfied?"

"I should leave?"

I would have rather felt his arms around me. Had a long sit on the couch. Watched part of a TV show. But if things went sideways between us, we wouldn't have a way to start over.

Best to be sure. "You should leave."

He nodded. He gave me an extra long hug and slipped out the door. I watched until he was out of sight.

I didn't stop thinking about him.

Chapter Thirty-One

Just past eight a.m., my cell phone buzzed. I would have let it ring, but not even telemarketers from different time zones bothered Arizonans this early, so I checked the caller I.D.

"Tommy?" I grabbed the comforter and pulled it around my shoulders. I didn't have to be out of bed for another twenty minutes, and I wanted to enjoy at least nineteen of them.

"Need to ask you another favor."

At the crack of dawn? Since he was my employer of sorts, I let it slide. "Costume repair? Set painting?"

"Worse. Isabel is out of commission. She can't do the play."

"She can't pull out two days before you open!"

"That's what I told her. She said, 'No way.'"

"What excuse—I mean, reason—could she possibly give you?"

"Women's thing! Says it lasts three days and there's nothing she can do. Claims she won't be out of bed until Saturday."

Tommy was naïve enough to buy such nonsense? Now I could list cop-outs as another thing I didn't like about her. "Tell Isabel to buck up and take painkillers. That's what the rest of us do."

"Normally I would agree, but she sounded so crazy on the phone I was ready to have her committed."

What a baby! "Tell her to save her acting for the stage. She wants sympathy. No. Permission to walk in front of the coffee table. If she groans enough, she figures she'll get her way."

"She sounded like a dying coyote. Her dad took the phone and apologized. He spent the night trying to get her to Emergency but couldn't get her out of bed. She just rolls and clutches her stomach."

Her stomach. No, wait. No. Not possible. I threw off the comforter and jumped to my feet. Emil. Laney. Isabel. They couldn't all be coincidences, yet how could they be anything else?

The wind brushed a mesquite branch against the window. I was like a tree, connected to everything, part of a cosmic chain I never asked to join.

"Dervla, are you there?"

"What were her symptoms?"

"She's in such pain she won't leave her bedroom. Never mind! I need you to take over for her. I need you to play the maid!"

The nanas had been right all along. I had known better than to question them. But now what? The only people I could talk to were Mari and Lula and maybe Joachín. That's what we needed. A club for people with special powers. So they could share their stories. Pool their strengths. Make use of their energies. The nanas should have set up shop years earlier.

Or maybe they had. They had a wide range of friends who dropped in at unexpected times. They had money but no visible income. They kept late hours for no apparent reason.

Maybe they did have one. I would grill them as soon as I had the chance.

I ran down the stairs, nearly tripping in the process.

"You wouldn't have time to learn the lines," Tommy said.

I eased out the first pin. Then the second.

"The rest of the crew can coax you through the part," Tommy continued.

I pet Isabelita and smoothed her belly. I set her next to Emilito. Stupid doll! How was I to know that anything so far-fetched could be real?

"They can fill in with extra dialogue or improvise if they have to," Tommy said. "But we need you. We're desperate."

I needed to throw the dolls away. Get them out of my house. I grabbed all three, tossed them in the garbage bag, and headed for the trashcan outside.

"You're probably thinking we should postpone opening night, but that would be a disaster. We sold tickets. Spent a ton on advertising!"

I only went halfway down the path. What if throwing them away killed them?

"I'll hire you a substitute teacher so that you can spend every moment rehearsing."

I fished all three back out of the bag. What could I do with them?

"I'm begging you here. You're our only hope."

If the dolls were in sight, they were a menace. Maybe I could tuck them up in the cupboard so high that no one would ever notice them.

"Tell me you'll do it!" Tommy cried.

Poor man. All my fault. I hadn't believed because I hadn't wanted to.

"Joachín says you can memorize easily, and he'll help you," Tommy said. "We all will! But you have to help us! I'll pay you double as long as you promise not to tell anyone."

"You're wrong about Isabel," I said. "I predict that she'll have a full recovery within a couple of hours."

"You didn't hear her wail!"

I took a deep breath before diving into the lie pool. "Sorry this is TMI, but I have pretty bad periods myself. There's a new drug on the market Isabel probably hasn't heard about, but it's real good. I'll take her some. If she's not better by this afternoon, I'll be your new maid. Deal? Give me her address."

"She's in so much pain she won't even see a doctor, let alone you!"

I wanted to share the truth. Tommy was open-minded. Worldly. But a magic doll was too much for a regular person. Poor soul, he was merely normal.

"This is like a miracle drug," I said. "It really helps, okay? Trust me here."

"If it's so helpful why doesn't Isabel know about it?"

"It's not FDA approved. Emil's relatives brought it from Mexico."

"I still don't see how —"

"Give it a few hours all right?"

"You're wasting time. You could start rehearsing now!"

"Bring me a copy of the script and I'll start. But you won't need me. I swear."

"My career is on the line! So is the whole theatre!"

"Give me two hours from when I get to her house. And I have to hit a pharmacy first. What's her address?"

"But —"

"Address? She's close to the theatre, if I remember right."

"She's at 620 S. Santa Rita. That's near 15th Street. But it won't help. She's too far gone."

"Don't be so sure about that."

"I can bring you a copy of the script in the meantime?"

"If it makes you feel better, be my guest. Leave it on the back porch."

He was in such a rush that he hung up without saying goodbye.

I didn't take more than ten minutes to get dressed. I threw a handful of vitamins in a baggie, tucked Isabelita into my purse for safekeeping, and headed to her namesake's house.

***

Joachín's dad, whom I'd met on a couple of occasions, opened the door holding a section of newspaper. Although he was wide awake, he wore threadbare blue pajamas. Given his white hair, wide forehead, and fair skin, he didn't look one thing like his son.

"Whatever you've got, we don't want to buy it."

I couldn't remember his first name. "Mr. Gómez, I'm Dervla, I'm from the theatre. I came to give Isabel some medical advice."

"Oh! Well, she needs some." He opened the door and ushered me inside to a crowded living room commanded by a TV. Coffee tables sprinkled with coffee cups held stacks of newspapers and magazines. "We spent an hour trying to get an online nurse and gave up. Isabel?"

He led me down a hallway whose once-white paint was flaking off. Framed photographs, mostly of Gómez Senior standing before various cars, graced either side.

As we reached the bedroom door, he held out his hand to hold me back. "Let me peek inside to make sure she's awake."

"Of course I'm awake," Isabel sobbed. "I'm in pain!"

The little bedroom was crammed full. To the right, a closet door dangled open. A narrow dresser hugged the adjacent wall. The twin bed in the corner demanded a full third of the room.

Isabel lay amidst a series of pillows. Fuzzy blankets in blue and green were strewn across the bed and over the floor as if, among other problems, she couldn't find the right temperature. She wore no makeup, so her face seemed unusually naked. Her hair was messed up from lying in various positions.

"You came for the script, didn't you?" Isabel asked. "I can't be in the play!" Her eyes were wild. She glanced around the room as if expecting goblins to jump in from the windows.

Her dad stayed at the door, but I knelt by the bed. "That time of the month, right? Tommy told me."

"He tried to be nice, but I ruined everything!"

She grabbed my hand so hard I had to wrestle it away. "I'm going to help you feel better."

"You can't!"

I put my other hand to her forehead. "I don't think she's running a fever," I told her dad. "Let me talk to her alone for a few minutes?"

Mr. Gómez was happy to retreat. I didn't blame him.

Isabel teared up. "I shouldn't be getting my period until next week, but I know what's coming! Three days of pain. My body screwed me up." She covered her face with her hand. "It's my fault for being a bad person!"

No, my fault for disbelieving the nanas, but if Isabel learned a lesson in humility, the experience was valuable. "I'm here to help. I get bad periods too. Did you take anything?"

"Midol, Advil, and Motrin." She clutched the cross around her neck. "God's punishment!"

She pointed to the two-feet-long crucifix hanging over her head. The wall to her right sported posters of Pope Francis and the Virgen of Guadalupe. In Isabel's place, I would have suffered from claustrophobia, not because of the physical space, but because I was being watched.

"These are normal problems," I said.

"Yesterday I ruined the set! I hate myself! No wonder the others hate me too."

"You didn't ruin a thing, and I'm sure you can rally." I took the Baggie out of my purse. "I'm on a special trial for a new drug for menstrual pain. It helps a lot, so I brought you some. Have any water?"

"Won't help!"

All the nightstand contained was an alarm clock and a box of tissues, but a water bottle lay beside it. Some water had oozed out onto the carpeting because the cap wasn't screwed on all the way.

I handed her the bottle and a vitamin. "Try one of these."

"Useless."

"Just try."

She sat up long enough to do as I asked.

I took the water bottle and set it back down beside the nightstand. "Give it a few minutes. You'll feel better. I'm sure."

She grabbed one of the pillows and buried her face into it. "Dimeenhrer!"

"What was that?"

"Didn't mean to!"

Who would purposefully destroy the set? "Of course you didn't."

She turned her head as a swimmer grasping for a quick breath of air. "Dimeenhrthimther!"

"You didn't mean to hurt him either?"

"No!"

Finally she acknowledged that she'd hurt her brother. The realization was a decade and a half late, but there was still time to make amends.

"Things . . . never . . . same. Hate me forever!"

She was right in that Joachín was rooted in the past, but forever was a long time. If Isabel continued to show the slightest good will, I would help him come around.

They were siblings, after all. For their father's sake, they needed to attempt to get along.

"Going . . . straight . . . hell!"

"We all make mistakes."

Again she dove into her pillow. What she needed was a good psychologist and a few years of therapy. I was way out of my league.

"Don't you feel a little better?" I asked.

As she mumbled into her pillow, I heard the minute hand click. 9:32. I had twenty-eight minutes to get to class.

I set the rest of the vitamins on her nightstand. "I want you to take one of these pills every three hours. Got it?"

She nodded faintly.

I took a step toward the door. "I'll call in an hour to see how you're doing. By then, you'll feel strong enough to do the play."

She didn't answer, but I sensed that she heard me. By now the pain was subsiding, but she was responding to its memory.

Note to self, I thought as I ran to the car. No more pins. Or dolls. Ever.

Chapter Thirty-Two

The nanas were both drawing crude diagrams on the whiteboard by the time I reached World Lingo. They wore their nicest teaching outfits: pastel skirts with matching jackets, and comfortable walking shoes.

I gave them my cheeriest wave, but I hadn't even set down my purse before they crowded into my office and pulled chairs up to the desk.

"What's wrong?" said Mari. "You're upset."

"You can't hide from us," Lula said.

They were the perfect tag team. They even wore dabs of complimentary perfumes. Flower-based, I guessed. Light and airy.

I clasped my hands together as I sat behind the desk. "Okay. I give in." I spoke softly in case any students came around. "You were right."

Lula and Mari nodded in slow waves.

"About the special powers, I mean."

They kept nodding.

"I didn't want to believe it."

Lula brought her chair forward. "No one does. Not at first."

Mari scooted forward as well. "Later you realize you don't have a choice."

"Did you two notice early on? I mean, I don't see how I could have missed it, but you realized when you were kids, right?"

"Teens," Mari said.

"I'm an adult. Shouldn't I have noticed before now?"

Lula shook her head. "Something kicked in when you were in New Orleans."

"You understood that when you saw the dog-cat at my house."

"We suspected," Mari said, "but we weren't sure. Why are you upset? Did you hurt somebody?"

"We all make mistakes," Lula said. "That's how we learn."

"What did you do?" Mari asked.

I waved as the first students—the nanas'—headed into the classroom. "I made a doll for Joachín. He begged me."

Mari put her hands to her temples. "You tried white magic, and it backfired. Is Joachín in the hospital?"

"He's fine. But he asked me to make a doll to represent Isabel. We were playing around."

"That woman deserves a doll," said Lula. "She's spent her whole life being as unpleasant as possible."

Mari tsked. "She's not bad at the core. Someday she'll learn to stop blaming everyone else for her problems."

"I doubt that very much," said Lula. "She didn't learn anything the whole time she came to our house for lovely free dinners. Did she ever bring a casserole? A dessert? Fresh bread?"

"Wait," I said. "I never bring anything."

"That's not true. You and Emil have always kept us in brandy. Leave the cooking to people who are better at it."

"What did you do to the doll?" Mari asked.

Antonio waved as he held the classroom door for Ginger.

"We jabbed Isabelita—the doll—in the stomach a few times. Isabel woke up with such cramps she thought she was dying."

Lula laughed. "A little pain might do her good."

"Lula!" Mari said sharply.

"Well? Sometimes pain shows people how wonderful their lives are. How much they have to be thankful for."

I waved as several students greeted me before walking into their respective classrooms. "Listen, the point is that she's in hysterics. She panicked so much that she called Tommy and said she couldn't do the play."

"You removed the pins, correct?" Lula asked. "The pain should subside right away."

"She can call Tommy and explain that she's better," Mari said.

"That sounds great in theory. I went over to check on her, but she's gone crazy. Her bedroom is all full of religious stuff. God is punishing her and I don't know what all. She was too upset to know whether she was in pain or not."

"That's unusual," Mari said.

More students. Ten o'clock, class time.

"She was delirious. Like she was possessed."

"That feeling will pass in no time," Mari said.

"But there is no time! Now Tommy is panicking too. If Isabel can't perform, Tommy wants me to do the part."

"You're an expert on theatre," said Lula. "Emil always said you should audition for the stage. I'm sure you'll do a wonderful job."

"The show opens on Friday! I can't learn the part in two days. I messed up. Please come visit her with me after class?"

"She'll be fine by then," Lula said. "We can save ourselves the bother."

Mari nudged her sister. "You don't want to see her, and I don't either, but Dervla can call her after class. If she

271

hasn't bounced back, we'll visit her together. While Lula asks questions, I'll watch her aura. If she still needs help, we'll probably understand what to do."

"Thanks. A lot."

The nanas rose and went to greet their students. I did the same, but I taught mechanically and wrapped up a few minutes early. I had to get back to Isabel. She was so volatile that I couldn't outguess her next direction If she were drastic enough to hurt herself, it would be my fault.

***

Mr. Gómez answered the door before I could reach my hand up to the doorbell. "Come in! Thanks for coming to help my daughter. Have you brought nurses?"

"You probably remember Emil's aunts."

The glaze on his face said that he barely remembered the name of Emil. "Yes, yes."

"They know almost everything about women's health. Homeopathic stuff. You know."

"Yes, yes." His eyes retreated into his face. He had no idea what I was talking about, but he knew he needed help. "Please come in."

The nanas exchanged glances before we all crowded the living room.

"Isabel is a little better?" I asked.

"She's still crying nonsense, but your pill calmed her down." Mr. Gómez gawked at the nanas' plastic bags. "I hope that's not medicine. We won't be able to pay for—"

"No medicine," Mari said. "*Caldo de pollo.* You know that chicken soup is the best thing at times like these. May we visit Isabel now?"

Mr. Gómez rushed us down the hall. "Visitors!" he called out. He stopped outside the bedroom door. "I'll leave you ladies alone. I know it's girl talk."

"May we join you?" I asked as I opened the door.

The nanas and I squeezed inside. Isabel was still in bed, but she was sitting up. She held the script in her hands.

"We're sorry for intruding," Mari said as she approached the bed, "but we know how you–" Mari suddenly backtracked into Lula. They both stumbled. I barely managed to steady them.

"It's nice that you came," Isabel said softly. "I'm sorry I've been so much trouble."

Mari pushed Lula and me forward while she retreated to the doorway. I knew what that meant: a bad aura.

"When Dervla explained your problem, we knew exactly what you needed," Lula said. She set her bags on the foot of the bed.

"Thanks," Isabel said faintly.

Lula opened the bag. "It was nice to see you the other night. Joachín keeps us up to date, so we never felt that we lost touch. You used to be part of our family. All those lovely dinners you had at our house! I suppose you stopped thinking of Emil long ago."

Isabel fingered her cross. "Right."

Lula fished around in her bag without removing anything. "I realize my grandson didn't treat you well. He should have been up front. Honest. That was a mistake on his part. Men!" She winked as if every woman understood men's mistakes the same way. "You probably forgave him long ago. You did love him, didn't you? At least for a while?"

Isabel stared at the closet door behind Lula as if in a trance. "Loved him."

In contrast, Lula might have been Mary Poppins, full of peppery advice. "I know it's hard, but you have to let people go. Otherwise, they stay inside your stomach and make wars. Like right now."

"Can't let go."

"You only think you can't, but you'll have to. Have you tried writing down some of your feelings? Recording them helps you get rid of them."

"Diary," Isabel said.

"Exactly. Right, Mari?"

Mari retreated through the doorjamb. "I'll wait outside."

"Let me explain." Lula took out a plastic container. "We brought some of our special homemade soup. Our grandmother's recipe. Rich with the right blend of spices. Are you hungry?"

"No."

"But you will be later." Lula pulled out another container. "We also brought our *pico de gallo*. This too we make a special way. Only eat a little. Let your stomach recover a bit first. All right?"

"*¡Vámonos!*" Mari called out. She never rushed anyone, yet she was already out of sight.

Lula opened the other bag. "Since you need to spend the day in bed, we brought something to read." She took out a couple of Spanish-language magazines, the kind with fake gossip.

I tapped on the script. "Did you call Tommy? You can't give up the play."

She clasped her stomach. "What about when the pain comes back?"

"It won't," I said. "Keep taking that medicine. And call Tommy."

"Lula?" Mari called from down the hall.

"I'll check in with you later," I said.

Isabel stared at the closet door as she slowly bobbed her head.

Lula and I met up with Mari in the living room, where Mr. Gómez was still thanking her.

Mari extricated her hand from Mr. Gómez's. "We have daughters ourselves. We've been through these things before."

Mr. Gómez opened the front door. "I know it's the mental stress. She lost a classmate the other day. That's always hard. Up until you lose somebody your own age, you think you're invincible. Afterwards you realize well enough that you're not."

Agreed. It was the sensation of "if not for the grace of God," it might have been me. I'd gone through the same emotions a year or so earlier when the most popular girl from my high school, whom I barely knew, passed after suffering a brain tumor. I didn't know her well enough to mourn her, but I paused long enough to realize how fortunate I'd been so far.

"Car accident?" Mari asked.

"Worse," Mr. Gómez whispered. "That gal who died over there on Seventh Street. I heard she was murdered."

Twinkle. One of Isabel's own classmates. It wasn't surprising given that they lived in the same part of town.

"My daughter hasn't been the same since then," Mr. Gómez said.

I herded the nanas toward the door. "I can imagine."

Mr. Gómez walked us out to the car. "How can I thank you all?"

Lula patted his arm. "We're happy to help. God knows it's hard to be a woman."

"Have Isabel call Tommy," I said. "She needs to let him know that she can do the play. Maybe you can help her study her lines."

Mr. Gómez opened the front passenger door for Mari. "I'm not good at that sort of thing, but I'll do my best. And thanks again."

Thanks for nothing, since it was my fault in the first place. But if Isabel went to school with Twinkle, and

Twinkle's death affected her, they had some kind of connection.

One I needed to learn from.

Chapter Thirty-Three

By the time I turned on the engine, Mari had slumped back against the seat. She took a Tucson roadmap from the car door and fanned herself so quickly she sounded like a trapped moth.

I took a water bottle from my purse. "Take a sip?"

Mari shook her head.

"That bad?" I asked softly. "How can we help?"

She pointed ahead. "Go!" The woman hadn't been that pale even when she was in bed with the flu.

"Should I stop at a pharmacy?"

Mari held her hand near her shoulder, and Lula slipped her a small black bottle with a polar bear on it.

"No, dear," Lula said. "I have smelling salts right here."

Mari took a strong whiff and gasped.

"What happened?" I asked.

"She'll be all right," Lula said. "Get us home."

I waited for a red light to turn to Mari. "Can you talk about it?"

Mari shook her head once while Lula positioned herself in the middle of the backseat. "I can start. Isabel is envious of you and furious with Emil for leaving her. She wants him back. That's what I got. Mari?"

Mari briefly waved her hand.

"She lied about Emil every time I asked a question," Lula continued, "She still thinks about him, she's still mad at him, and she's still in love with him. Maybe she can't help herself on that last one. Mari?"

Mari closed her eyes. "You talk."

Lula patted my shoulder. "It's rare, but if it's bad enough, this is what happens to her after."

I was the one who had put Mari in this terrible position. I'd jumped right in without considering the consequences. I'd put her at risk, and for that, I blamed myself first but Emil a thousand percent. "Mari, I'm so sorry about all this."

"Not your fault," she said softly.

I drove east before turning north to travel up Campbell. "Isabel feels bad about messing up the play?"

"Did you see black?" Lula asked. She tapped me on the shoulder. "That would have to do with unreleased grief."

Mari shook her head.

"Dark green?"

"Jealousy and lack of esteem. Our little Isabel certainly has both of those."

Mari put her hands to her throat.

"Oh," Lula said. "You saw blue."

Mari nodded vigorously.

"Dark, dark blue," Lula said.

Mari coughed so hard I nearly stopped the car.

"A fear of expression," said Lula. "I suppose Isabel is afraid to be in the play. Probably knows she can't learn the part fast enough, so she'd merely be making a fool out of herself."

Mari shook her head.

"But she's terrified of words, somehow," Lula said. "That's why she would hardly speak."

"Kept staring at me," Mari sputtered. "Like a ghost. Had to leave the room." She leaned back against the seat. "Let me rest."

I stepped up the pace and slid through a yellow to reach Third Street. I drove into the nanas' driveway and held Mari's hand as we made our way between the car and the porch.

Once seated, Mari rocked, her hands over her eyes.

"She'll be fine, but sometimes it takes all day for her to recuperate," Lula said. "I'll fetch some cookies."

I poured Mari a cup of coffee from their ever-ready Thermos. "How can I help you?"

"Need time."

But we didn't have any. I had too much to do. Get back in touch with Tommy. Let Joachín know what was going on. Reassure Isabel. Wasn't I also running a business? I probably had at least fifty unanswered emails and a dozen pending bills.

I gestured toward the kitchen. "Did you know Isabel better than your sister did?"

"The same. Disliked her equally. Hid it better."

Of course she did. Mari was more polite, more restrained. She was the mediator whereas her sister was the instigator. That was one reason they made such a successful pair. They projected the ying-yang effect.

Lula came out with a tray of Vanilla Thins, which was a big departure from their usual quality of bakery goods. "Isabel avoided me because I scolded her about ignoring Joachín. She didn't care to hear it."

I imagined a younger, thinner version of Isabel intent on intimidating other women. She would have curled her hair more tightly and worn brighter colors of mascara. During high school, where she would have ignored academics, she would have routinely competed for the cutest boys and gotten them. She would have been the cheerleader and the prom queen, the first among her peers

D. R. Ransdell

to have breasts and feel the magnetic pull to the opposite sex.

The woman I'd seen today was a shadow of herself, one so traumatized she couldn't perceive her own emotions enough to realize that her stomach no longer hurt and that she could get out of bed. That when visitors entered her room, she could look them in the eye instead of staring ahead self-consciously.

Or wait.

"Am I crazy," I asked, "or was Isabel staring at the closet a lot?"

Mari snapped her fingers. "She was."

"Think that means anything?"

"I only know what I saw," Mari said. "I can't tell you anything else."

Lula set down her coffee cup. "But we can guess that what she felt was guilt. Pure and simple."

"She was hiding her guilt in the closet? Symbolically, I mean?" I asked.

Mari rocked harder. "She might have something of Emil's. Something she never gave back."

"Something she stole out of spite," Lula said. "Knowing her, that's exactly what she did. I can't believe we even went to help her. I even gave her good advice. Sometimes, if you write something down—"

"Diary," I said.

Mari sat up a bit straighter. "What?"

"A lot of women keep diaries," I said. "Maybe Isabel has one in the closet, and she subconsciously didn't want us to find it. Or didn't want me to find it."

What might Isabel have written about me, that stupid white woman? That I was too naïve to see that I was losing my partner? That where Emil was concerned, the phrase I needed to repeat to myself was "What goes around, comes around?" That if he were willing to give

Isabel up for me, he'd soon be giving me up for someone else?

When I started dating Emil, Keevah warned me: He's Hispanic. He belongs to a different culture. Watch out because you don't know what you're doing. For an equally long period of time, I told her, don't worry, Emil doesn't fit any patterns.

But his old girlfriend fit some patterns I was familiar with. She was jealous. She was angry. She had probably tried outlandish ways to get Emil back that I wasn't aware of.

She and Twinkle might have grown up together. They might have started writing diaries at the same time and used them to giggle about boys at slumber parties. They would have been two cute teens gossiping over the boys they liked and how they might attract them.

I poured myself more weak coffee. Better than nothing. It was too weak to hurt anything.

"Have another cookie," Lula said.

I snatched up two while Mari retreated to the depths of her chair. "This might be bigger than we can handle," she said.

"Nonsense," said Lula. "It couldn't have been that bad. She's a liar, of course, but many women do lie."

"Her aura was more serious than I can explain," Mari said. "It was so heavy I couldn't stand to be next to her. It nearly burst while we were in the room."

"She was in pain," I said. "I put her there."

"She's too much of a mess," Mari said. "You should avoid her."

"Can't do that at the theatre," I said.

"She's unstable," Mari said. "Don't be alone with her. Don't go out to the parking lot if Joachín isn't with you."

Mari was hanging off the deep end, but I didn't know how to pull her back.

"Isabel is a mess," Mari said. "She's on a dark path. She doesn't know how to get off it. Stay away, or she might pull you down with her."

"We should find out more about her connection to Twinkle," I said.

"Too dangerous," Mari said. "Promise not to ask anything that will make her mad."

"That might be anything," I said.

Mari waved her hands in front of her body. "Stay away. That's the most I can tell you."

I appreciated her warning even though it was overkill. When she made me promise to stay away, I agreed. I wasn't completely unarmed. I merely needed to send in Joachín to find out more.

***

Joachín sped up to reach World Lingo's front door just as I did. He was fresh in the morning light: tan pants, a long-sleeved white dress shirt with light blue stripes, black hair that sparkled in the sun, a spring in his step more childish than professional. He claimed that he was uncomfortable teaching, but he had enthusiasm for it. That counted more than anything else.

"I have bad news," I said.

"You look awful," he said simultaneously.

I stepped back and grinned.

He put his fingers to his lips. "Sorry. Should have kept my mouth shut."

Emil had never noticed how I was doing until I made a point of telling him. Joachín and I had spent little time together, yet he hooked into my mood automatically. Not only was he more sensitive than Emil, but he didn't need cues. He read people. It came from caring about them. From putting them first. What he said was perfect.

"I'm okay." I squeezed his outstretched hands. "It's been a rough morning."

"How so?"

"To start with, Isabel called Tommy and told him she couldn't do the play."

"That's ridiculous! She can't bail on us like that! It's unprofessional! It's—"

I opened my purse and set Isabelita on its rim.

Joachín's eyes lit up. "The pins."

"Yes. Or something."

He stretched to open the door. "Or the pins."

Silently I thanked him for not saying *I told you so*.

He followed me inside. "But you took them out and now she's okay. That's how it works, at least generally."

I led him into the office and sat on the desk. I tapped my forehead. "She worked herself up into some kind of loop, how she's terrible and let us down. Those ideas spun around in her head until they wrapped her up like a mummy."

"I love it," Joachín said. "I do."

"Come on," I said. "You can't hate her that much."

Even the most sensitive person in the world could have a vulnerability, especially when it traced back to childhood. Joachín wasn't alone. I needed to forgive my siblings the same way. So what that we'd fought throughout childhood? That they'd constantly made fun of my graduate studies? It wasn't their fault that they couldn't see past their limitations. They had my parents to thank.

"Isabel has always been only about Isabel," Joachín said. "Do I have trouble with that? I do. Should I? Maybe not. But I love the image. Her doubled up in her bed in pain, praying to the Pope to forgive her for everything she's ever done wrong. No saint would have the patience to listen to that crap. But you must have talked sense into her eventually."

"I went over there with fake pain pills and both nanas."

"Mari and Lula could convince a chicken to walk into its own pot."

"Exactly! But this particular chicken kept staring at her closet door. And guess what, she knew Twinkle. They went to school together."

"That's interesting. Learn anything concrete?"

"Mari felt such a bad aura that she nearly passed out."

My three Japanese businessmen, who always arrived together, waved as they continued to their classroom. As usual, they arrived ten minutes ahead of time. Thankfully, I'd already planned the day's session.

"Listen, here's the short version," I said. "We think Isabel is hiding something in her closet."

Joachín laughed. "A small child? A pet dog?"

"More like a diary. A high school yearbook."

"I'm not following you."

I took the Business English folder out of the middle drawer. "We suspect she knows something important about Twinkle that will help us with Emil."

A student waved on her way into Joachín's class. Four students trailed her.

Joachín stepped closer to the door. "I don't see how this helps us."

"This is where you come in."

He took another step. "Tell me how."

I sighed. The long shot was my best clue for the moment. "During rehearsal tonight, the nanas and I were hoping you could slip into her room."

"Isabel's room? At her house?"

"Yes?"

"I would do that how?"

I picked up the folder. "Not sure."

"I don't go over there often, you know. For holidays. For quick visits."

"You have a key?"

"Sure, but—my dad is nearly always there."

Outside the office, students milled past. Time to get started.

"Tell your dad that Isabel sent you. That she forgot her script and you had to retrieve it for her."

"Why wouldn't she do that herself?"

"Because . . . she's in the first scenes of the play and you aren't. So she asked you to run home and get it for her."

"My dad is supposed to buy that?"

"Wouldn't he?"

"He knows Isabel and I aren't close."

Did I have to think of everything myself? "He seemed clueless to me this morning. He probably likes to think that you're close, doesn't he? He'll buy it."

"But—"

"You're an actor. Sell it."

I hurried into my classroom before he could offer another excuse.

Chapter Thirty-Four

Tommy approached my car door as soon as I pulled into the theatre's parking lot. He was hunched over as if he'd spent too much time waiting to exit a small plane. He squeezed Havie as if he were stuffed, but the terrier was putting up with him—for now.

He opened the door before I turned off the engine. "Thanks for coming. I appreciate it. A lot."

"I'm going to stop reading my texts."

"Twice in one day, right? But thanks, thanks, thanks. I really appreciate it."

I followed him across the parking lot. "I ran over as soon as I saw your text. Another costume disaster? I have enough time to make an adjustment before rehearsal starts."

He stopped outside the back door. "Isabel isn't convinced she can do the play. I need you to talk sense into her."

"But she's not in pain."

"Her nerves are shot! I know you spent the morning with her, but she needs an extra jolt of encouragement."

"That's silly."

"Please. We're desperate. If we wrote the maid out of the script, the story would fall apart. I'd ask Holland or Désirée to talk to her, but they went through the change a while ago. They're not patient with Isabel about that or anything else."

I'd been blessed with mild periods. Yes, I'd taken a painkiller from time to time. Felt irritable. Yelled at a grocery boy for putting cans on top of produce. Snapped at my mother once, which backfired since she then smacked me. But generally, I could manage those four days a month without disrupting my original plans, no matter what they were.

Several of my friends suffered opposite experiences. One spent the first day of her period in bed. Another curled up in a dark corner to wait out the worst of the pain. Isabel shouldn't have needed so much coddling, but I understood where she came from.

"She's embarrassed, you know," Tommy said. "Some women have trouble talking about stuff like that."

They did indeed. "She's here?"

"Yes."

We slid through the lobby and entered the theatre.

Tommy pointed to the stage below. "She feels bad about busting the stairs, so she came in early to help nail them back together. She went to the rehearsal room to change clothes."

Isabel had no idea what I knew about her, which was practically nothing. If she saw me as a stranger, such as a fellow passenger on an airplane, she might open up. "I could give it a try."

"She'll listen to you."

"I doubt it, but deep down, she wants to be on stage. She likes acting."

"She probably has a deep-rooted need to play out different roles."

"She might indeed." I doubted that as well, but it couldn't hurt to appeal to her thespian side.

Willard entered from the lobby. "Hi, guys. You said you needed help with the set?"

The last thing Isabel needed was a few men hanging around. "Isabel's upset," I said. "Woman stuff. Why don't you and Tommy take Havie for a walk so that I can talk to her alone for a few minutes?"

"Are you sure?" Tommy asked.

"The conversation will seem more natural that way. I'll gradually get around to the subject of her acting. Either I can help calm her down or not."

"Dervla, I can't say how much I thank you."

"Keep me employed." Not that didn't have enough jobs already. But for Joachín's sake, and for the company's sake, I would try.

"Funny you should say that," Tommy said. "I was hoping you'd join us for *March Murder Madness* I have the perfect part for you."

"I'll definitely consider it. But let's get through this play first."

"If we possibly can."

"Go! I'll see what I can do."

I descended the last steps into the cool, dark space of the theatre, threw my purse on a front row seat, and continued to the stage. Spotlights lit the ruined stairs. A set of fresh boards had been placed beside them along with an industrial-sized toolbox.

I ran my index finger over the top board. I could pass as a makeshift seamstress, but I knew nothing about carpentry. The last thing the company needed was for me to nail two boards together that later flew apart, sending an actor careening into the audience.

Heavy footsteps plodded toward me. "Isabel?"

The woman peeked around the corner. "Thank God it's just you." She came into full view wearing sweatpants and a holey T-shirt. "What are you doing here?"

"I offered to help with these steps."

"I ruined everything."

"You found a flaw in the set."

"Everything."

Seamstress, carpenter, and now psychologist. What would this drama company ask of me next?

"I bet we can fix the stairs together. It shouldn't take that long." I tried to pry apart two of the ruined boards, but they wouldn't budge.

Isabel took them from me. With a grunt, she pulled them apart and flung them down. "We can use some of the new ones first." She knelt beside the pile of wood. "But that's me. I ruin everything."

"Everybody makes mistakes."

"Not like the kind I make."

When people were set on blaming themselves, they wound up in quicksand. I wasn't sure how many ropes I would have to throw before I found one she could hang onto.

"Tommy says you're a great actor," I lied. I had to start somewhere.

"He contacted me because his other actress had an accident!"

Right. An accident. Not that I would know anything about it. I must have had a healthier ego than Isabel. In reality, I was the one who had ruined everything. But I hadn't meant to. I would have never guessed I could have. I exonerated myself on the basis of stupidity, which didn't sound positive either.

I picked up the nearest board. "Your father adores you." At least I had to assume he did. But who wanted their grown daughter living at home forever?

"You're probably a wonderful friend," I continued. Most people spent lots of time on social media—that meant they had digital friends at least, right?

Isabel shook her head. How many layers would it take to get through to this woman?

"You've always lived in Tucson, right? You must have friends from elementary school, junior high, high school."

"I've ruined every friendship I've ever had!"

She was a drama queen at heart. No wonder Joachín had little patience for her. It was exhausting to have to spend all day building up someone's ego.

"My parents were so unstable that I wound up at three different high schools," I said. "But you grew up in the house where you live now, right? You must have tons of friends who went to your high school. Like Twinkle, right?"

"Twinkle!"

"Poor woman. May she rest in peace and all that." If thinking about Twinkle's life didn't make Isabel feel better about hers, there was nothing I could do.

"Twinkle!"

"Did you know her well?"

Isabel sat on the floor. "You could say that."

"Her tragic end is a sharp reminder that we have to appreciate what we have. We lucked out because our lives aren't as cursed as hers."

"Not as cursed?"

"Well, Emil's might be. The police think he did it, you know. Killed Twinkle. Were you good friends with her?"

"What?"

"Is there anything you know about her that might be helpful? To Emil, I mean. He swears he didn't kill her. I've been trying to help him get out of jail."

"Emil wouldn't kill her!"

"Nonetheless, it looks like he did. To an outsider, I mean. To someone who doesn't know better."

"Not Emil! No!"

I rummaged through the toolbox for a nail that was long enough to be useful.

"He asked me to help him get out of jail," I said. "Can you believe that? He dumps me, moves in with her, and she's murdered the next day. We live in a strange world. Who knows? Maybe Emil really did kill her. What do I care?"

"Emil would never hurt anyone!"

"He hurt me all right. You too, I take it." I only knew what Emil had told me: they'd gradually grown apart until it was silly to continue.

That was Emil's version. Short and sweet. But any decent story had more than one side.

"He wasn't a perfect boyfriend," I said. "If you get right down to it, he was impatient and selfish. Was there a specific reason you guys broke up?"

"Because he started seeing you!"

Emil, Emil. I should have seen through his facile explanations, but it was clever of him not to leave me until he was sure about the next one. That way he always had a warm bed.

"Honestly, Isabel, if I'd known he was still seeing you, I wouldn't have gone out with him." Well, maybe for coffee, but that didn't count.

"I know."

"He said he wasn't seeing anyone."

She picked up a hammer and hit it against the palm of her left hand. "I remember the day he met you like it was yesterday. He came home that night and went on and on about his classmate from the East coast who knew the same plays he did."

I remembered too. It was the first day of the Irish Drama class. When the professor asked who had seen Yeats' "Words upon the Windowpane," the obscure one-act about Jonathan Swift and his two lovers, Emil and I both raised our hands. We exchanged glances until the end of the lecture. After class, we went for coffee. I was thrilled to meet a local man who read plays, who was so handsome I couldn't look away, and who was more mature than the disastrous boyfriends I'd suffered back home.

Stupid thinking. I'd been incredibly naïve.

Isabel switched hands and tapped the hammer against her right palm. "Twinkle's death is all your fault."

"Mine? Excuse me!"

Isabel took two boards and firmly nailed them together. "Emil looked elsewhere because you neglected him."

"I did not!"

I had not come here to help Isabel only to be psychoanalyzed myself. Carpentry had helped her recover from self-doubt, so she didn't need to chat with me anyway.

"He felt alone," Isabel said.

Poor Little Emil. I could hear the "pity me" chorus in the background, but I didn't buy it. "I've worked my ass off to keep our business going. If that's neglect, he deserved it. It's not my fault he met some woman in the meantime."

Isabel hammered a third board, but the nail went crooked. She took a handful of nails and set them next to the board. "Don't you understand anything? Emil met Twinkle through me!"

"Oh! So you were friends."

"She was my best fucking friend!"

I thought back to Twinkle's diary. *Great to spend time with B again. She hasn't changed since middle school.* B. Bel. Isabel. Of course.

"Wait a minute. When did you have a chance to introduce Twinkle to Emil?"

"A year ago when you went back at Christmastime to see the family Emil said you don't even like. How could you leave him alone for December Twelfth?"

"His birthday is the eighth. I left the day after." I'd carefully arranged my travel plans around a special dinner. A romantic one.

"December Twelfth is for la Virgen de Guadalupe! It's a holiday!"

How could I forget about the holiday that kicked off the Christmas party season? Meanwhile the fire alarm finally went off in my brain. "You were trying to get him back."

"I invited him to my party because I knew he was lonely."

On the surface, she could have been doing a good deed. From everything Joachín said, she wouldn't be. Possibilities slid through my mind like a slot machine, but three pictures came up, little boxes that said "Get. Him. Back."

She would have greeted him at the door in her slinkiest black dress that was too tight and too short. She would have flashed her biggest lipstick smile and batted eyelids loaded with three shades of shadow. When she sat with him on the couch, she would have parted her legs a few inches, enough for her skirt to crawl up her legs the way she wanted Emil to. Sneaky.

But I knew Emil well enough to know that he didn't backtrack. If he didn't like every aspect of a new exercise routine, he tried a new one. New recipe that wasn't quite right? He never tweaked it. He moved on. Why would he have reacted to women any differently? Things weren't quite right between him and me. Without warning, off he went.

At the party, Emil wouldn't have been enticed by Isabel no matter how much she played him. He would have moved on.

"He left with Twinkle that night, didn't he?" I asked.

"You have no idea."

"I'm starting to get one." I had yet another reason to leave Emil in jail permanently. "We both have reasons to be mad at him. But look on the bright side. His new lovers will all be male."

He would be popular in a communal shower: wet, soapy, vulnerable. I chided myself for having a flicker of pleasure. Do onto others. And he did and did and did.

But I had a job to do. Get Isabel back on her feet. "Finish the stairs?" I asked.

She threw a broken board across the set and picked up two more pieces of lumber.

"You don't have to be so upset about it," I said.

"What the hell do you know about how I should be?"

Uff. I was supposed to help, not make things worse. Tommy would be better off not hiring me after all. "You're nervous. That's all."

"I'm pathetic!"

True, but what could I do? I wasn't a psychologist. Best to leave it to the theatre director. He got paid to deal with ego. "You'll be all right. You just need time."

"I handed Emil his new lover on a silver platter! I might as well have tied a bow in her hair!"

It was ill-advised to have introduced them, but how would she have known? Emil probably hadn't planned to go to the party. It would have been a casual "Say, I'm having a party tonight, why not come over?" type of thing. Isabel couldn't blame herself for putting Emil and Twinkle together. They might have met at Walmart. But Isabel wouldn't conquer her emotions until she met them head on, wrestled with them, and threw them out the window.

"Blaming yourself won't help," I said. "Blame Emil and Twinkle. How could you know some deranged idiot would sneak into Twinkle's house and murder her while her lover was out running? How random is that? It's crazy. It's not like you have a crystal ball or anything."

Isabel placed her foot on top of the pile of boards. "You know what Twinkle said? That she'd met exactly the rightest man."

Rightest. Ugh. As if that were a word. She'd written the same thing in her diary. Emil would have been on his best behavior. He would have been suave. He would have listened. Made compliments. Jerk. If he got out of jail and I strangled him, no one would blame me.

Isabel kicked the top board off its stack. "She said she'd been waiting for him her 'whole darned life.'"

In sprawling loops, she'd penned that in her diary too. Ridiculous. At most, she'd been waiting a dozen years.

Isabel kicked two boards off at once. Evidently her stomach was more sensitive than her foot. "Twinkle's excuse was that he made her feel wonderful about herself. Can you imagine that?"

Ah, yes. Needing a man to feel wonderful about yourself. It did help to have a show of support, but Twinkle might have been needier than most. That had been the January 5 entry, if I remembered right.

Yes. That was exactly the way Twinkle wrote it in her diary.

Finally the meteorite landed on my head. Isabel knew the exact words in the diary because she'd seen it.

By now it was probably in her closet.

Because she'd probably stolen it from Twinkle's house.

Because she'd probably —

Oh.

She held the hammer with both hands. "God are you slow."

I inched backwards. Isabel had found out about the affair. Trailed Emil. Waited outside Twinkle's place for the right moment.

"I'd be angry too," I said quietly. "Emil did wrong by you."

"Shut up."

I was so dazed that when my cell meowed, I checked Joachín's text automatically. *found T's diary in closet. Get out of there.*

It was like someone telling you to watch out for that— tree. I took a step back toward the set's living room. Where were Tommy and Willard?

"You took me off guard. The way you swept Emil off his feet without trying to."

"I never meant—"

"I get that or you'd be as dead as Twinkle by now. As long as you're alive, you're my worst competition. Why put up with that?"

"You killed your own best friend."

"We weren't best friends. Not anymore."

Where had Tommy and Willard walked to, Phoenix?

"Temporary insanity," I said. "You didn't mean to."

"How stupid are you?"

At the moment, incredibly stupid. Unimaginably. What had the nanas said about being alone with Isabel?

"I would have never guessed that—"

"Look. I never meant to kill her."

In the distance, I heard a dog bark. Havie?

"What was your plan, to saw her arm off?" No, no, no. Never taunt a killer. What was wrong with me?

"My only plan was to threaten her. Explain how things were."

"You spotted the saw outside her neighbors.'"

She waved the hammer like a wand. "It's easier to make a point with a weapon in your hand. All I needed was for her to leave Emil alone so that he would come back to me."

"When she said 'no,' you sawed through her neck?"

Isabel's eyes rested on the ruined staircase before she turned away.

Then I knew what happened. Isabel hadn't set out to kill Twinkle. She turned on the saw, tripped on the rug, and tumbled right onto her.

"You didn't mean to hurt her," I whispered.

"I couldn't turn off the damned saw! Blood went everywhere! I finally threw it across the room, but by then it was too late!"

"So you ran."

"Of course I ran! You would have too!"

I heard faint voices in the lobby. *Come on!*

"You wanted Emil back, but now you're willing to let him pay for your crime?"

"They can't convict him. They don't have proof. I'm the only witness!"

"But I know what happened."

"You won't have much time to think about it."

She hurled the hammer at me but missed. When she reached into the toolbox, I turned and ran. Tools thudded around me as I dashed through the set. Then my heel caught the coffee table. While the replacement vase hit the floor and shattered, I twisted my ankle and flopped.

Pain choked me so hard I ignored the screwdrivers flying past.

"Isabel! Put that thing down," Tommy yelled.

Tommy and Joachín ran toward the stage while Havie danced beside them.

"Watch out!" Joachín yelled.

The woman was running toward me with an ax. Its foot-long blade shimmered in the light.

"I'm calling the cops," shouted Tommy.

"You can't stop me!" Isabel cried.

"Joachín! Purse!"

Joachín tossed my purse so high I had to stretch for it. I snatched it like a goalie, ripped out the doll, and drilled both my thumbs into its stomach.

"Ow! Ow! Ow!" cried Isabel.

I laid the doll on the ground and pounded it with my fist. "Get her!"

"Ow!" She balled into a fetal position and clutched her stomach. Tommy held her shoulders while Joachín grabbed some rope and tied her like a calf in a rodeo.

Willard came running. "The police are on the way!"

When Havie barked, I imagined sirens. I lay back and put my hands over my eyes.

A few moments later Joachín gently scooted his lap under my head. He brushed back my hair and ran his fingertips down my cheek. "It's over."

"Let's hope."

Tommy knelt at my side. "You're okay, right?"

My ankle throbbed, my head ached, and my heart beat at triple time. "Perfect."

Tommy took my hand, kissed it, and set it back down. "That's great. Because you're going to have to play the maid."

I closed my eyes and laughed.

Chapter Thirty-Five

Given the frenzied rehearsals, the weekend performances of the play, and the parties thrown in my honor by Tommy and the nanas, it wasn't until Monday morning when I arrived at school that I finally saw Emil. He had wisely chosen to sit in his own classroom rather than at the office desk I now considered my own. When he saw me, he rushed over as a mutt happy to see its owner. He'd lost weight in jail, so he was gaunt, and his haircut was way too short to show off his rich black hair. He wore fresh clothes, though, probably courtesy of Orlando.

Scenes of romantic dinners followed by lovemaking flashed through my brain. They evaporated, replaced with flashes of Isabel.

I sat behind my desk and propped my swollen ankle on a stack of books. "Have a nice run this morning?"

"No more running. I'm considering a different sport."

I smiled as if expecting that very answer. I plunked my elbows on top of my attendance lists. Since I'd cancelled two days of classes to study my lines for the play, I'd extended the students' tuition for an extra week. Emil would have never approved such a decision. However, he was no longer in charge.

"The nanas and Joachín left notes for you about your students' progress. Do you have any questions?"

His eyes showed surprise. Evidently he expected a more personal question. He wasn't getting one. How was he? He was out of jail, so he was doing fine.

"No questions. They left clear notes for me."

I knew they had; I'd reviewed their work myself. Although the nanas had spidery handwriting and Joachín rarely finished a sentence, they'd left plenty of clues about the material they'd covered with Emil's students.

Emil stood expectantly, but I clasped my hands and smiled. I wasn't giving him anything for free. Any information he wanted from me he would have to work for.

"You handled things beautifully while I was . . . away."

Several responses crossed my mind, most including expletives. I hadn't had time to categorize my charges against him. What was worse: the lying, the cheating, or inadvertently causing Twinkle's death and Isabel's consequent crimes? In the end, Emil was still the nanas' grandson and nephew. He'd still show up at family dinners. We still owned a business together. It was well and good to be angry, but it was more important to be practical. So I kept to the script I'd written for myself. I concealed my anger and focused on the school.

"When you own over half of a business, you take care of it, don't you?" I asked.

He smiled meekly as if he weren't sure he had permission to do so. No doubt he had conflicting thoughts. Was he wondering how we'd found a witness? When pressed, the dog owner admitted to spotting Isabel entering the house the morning of Twinkle's demise. With any luck, the police found telltale fingerprints on Twinkle's wall, the power saw's electrical cord in Isabel's trunk, and Twinkle's diary in Isabel's closet. Emil owed his freedom to a team of dedicated volunteers. And to me, of course. I hoped he realized how lucky he was.

He stepped closer. "Dervla, I don't know where to start."

I could have helped, but I loved seeing him stuck for words. He might have started by apologizing. But no. Mordy had his tongue.

"I feel so bad that— Well, I feel bad about a lot of things," he said softly.

Bad? He should have felt awful. He should have been so horrified by his own stupid, immature, egotistical actions that he couldn't stand himself. He should have been ready to throw himself off a building for a quick, merciful demise.

Overkill. At the very, very least, he should have realized that he owed me the universe for the rest of his life. I refrained from pointing that out. I needed to heal too, and if I started listing the many ways he'd failed me, I wasn't sure I would have time for anything else.

He pointed vaguely toward the classrooms. "You did a tremendous job."

I nodded.

"I mean, both with the school and with . . . ." He trailed off as if he thought I'd finish the sentence for him.

I did not.

"You never thought I killed Twinkle, right?"

Not really, but he didn't need to know that. "The nanas asked me to help. I did. They're the ones you need to thank. And Joachín. He helped save me from Isabel."

"He was a godsend."

"He sure was. If Isabel had killed me, you'd have to teach all the classes yourself, English and Spanish."

He wasn't sure whether or not to smile. I embraced his confusion.

"I can never thank you enough," he finally said.

So true.

D. R. Ransdell

He rested his hands on the desk. "I was hoping—I mean, there's no rush, right? But in jail I realized something important, something I should have realized before. You're the best thing that ever happened to me. You're the best life partner I can hope for. I fouled things up, and I want you to know that I'll never do it again."

A nicer person might have pretended to take what appeared to be an apology seriously, but I owed myself some levity. "Actually, you screwed up. Many, many times. Or simply screwed."

He smiled as if offering me a ray of sunshine. "When you're ready, and I know that might be a while, maybe we could go on a date together."

He was worse than a language student who thought successfully memorizing ten words meant knowing a foreign language. "A date," I said. "With you."

"Come to dinner on Sunday," he said. "I'll ask the nanas to invite you."

The nanas had already invited me. They had a friend who might need my help. "Actually, you're the one who might need an invitation."

He grinned as if I had gone into a comedy routine. I didn't mind. He would understand soon enough that he had wrecked his life so completely that he would need a few years, maybe even a decade, to bounce back.

I fished inside my purse. "I brought you something." I tossed him Emilito. Since Havie had gnawed the photo off his face, the doll was more like a rag. I had stitched him back together and added two shirt buttons for his eyes, but the teeth marks were still visible.

Emil squeezed his namesake's belly. "What's this?"

"Your souvenir."

"Uh, thanks." He rotated the doll and examined it from all sides. "Did you make it?"

"The nanas, actually. But they gave it to me, and now I'm giving it to you."

302

He continued rotating the doll, no doubt trying to figure out what was interesting or beautiful about a rag. *If he only knew.* But alas, none of us, not the nanas, not Joachín, and certainly not I, would be explaining it to him.

Finally he looked up. "When I was in jail, the other guys said there was no way I was ever coming out. You saved me, and I know it. How did you find the strength?"

My eyes traveled to Emilito. "Let's say it was a little daily magic."

He brightened. "I guess that's as good an explanation as any."

Good enough for him, at least.

My cell phone meowed with a new text.

"Important?" Emil asked. His insinuation was that we were having a conversation. In the old days, I would have turned off my phone to devote my undivided attention to my lover. That was still true. It was the lover who had changed. Or rather, the potential, perhaps tonight-for-the-first-time lover.

Six at your place? Joachín had written.

I texted back a smiley face.

"Important?" Emil asked.

"Only my future." I folded my hands back over my papers.

Emil leaned on the desk. "Busy tonight?"

"Very."

My cell rang with a jazzy ringtone.

"Your cousin?" Emil asked.

"Yes. That's Keevah. I better take it. Family stuff."

Emil smiled as he retreated to his classroom.

"Cuz! How are you?" I asked.

"Miffed. You said you found the perfect spot for the dog-cat I gifted you, but you never sent me a picture."

"About that. I have a bit of a story. It might even call for a visit." I leaned over and repositioned my ankle. Then

D. R. Ransdell

I sat back and smiled. It was probably time to start sewing a few more dolls.

Acknowledgements

Many thanks to early readers including Elise Ransdell, Brenda Windberg, Lorin Oberweger, Don Maass, and especially to David Loeb. Another big thanks goes to Glinda Mantle for sharing the magic of New Orleans.

About the Author

Originally from Springfield, Illinois, D.R. Ransdell now resides in Tucson, Arizona. During the school year she teaches writing courses at the University of Arizona, but during the summers she travels, sometimes to New Orleans. Dervla's story was inspired by stories D.R. heard when she taught English down in Durango, Durango, Mexico, but that's another story. Please visit her online: http://www.dr-ransdell.com

Dear Readers:
Drop me a line at drr@dr-ransdell.com.
If you enjoyed Dervla's story, please leave a review on your favorite social media site.